The Division
Bell Mystery

The Division Bell Mystery

Ellen Wilkinson

With a Preface
by Rachel Reeves
And an Introduction
by Martin Edwards

Poisoned Pen Press

Originally published in 1932 by George G. Harrap & Co. Ltd., London. ©Ellen Wilkinson 1932
Preface Copyright © 2018 Rachel Reeves MP
Introduction Copyright © 2018 by Martin Edwards

Published by Poisoned Pen Press in association with the British Library

First U.S. Edition 2018

10 9 8 7 6 5 4 3 2 1

Library of Congress Control Number: 2018948399

ISBN: 9781464210853   Trade Paperback
ISBN: 9781464210860   Ebook

Poisoned Pen Press
4014 N. Goldwater Blvd., #201
Scottsdale, AZ 85251
www.poisonedpenpress.com
info@poisonedpenpress.com

Printed in the United States of America

*Dedicated with sincere apologies to
my good friends among the police and
kitchen staff of the House of Commons*

Preface

When I first stumbled upon *The Division Bell Mystery*, it was with the rather instrumental intention of finding out more about the culture of the House of Commons during the inter-war period and the status of women in Parliament. Yet by the end of the first chapter, I had become hooked on the fusion of whodunit suspense and political commentary that Ellen Wilkinson so cleverly creates.

Wilkinson was one of the first Labour women in Parliament, being elected for Middlesbrough East in 1924 during a general election in which the three incumbent Labour women were defeated in the opposite of a landslide for MacDonald's embattled minority government. Wilkinson grew up in an impoverished mining community in Manchester where she remembers that even the leaves were grey from the soot. She quickly developed an all-consuming passion for social justice. Having managed to win a scholarship at Manchester University—no mean feat for a working-class young woman—she became a political organizer, suffragist campaigner, and councillor for Manchester City Council.

When she entered Parliament in 1924, it was just five years since the election of the first woman MP to take her seat (Nancy Astor). Wilkinson was alone as the only woman on the Labour benches—one of the "Orphans of the Storm" as she jokingly put it in her Maiden Speech—and yet it did not impede her limitless confidence, enthusiasm and commitment to parliamentary politics. Standing at just 4'10 with flame-red hair that matched her left-wing politics, she earned the epithets "Red Ellen", "The Fiery Particle" and the "Pocket Pasionara" (for her involvement in Spanish Civil War campaigning). Wilkinson quickly developed something of the celebrity about her—with her penchant for colourful outfits, her various love affairs with married men, and her strong independence of mind. In the chamber, she spoke the most of the women MPs and cast the most votes, despite bouts of ill health. While Nancy Astor sported a minimalistic black and white suit with a tricorn hat, Wilkinson ignored her advice and sported a range of eye-catching outfits. She was also the first to venture into the male fortress that was the Smoking Room. When accosted by a policeman who informed her that ladies did not usually frequent the Smoking Room, she quipped "I am not a lady—I am a Member of Parliament," as she pushed the door open defiantly.

Yet despite her early success as a woman pioneer, Wilkinson was, like her colleagues, swept away in a greater storm than the one she had weathered previously: the 1931 election. She would return to Parliament four years later, but in the meantime she took to writing—both fiction and political works. An avid murder mystery fan who named her kettle "Agatha" after her heroine Agatha Christie, Wilkinson now ventured into the genre herself as boldly and zestfully as she had ventured into the parliamentary Smoking Room. The book was written at the precipice of a transition within the Golden Age of crime fiction, at a time when the genre was gradually replacing cosy escapism with politicized dramaticism. The plot draws heavily from the political climate of the time: the crucial loan being negotiated between the government and Oissel, an American financier, is an unconcealed allusion to the difficulties experienced by the British government in the wake of the Wall Street Crash of 1929. Political commentary is interlaced throughout the story, and yet despite the strength of Wilkinson's political ideology, she never descends into political point-scoring. Instead, her political experience gives colour and warmth to the drama that unfolds. Indeed, her main character—a young and impressionable Tory Parliamentary Private Secretary at the lowest ranks of a ministerial career—is presented as utterly decent. No doubt Wilkinson's own experience as a Parliamentary Private Secretary under Labour MP Susan Lawrence from 1929–1931 informed her portrayal of his character. Despite Wilkinson's (perhaps tongue-in-cheek) assurance that "All the characters in this book are entirely fictitious," there are clear parallels between Wilkinson herself and the Labour MP Grace Richards, as well as between Lady Astor and the formidable and bubbly society hostess Lady Bell-Clinton.

The setting of Parliament and the political intrigue that Wilkinson so powerfully depicts can be seen in Parliament today. Every day or so, I walk down the corridor by the Terrace leading to what Wilkinson refers to as the "Harcourt Room" (which I believe to be the Churchill Room—a grand dining room now adorned with paintings by the wartime Prime Minister), with its various small "alphabet" dining rooms inspiring the ill-fated "Room J" (where the murder takes place). One evening, a while after having read Wilkinson's book, I was walking down the corridor late at night when most MPs had gone home, and I nearly jumped out of my skin when the division bell rang shrilly.

Wilkinson was a real character around Parliament, and her knowledge of the place comes through vividly in the book. Always in a rush, on the Parliamentary Estate she became known for her incredible propensity to fall over, hence why she dedicated the book to her friends among the House of Commons police and kitchen staff, who often helped her up. She was loved and admired across the party divide to such an extent that a group of Conservative MPs, distressed at how little care she took of herself, bought her an electric cooker (possibly to encourage her to cook rather than relying on her usual diet of cigarettes and chocolates). In 1935, she returned to Parliament as MP for Jarrow, and the following year, her status as a campaigner, a radical and a deeply passionate politician was galvanized by her role in organizing the Jarrow Crusade, a march of 200 unemployed men from Jarrow to London in protest against the 80% unemployment in the town after the closure of its shipyard and steelworks. Wilkinson would later become the second woman to enter the Cabinet as Minister of Education in Attlee's government of 1945, when she championed the raising of the school-leaving age and the introduction of free school milk. In the winter of 1946, Wilkinson died suddenly from an overdose of Medinal, one of the many medications she was taking for her increasing ill health. It was a terrible loss for Parliament, for the Labour party, and a tragic end to a dedicated and productive parliamentary career. Wilkinson's brother destroyed her papers, worried that her reputation would be damaged by the stories about her affairs—with illustrator Frank Horrabin and Home Secretary Herbert Morrison amongst others. But her speeches, newspaper clippings, articles and two novels survive. And what cannot be lost is her legacy, as a trailblazer for women in Parliament.

—Rachel Reeves
Member of Parliament for Leeds West

Introduction

Politics in Golden-Age Detective Fiction

Detective novels published during the Golden Age of Murder between the two world wars have long been undervalued. For many years, it was a critical commonplace to dismiss them as cosy, conventional, and conservative. This lazy stereotyping was (and, where it persists, still is) all the more regrettable because it led to the neglect of many enjoyable whodunits once they were out of print. Of course, Agatha Christie's work enjoyed enduring popularity, and the work and reputation of a handful of other writers, such as Dorothy L. Sayers, also escaped oblivion. But until the recent revival of interest in Golden Age detective fiction—fuelled, in part at least, by the success of the British Library's Crime Classics—most Golden Age authors were forgotten by all but a few diehard fans.

Yet the stereotype was not only facile, it was also misleading. There is nothing cosy, for instance, about the finale to Francis Iles' *Before the Fact*, for instance, or the closing pages of E.R. Punshon's *Crossword Mystery*. Or about Christie's *And Then There Were None* or *Five Little Pigs*, come to that. There is little that is conventional about *The Documents in the Case* by Sayers and Robert Eustace, *Sic Transit Gloria* by

Milward Kennedy, or *Lonely Magdalen* by Henry Wade. The examples could be multiplied.

Equally, the received wisdom (famously articulated by Julian Symons, the finest British crime critic of the second half of the century, in his seminal history of the genre, *Bloody Murder*) that "almost all" British writers of the Golden Age were "unquestionably right-wing" is very wide of the mark. Even the tiny band of leading writers who made up the membership of the Detection Club in the 1930s included Nicholas Blake, briefly a Communist, Lord Gorell, at one time a prominent figure in the Labour party, the Fabian Socialists Douglas and Margaret Cole, the former *Daily Herald* journalist R.C. Woodthorpe, and other left-leaning figures such as Punshon, Kennedy, Helen Simpson, and the Club's first President, G.K. Chesterton. Among the successful Golden Age writers whose politics might today be classed as "far-left" were Bruce Hamilton, Raymond Postgate, and the Marxist critic and poet Christopher St John Sprigg, while the most renowned crime publisher of the era, Victor Gollancz, was also the founder of the Left Book Club. The term "the Golden Age of detective fiction" itself is generally attributed to John Strachey, a Marxist critic who served as Secretary of State for War in Attlee's post-war government. In other words, Ellen Wilkinson was very far from alone as a detective novelist of the left.

Perhaps the explanation for the myth about the conservatism of Golden Age writers is that Christie, Sayers, Anthony Berkeley, Freeman Wills Crofts, H.C. Bailey, and Wade, who were arguably the most admired detective novelists of their day, were indeed essentially conservative in their outlook. The crime writing careers of their radical colleagues tended to be shorter and much less celebrated. Sprigg and Simpson, for instance, died young, while Woodthorpe, Hamilton, and Kennedy were far from prolific. The preoccupations of politics in real life evidently (and regrettably) prevented Ellen Wilkinson from writing a follow-up to *The Division Bell Mystery*. Yet even Christie wrote one novel in which the "least likely person" murderer is a pillar of the political establishment, and the cricket-playing baronet Wade was not afraid to glance at police brutality and corruption in the course of his inventive and often highly sophisticated mysteries.

As politicians who wrote classic crime fiction, Ellen Wilkinson and Lord Gorell were exceptional, but reading detective stories seems to have been a favourite pastime of leading political figures on both sides of the Atlantic. The career of the prolific Yorkshire-born author J.S. Fletcher was boosted by publicity given to the U.S. President Woodrow Wilson's endorsement of his work. Conversely, Stanley Baldwin, three times British Prime Minister, revealed in a speech in 1928 that he regarded *The Leavenworth Case*, by the American writer Anna K. Green, as "one of the best detective stories ever written". When invited to a Detection Club dinner as a guest speaker, Sir Austen Chamberlain, half-brother of Neville Chamberlain, and a man who had himself narrowly failed to become leader of the Conservative party, told guests that he was a "greedy, interested, and passionate" fan of the genre. Victor Gollancz even ran a short-lived imprint called "The Prime Minister's Detective Library", although why he thought such branding would have widespread appeal is itself a mystery.

In fact, the main contribution that political class made to the classic detective novel was to supply a reliable and plentiful source of victims. Together with rascally financiers, disagreeable misers, and rich folk unwise enough to announce an intention to change their wills, politicians crop up again and again in Golden Age novels—as corpses unlikely to be widely mourned. Titles of the era included Robert Gore-Browne's *Murder of an M.P.!*, Alan Thomas's *Death of the Home Secretary*, and Helen Simpson's *The Prime Minister is Dead* (this being the American edition; in Britain, the book was called, more cryptically, *Vantage Striker*). Nor was Ellen Wilkinson's sole detective story unique in its parliamentary setting; Anthony Berkeley's *Death in the House* features an apparently "impossible crime" in the House of Commons.

During the 1920s, the Golden Age whodunit represented a reaction from the slaughter of the First World War. People amused themselves with puzzles as a means of escape from the horrors that had left few families in Britain untouched: hence the supposed "cosiness" of the classic mystery, with its focus on a battle of wits between reader and writer. But during the 1930s, it became increasingly difficult to ignore the grim realities of the international political scene, as dictators flourished, and the existing order came under threat. Golden Age writers did not turn a blind eye, and their work reflected the world in which they lived in a variety of ways.

Woodthorpe and Punshon poked fun at Fascists in books such as *Silence of a Purple Shirt* and *Dictator's Way* respectively, while other authors grappled with a growing awareness of the fallibility of long-cherished systems of justice, not only overseas but closer home. The anxieties of the age are captured towards the end of Kennedy's *Sic Transit Gloria*, a book he described in a dedication to Gollancz as an "experiment":

"British liberties, fair trial, justice, freedom of speech—shibboleths were as easy as clichés…A jury could only have secured injustice. What did the law matter—if the law could not have secured justice? People talked of judicial murder; was not judicial failure to secure the just punishment of a murderer just as bad?"

Kennedy's story deals overtly with the political dimensions of injustice, but his more renowned and conservatively inclined contemporaries addressed similar issues more obliquely, and more successfully. Christie integrated daring ideas about how best one may achieve justice with ingenious plots in two of her masterpieces, *Murder on the Orient Express* and *And Then There Were None*. Berkeley approached similar themes with irony and flair in *Trial and Error*, and John Dickson Carr wrapped them up within the confines of a "locked room" mystery in *The Reader is Warned*.

Bruce Hamilton's *Rex v. Rhodes: the Brighton Murder Trial* was an equally inventive novel, highly political written in the dispassionate, factual style associated with the *Notable British Trials* series. Published in 1937, but supposedly written in 1950, the Foreword to his book begins:

"In these days of expansion and activity the eyes of Soviet Europe are turned towards the future rather than the past. The history of the revolution which a short three years ago began its enormous task of liberating the energies of the working masses are yet to be written...[the Rhodes trial] was the first occasion in England on which a clear-cut issue, of whether a man did or did not commit homicide, was permitted, with an almost disarming frankness, to be judged in the light of the political sympathies of the ordinary middle-class jury."

Hamilton's vision of the future proved to be as misconceived as his understanding of the Soviet economic system, but his novel—for all its naivete—illustrates the ambition, originality, and social and political awareness that was evident in much more Golden Age fiction than has generally been acknowledged. The books by Hamilton and Kennedy suffer in comparison with those by Christie, Berkeley, and Carr not because they are less interesting, or less well-written, but because the storylines are less well-balanced, and prioritize the message over the mystery.

This is not a mistake that Ellen Wilkinson made. Nobody who knows anything of her life and career can doubt that her political views were passionate and deeply felt. But far from being didactic, *The Division Bell Mystery* is highly enjoyable, despite a few flaws typical of a first crime novel—notably the incompetence of the original police investigation of the murder scene. To her credit, Wilkinson avoids falling into the trap of scoring cheap political points in her portrayal of the Conservative PPS and amateur sleuth Robert West. This avoidance of bigotry and narrow-minded sectarianism sets an example to other members of the political class in any age. And it's one of the reasons why it is such a shame that this lively "impossible crime" puzzle had no successors.

Martin Edwards
www.martinedwardsbooks.com

All the characters in this novel
are entirely fictitious.

—E.W.

CHAPTER I

No matter how exciting the day, the House of Commons loses all interest between the hours of 7 and 9 P.M. The big speeches of the day have been made. The battle of the bigwigs is resumed after nine o'clock. M.P.s must eat. They drift out of the debating-rooms, and leave the long green benches to those agonizing souls who have to work off a maiden speech or who must catch the Speaker's eye occasionally to let an otherwise uninterested constituency know that they are alive.

Robert West, lolling on the second bench behind the Government in virtue of his high-sounding title of Parliamentary Private Secretary to the Secretary of State for Home Affairs, divided his attention between the clock and the sufferings of one of the Opposition Members, perspiring with his efforts to raise the roof, and encouraged by the malicious shouts of "Speak up" from his tormentors.

"Too bad," said West's neighbour.

"We ought to film this place," chuckled West. "Would any of us ever make a speech again if we could see how funny we look when we are doing it? Damn Murray Grey," he continued, thinking aloud; "the rotter promised to relieve me by a quarter to eight."

"Got a dinner-party?" queried his colleague sympathetically. "But you aren't bound to stay, are you? This isn't your Minister's show."

"No, it's Treasury, but Murray Grey was gasping for a drink, so I promised to keep guard over his Minister while he had a couple. The blighter could have mopped up the entire bar by now."

It is the unwritten law that a Minister must have a Parliamentary private secretary on the bench behind him during a debate in which he is leading, to get papers from the library or the answers to awkward questions from the experts' box under the Press gallery. It is an irksome duty, and Robert West was feeling aggrieved that having volunteered to relieve a friend he should be left in the lurch like this.

"Is the lady very pretty?"

"It's not a she, it's a he. Fact is, my oldest friend is coming to dinner at a quarter to eight, and as we've all got to be back for the division at nine it doesn't leave me much time. I haven't seen him for five years."

"Clear off, then," said the older man. "I'll keep guard on the Chancellor."

"Bless you, will you? I hate leaving you like this, but I'll boot Murray Grey in if I see him."

West gathered the official papers together and dumped them on his neighbour's knee, as though he were afraid the other would repent of his offer.

A good many eyes in the public galleries followed him as he made his bow to the Speaker and walked down the centre aisle out of the Chamber. Robert West was quite worth looking at. He hadn't the disadvantage of those tailor's mannequin good looks which make other men slightly contemptuous and cause women to speculate rather petulantly as to the probable queue of female admirers. But he looked interesting, with heavy black hair waving over a good head, a square jaw, a clean complexion, and a pair of large brown eyes that only partly admitted the hot temper which was his chief weakness.

At twenty-nine he was comfortably fixed in a fairly safe Parliamentary seat, and being fortunate enough to be entirely without private means he had to keep his wits alert to earn money for his luxuries. The meagre Parliamentary salary barely sufficed for the necessities of even such a comparatively frugal bachelor as he was.

Like most young politicians (male) he had given as much thought to the *rôle* he should assume when he entered Parliament as a newly elected woman M.P. gives to the costume to be worn on her first appearance. After considering several models he had decided that a slightly cynical air of detachment from the worries of common man, an unruffled calm amid political storms, coupled with a keen watch for the right moment to intervene, was to be his special *rôle*. As he kept these decisions carefully to himself no one could tell him that every young politician (male) had made a similar decision during the days between the count at his winning election and taking his oath in the House of Commons.

Actually Robert West could not maintain the slightest detachment even from a street dog-fight. It was as a dog-fight that politics interested him, though he was always assuring himself that some time or other he would settle down to find out how the country ought to be run, and why politicians made such a mess of running it. But as a popular young bachelor he found life too interesting at any particular moment to acquire sufficient of that knowledge to be awkward to his party whips.

That was why, at twenty-nine, in his second year in Parliament, he was Parliamentary Private Secretary to the Home Secretary, was known to every one as Bob, and was well inside the comfortable fairway which leads in due but long course, when the tides of youth have ebbed, to that placid company of politicians who decorate the Front Bench of any particular Government, whose names are seldom remembered during its lifetime and forgotten the day after the dissolution.

On this particular evening in June, West walked a little self-consciously down the short but important corridor that separates the selective privacy of the central lobby of the House from the Strangers' Lobby, where constituents, lobbyists, guests, and the men who have come to borrow half-crowns are herded together indiscriminately by gigantic but amiable policemen.

West paused at the barrier while the policeman called out his name. His eyes impatiently searched the crowd. Donald Shaw, for whom he was looking, had never been easy to pick out in a mob. He had always been of the type that prefers to be part of the scenery. It was with a little twitch at his heart that West recognized in the man walking towards him the adored companion of his school and college days—still the same tall thin figure, browner in the face, but with the same humorous apology in the blue eyes for being in the picture at all.

"Why, there you are! I say, it *is* good to see you again after all these years. Found your way all right?" West covered the real emotion he was feeling after a separation of five years by his almost too hearty manner.

"Perfectly, thanks to your admirable instructions. I mentioned your magic name and bobbies stood stiffly to attention in rows."

"Draw it mild, my son. I told you in my letter that a P.P.S. is the humblest of God's creatures—but"—a little self-consciously—"it does get one through quicker to give the policeman a name they know. Now what about dinner? I've ordered a meal in the Harcourt room. Want to wash?"

"No, thanks. I'm in a faultless state of preparation for the great occasion. It's my first meal in the House of Commons. I can assure you I'm feeling properly impressed."

"You wouldn't be impressed with this outfit long if you were in it." Don smiled at this remark, for Bob himself was so obviously impressed with it all.

The Harcourt room to which West led his guest is the fashionable 'Society' part of the House of Commons. Members themselves dine in comfortable and inexpensive shabbiness in their own dining-room upstairs, and there is an equally shabby Strangers' room for the hurried business meal. But West rather wanted to show off his new dignity to his friend, besides standing him the best possible meal the Commons *cuisine* could provide. He had booked a table for two which gave the best view of the lights and flowers, the celebrities and their guests, and the general atmosphere of what has become, since the War, probably the best mixed club in the world.

He had a good many friends to nod to as he piloted his guest to their table.

"It's rather full to-night," he said as they took their seats. "There's another of these financial crises hovering in the wind. Important division at nine, so people are dining in. I'll have to leave you then, just to dart up to vote."

"Don't let me interfere with the government of the Empire or what's left of it," begged Shaw. "Now tell me which are the bigwigs."

"Ministers don't come down here much. They have a dining-room of their own. Unless they have guests, of course. That grey-haired man with the hooked nose entertaining all those ladies—seems to have a different set here most nights and has got all the oof most mortals could do with—is Samuelson the racing man. That tall dark man with a heavy jaw is Joshua Stoneleigh. Did incredible things in the War." West punctuated each mouthful with a catalogue of the people around.

"Who is that good-looking fellow with the Jewess in green?"

"Philip Kinnaird. Adventurous card, that. Collected a pile out of that rather unsavoury Regal Irak affair. You ought to know all about it. You were out in Irak at the time, weren't you?"

"Yes, I know quite a lot about the Regal Irak Company," said Shaw quietly. "It's one of the reasons why I am in London now. So that's Kinnaird!"

"Awfully nice fellow really," said West.

"That's not his usual reputation, is it?"

"People are jealous of his cash, and saddle him with the sins of old David Davies, his unspeakable chairman. But people here like him all right—at least, those who know him."

"Does he do much in politics?"

"No, hardly ever here. Safe seat, properly bought and paid for and all that. Can't think what he wants to muck about the place for."

"Oil is supposed to have some occasional connexion with British foreign politics, isn't it?" said Shaw quietly.

"Well, there's an awful lot of rot talked about that. Britain isn't America—and any big interest that tried to pass palm-oil along our lobbies would soon be told where it got off."

"Yes? No doubt there is a somewhat subtler atmosphere here. Thanks, I *will* have a little more of that Hermitage. Pretty good, isn't it? I hope I'm not consuming your substance in this grand meal?"

"It's a binge to-night," laughed West as he ordered another bottle and went on with a gossiping list of the other diners in sight.

"But the most interesting dinners, of course, are not given in here," he said. "The private ones take place in the little dining-rooms off the corridor we came along. Some history has been made in them, I can tell you. In fact there's probably a bit of history being made in one of them now."

"That's interesting! State secret, or am I allowed to know?"

"Well, to be honest, I don't know much myself, but the Home Secretary—that's my Chief, you know—has got Georges Oissel to dinner *tête à tête*, and the Prime Minister is dropping in on them for coffee after the nine o'clock division."

Don Shaw looked humorously humble. "I know I ought to be impressed, but I've had my head in Irak sands for five years. Who is Georges Oissel? Don't tell me he's the French Premier or the President of the League of Nations or some other household word."

"Oh, no! No one knows much about Oissel. He's not one of those well-advertised mystery millionaires. He's just a plain American 'multi'—French extraction, obviously, from his name. He's head of one of the firms that deal in big Government loans, but he's a cripple and a recluse and mighty hard to dig out of his shell. I consider it's one chalked up to me that he's here at all."

"Did you do the trick, then?"

"In a way—I had to make all the arrangements. It's not Home Office business, of course. My Chief is in it simply because he's a pal of the Premier's and rather takes a hand in any confidential business that the P.M. may want to drop out of later. You see?"

"Perfectly."

"In addition, by the greatest luck, Oissel happens to have been friendly with my Chief in the long ago. Spent some holidays together in a log camp or something. So Oissel made an exception to his rule never to accept invitations. He would have been a surly dog not to, for I must say the Chief's been awfully decent to him. Lent him Jenks, his own private detective, because the regulation Scotland Yard variety got on his nerves, and the Government would not agree to his being without some kind of protection just now. But I wish I knew what was in the wind. The Chief's been as surly as a bear with a sore head ever since Oissel's appearance in this happy land."

"And don't you know?"

"Only in a general sort of way. I know that we must get a big loan and for longer than we usually have borrowed. Oissel is here negotiating on behalf of the only group who are likely to lend us the money for the length of time we want it. I've rather gathered that the terms are pretty stiff, but what the Chief expects to be able to do about them I don't know."

"Perhaps he's giving him a good dinner to soften his heart."

"Wouldn't appeal to Oissel. Lives on charcoal biscuits and fruit and that sort of stuff. And you may accept a chap's invitation because you went logging with him as a lad, but I can't see that being allowed to make even an eighth of one per cent. difference to a big loan, can you?"

"Can't say. It would in all the loans I've ever had anything to do with, but they amount to about a couple of dollars."

West grinned, and then said rather sheepishly: "Of course, all this is deadly confidential. I expect you think I've been opening my mouth pretty wide, but then I always did tell you everything that went through my head."

"And it was all right, wasn't it?"

"Rather, and forgive my saying that. I know you are as deep a well as your navvies ever dug. I *am* glad you are back in England. I'll see a bit of you before you hop off again, won't I?"

"Sure. Probably more than you want to. I'm one of the great unemployed now. I have to thank the Regal Irak ramp for that. I'll tell you the story some time…"

"But look here, old chap… I mean… if I can do anything…"

"Oh, I didn't mean I was joining a Labour Exchange queue just yet. It's not the cash I mind, but having to give up a job that was really worth while doing. But a quiet time in your respectable London will do me a lot of good… Kinnaird is trying to catch your eye, by the way."

While West went over to be introduced to Kinnaird's vivacious Jewess, Shaw sat watching the scene with a wry smile behind the smoke of his cigar. This was the House of Commons. This was Home, and the centre of Home. For the dividend to be spent by these men and women dining in comfort he and his men had sweated among Irak flies and dirt. He felt no resentment against them. It was rather pleasant to sit at his ease and contemplate his share in building all this. After all, it was this Parliament and what it represented that had stretched a protecting arm over the loneliest outpost, that had given point and purpose to the hardest pioneering tussles. But at the thought of the Oissels and Kinnairds his mouth hardened. To have worth-while civilizing work held up indefinitely by irresponsible gamblers, to be a pawn in a financial *coup*—that made a man bitter. And there was no way of getting at these men; no revolution seemed to shake their thrones; revolutionaries had to go cap in hand to them when they had done the job of finishing off age-old dynasties.

West returned rather hurriedly, breaking into his reverie.

"Sorry, old man. Our manners here are the world's worst. Everybody butts in on everybody else, but it's nearly nine and I've got to go up for the division. If you'd care to come along I could stow you in a side gallery till it's over and then show you round."

The electric indicator showed that the Prime Minister had been on his feet some time, and most of the other Members had left their guests to be in at the last few minutes of what was expected to be an exciting speech and a close division. Even so it took a little time to push their way through the crowded room, and the bells of Big Ben had already begun the carillon of the hour as Robert West piloted his companion into the long Terrace corridor.

"That's Room J, where Oissel——" But his sentence was never finished, for as they reached the door the division bell began to ring. And through the double clamour of Big Ben and the shrill sound of the bell rang a revolver shot.

"Good God!" gasped Robert West.

CHAPTER II

For one split second the scene was photographed on West's brain. The brightly lit corridor, the hurrying waiters struck motionless at the sound of the shot, the waiter at the door of Room J, white-faced, the plates he was holding now in pieces round his feet. West's eyes met the waiter's. People in the corridor began to rush to the door. Shaw opened it, Bob rushed in, the waiter followed. Shaw slipped inside and stood with his back against the door to hold back the press in the corridor.

The multi-millionaire had slipped off his chair at the end of the table and was twisted into a heap on the floor, his shirt-front stained with blood. A revolver lay beside him.

"Suicide, my God!" gasped West. He picked up the revolver and put it on the table as he bent over the little crumpled mass that had been only a moment ago one of America's most powerful men.

There was an irresistible pushing on the door. Shaw opened it to admit a policeman. Dexterously he managed to keep the press of people outside while the policeman bent over the body with West.

"Better get a doctor, sir," said the policeman in a hushed voice. "There are always plenty about in here."

Shaw opened the door again. "Doctor," he called. "Some one get a doctor quick."

"Dr Reading is here now," called out several voices, and a tall thin man pushed his way authoritatively through the crowd that had gathered outside Room J. He knelt beside the body crumpled on the floor.

"Dead," he said. "Practically instantaneous, I should think. An awful mess. The bullet has struck a bone. Difficult to say more without a post-mortem. What has happened? Has he committed suicide?"

"The revolver is here. It looks as though he has," said West, "but I must get the Home Secretary at once. Mr Oissel was dining with him."

Again there was a banging on the door, and Shaw, who had constituted himself doorkeeper, which seemed the useful job at the moment, let in a powerfully built middle-aged man—a police-sergeant, one of the stalwarts of the House of Commons corps.

"Ah, Bourne, glad you've come," said Dr Reading. "This is more your job than mine now."

The sergeant knelt down beside the body. "Shot, sir? How has this happened? Who was here with him?" Bourne looked up at Bob West.

"There was no one with him, at least not when he was shot," said West. "The Home Secretary was dining with him, but he must have gone up to the division. We came in, Shaw and I, the moment we heard the shot. We were just passing the door at the time. We found this revolver on the floor. I picked it up," and West moved to pick it up again.

"Better not touch it again, sir. We'll have to examine it for fingerprints when the Inspector comes," said the sergeant. "He was dining with the Home Secretary, you said?"

West pulled himself together. "Yes, and I must get him at once, Sergeant. It is terribly important. I'd better tell him myself. It will be a terrible shock to him."

Any police officer in the House of Commons is always impressed with the danger of putting his feet where they are not likely to be welcomed by High Authority. Sergeant Bourne knew the House and its ways.

"That will be best, sir, if you'll see the Home Secretary while I phone up Scotland Yard. Would you like a constable to go with you? You look pretty shaky."

"I'll take Mr Shaw with me. There'll be enough sensation in the lobbies without my being escorted by a policeman."

Shaw took charge of his white-faced friend, and a policeman pushed a way for them through the throng of guests and M.P.s in the corridor. A dozen Members pounced on Bob, but his white face and staring eyes enabled the expert constable to get him through the crowd, which was left with the firm conviction that West was somehow the cause of whatever had happened.

The stairs and long narrow corridors of the House seemed endless. Shaw had all he could do to prevent Bob dashing along at full speed. As it was, they cannoned into several scandalized Members.

"It's like a nightmare," thought Don Shaw. The news had evidently begun to filter through as news does in the House of Commons, more quickly than anywhere except in an African forest. Hands tried to stop them as they rushed by. Heads were turned as they dashed along.

"He's sure to come out behind the Speaker's chair. He will have had to be on the Front Bench when the figures were announced," gasped Bob.

The division was over, and Members were pouring out

of the Chamber like bees out of a hive. In the centre of a group, yet coldly aloof, was the Home Secretary. Shaw caught a glimpse of the heavy white face, set high on a pedestal of starched collar, which was the joy of every caricaturist.

West seized his arm. The Minister looked at his Parliamentary private secretary in cold surprise.

"I must see you for a moment, sir," said West hurriedly. "Something dreadful has happened. Mr Oissel has committed suicide."

"Suicide! Mr Oissel committed suicide! What on earth are you talking about? He was perfectly all right when I left him."

"He's dead now, sir."

The Minister looked as though his secretary had taken leave of his senses. He drew him back into the division lobby. Shaw made to follow. A watchful policeman put out a restraining hand.

"Members only that way, sir."

Shaw gritted his teeth. It was maddening. The Home Secretary's face had interested him. He wanted to see how he would take the news. But the barrier between sheep and goats, between elects and non-elects, is Himalaya high in the House of Commons.

Shaw stood a few moments alone. The news was spreading. No one knew him, of course, and he heard scraps of conversation as excited Members went by him.

"Suicide in front of the Home Secretary, I hear."

"Does this mean a row with America?"

"I don't believe the story at all. It simply couldn't happen in the House…"

The dark-coated figures passed up and down the corridor, and somehow in the foreground there appeared to Shaw a twisted little figure with a red-stained shirt-front.

West came out of the division lobby with the Home Secretary. "This is Donald Shaw, sir. He was with me when we went into the room."

"I wish we met under happier circumstances, Mr Shaw," and the Home Secretary marched along the corridor with the two young men. "Simply inexplicable. I cannot understand why he should commit suicide at such a moment. And why choose to do it here? He knew my heart is bad. I really ought not to have shocks like these. Most inconsiderate."

"There hadn't been any difficulty… about the loan, I mean?" asked Bob hesitatingly.

The Home Secretary placed a dignified arm on Bob's shoulder without slackening his pace.

"If only the loan were in question," he said with just the ghost of a smile, "there would be more reason why I should commit suicide than he."

When they arrived on the lower corridor they found an excited mob of Pressmen, M.P.s' guests, and waiters in the entrance that divides the dining-rooms from the other part of the House. The police had cleared the Harcourt corridor, and they made a lane for the Home Secretary's party. As the Minister was recognized the crowd pressed respectfully back. His self-control was magnificent. With West, Shaw, and a policeman at his heels he walked up the empty corridor as one destined by Providence to take full command of any situation. The policeman on duty outside the fateful room saluted and threw open the door.

The body of Mr Oissel had been reverently covered by a white tablecloth brought in by the manager of the refreshment department, who stood suave and polite as ever, but with a slight protest in his manner at such happenings being allowed to disturb his cherished dining arrangements. The waiter, by this time under repeated questionings a mere mass of black and white misery, stood near the manager as one seeking protection from such assured authority. Sergeant Bourne and Dr Reading stood by the corpse. An awkward silence fell on the room as the doctor drew back the cloth from the dead man's face.

For a moment it seemed as though the awe-inspiring yet comforting self-control of the Home Secretary would break. He said nothing, but turned his back on the others and blew his nose violently twice. Dr Reading replaced the cloth.

"You think it was suicide, doctor?" asked the Minister.

"Of course, I can't say that definitely, without closer examination. But the wound certainly could have been self-inflicted," replied the doctor in low tones.

"Do you remember what the time was exactly when you left the room, sir?" asked Bourne, stepping forward.

"Perfectly. It was ten minutes to nine. I had promised the Prime Minister that I would be in for the last few minutes of his speech, and in any case my heart will not permit me to hurry, so I asked Mr Oissel to excuse me until the division was over. I had previously explained that the division was timed for nine o'clock. He quite understood that. He was perfectly happy and composed when I left him."

"And I know it was just nine as we heard the shot," added West, "because Big Ben was striking as we came along the corridor."

"Then the question is, was he alone during those ten minutes?" said Shaw.

Sergeant Bourne glanced at his notebook. "I've taken notes of the waiter's evidence. He says that he came into the room after the Home Secretary had left, to change the plates and bring in dessert, and that Mr Oissel told him not to bring the coffee till the Home Secretary came back."

Don Shaw turned to the frightened waiter. "Did Mr Oissel seem agitated as he told you that?" he asked.

The Minister's jaw set. "You will forgive my saying, Mr— er—er"

"Shaw," murmured Bob.

"Mr Shaw—that this does not seem the time or place for unofficial cross-examinations. The police have the matter fully in hand, I take it, Sergeant Bourne?"

"Certainly, sir. Of course we shall need Mr West and Mr Shaw as witnesses, and yourself, sir, I suppose. I telephoned the Yard. Inspector Blackitt is being put in charge—should be here any minute, sir. I can't have anything touched till he comes."

"The windows were closed, I remember," said the Minister, walking to them to try them.

"Yes, sir. Closed and latched from the inside as you see, sir. You hadn't had them opened during the meal?"

"God forbid! I hate draughts as much as Georges Oissel. Poor Oissel! Why ever did he do it?"

"If I may venture to ask, sir," said the sergeant with an enigmatic glance at Shaw, "I take it that your conversation, the—er—business, hadn't been of an unpleasant character?"

"Certainly not. We hadn't got to business. That was waiting until the Prime Minister came. We had just been talking about old times. I knew Georges Oissel in Canada twenty years ago, and we had talked most pleasantly. Of course, I don't know anything about his private worries. It's a sad business. But I must see the Prime Minister. He has been told, of course?"

"Oh, yes, sir—Mr Walters went to see him when Mr West went to you, and he has sent a message asking you if you would go to his room when you had seen the police, sir."

"Yes, of course, I am going now. I suppose there is nothing more that can be done at the moment. Oh, but what about the Press? They will make a scare thing out of this. Robert, you had better give out an official statement. There is no reason why the Press should make things worse by undue sensationalism." With this weighty utterance High Authority turned to the door, which was respectfully opened by one policeman while the others stood to attention.

Even in the midst of all the horrors Bob West managed a wry smile as the door closed behind his Chief.

"As though special editions aren't already on sale in the streets," he murmured to Don. "Well, you'll be glad to be rid of us, Sergeant, while I see the Press. Tell Inspector Blackitt I'm at his disposal any time. Thanks very much, Reading. Good night."

"Good night, West. By the way, has Mr Oissel any relatives? Oughtn't you to get into touch with them?"

"Heavens, I don't know. Don't know anything about him. But anyway I'll find out. Thanks for reminding me. I ought to see the Chief about letters of condolence, but they'll do to-morrow, won't they? I must see the Press now."

"That's a great responsibility, West. I should be very careful if I were you."

"Don't I realize I'm treading on egg-shells, doctor! But if we don't give out an official statement there'll be merry hell to pay to-morrow morning. Come along, Shaw. You'll see me through it?"

"Sure!" And the two men left the room together.

"Well, you *are* a blighter, West! Might give a pal the tip before you murder your friends in the House of Commons, or at least hand out the dope before our main edition goes to press."

West started. "Sancroft, you *are* the limit! You *would* get round the police somehow. How the hell did you get here when the police had combed every room along the corridor?"

Sancroft, the reporter of the *Daily Deliverer,* was evidently a friend of West's, for he slipped his arm through the other's and held him from going along to see the other Pressmen.

"Sheer luck, my dear fellow. There *are* places where the police are too modest to look. And knowing something was in the wind, there I stayed."

"You *would!* Shaw, this is the worst Pressman in London. He's always there. It's dreadful. You can never find him when you want him and never lose him when you don't."

Sancroft was a round, portly little person with twinkling eyes behind thick glasses. He looked cheerfully up at the tall, grave Shaw.

"And this is your accomplice in the crime, I suppose. Now, gentlemen, I want to warn you that what you say will not be used in evidence against you, so get along with the yarn."

"No, seriously, Sannie, you've got to help me," said West earnestly. "I'm in a devil of a hole. I don't know how much to tell the Press, and whatever I say there'll be hell's own row."

Sancroft saw the door of Room E opening along the corridor. With a swift gesture he drew the two men inside the convenient lavatory. He wanted West to himself for three minutes.

"Tell me the full yarn, Bob. It's no use trying to be diplomatic. Our chaps will ferret out the whole story and it will look bad if anything has been kept back. Besides, why shouldn't you? The Home Secretary can't be expected to know that his guests will commit suicide if he leaves them alone for a moment. Personally, if I were his guest I should commit suicide, or murder, if he didn't."

"But why must he do it here?" wailed Bob. "Hell! I had enough trouble getting the blighter here, without his serving this trick on me. And I know I'm going to be blamed for it somehow."

"Of course you are. That's why P.P.S.s are yanked out of their gooseberry bushes," said Sancroft. "But you'll be torn limb from limb if you don't get out to our lads and hand out the dope. My old mother's advice was 'If ye tell a lie stick to it and heaven itsel' can't get o'er ye,' but *my* advice is to tell the plain truth. They probably won't believe you, so it will do just as well as any lie you can think of at this moment."

As the two men turned to leave their retreat, after Bob had rapidly told his tale, Sancroft caught his arm.

"You are *sure* it's suicide."

"Of course."

"Then the only story is the *why*. Can I come round to your flat when I've seen this through, and talk a bit?"

"Yes, do. Shaw will be along for a drink. My God! I've forgotten I've had a dinner with all this happening!"

CHAPTER III

Shaw learnt why Robert West was a rising young politician as he watched his handling of the impatient Pressmen. There were one or two significant omissions in the tale he told, but all the journalists wanted was to get to their offices with the main facts. Clues and motives were the game of to-morrow.

"I'll have to go through the Members' Lobby," said Bob when the last question had been answered. "I'd rather dodge them down the back-stairs, but God knows what rumour will be out by now."

Shaw followed West along the locker-lined corridor to that octagonal space where the heart of Parliament beats. The House of Commons had risen soon after the nine o'clock division, and it was now ten-thirty, but groups of Members still stood excitedly discussing the sensation of the day—for the threatened crisis had disappeared with the announcement of the Government's majority. Again Shaw had to admire his friend's technique.

Every one made a dart at West, who somehow managed to deny rumours, to quieten agitated and elderly M.P.s and even to deal with a cynical young woman who wanted to know why he had only shot one poor little millionaire instead of turning a machine-gun on to the whole Front Bench.

"Cheeky young sprite," commented Don as at last he found himself being taken downstairs by Bob. "Is she a secretary or an M.P.'s daughter?"

"Daughter!" exclaimed Bob. "That's Grace Richards, M.P., our latest acquisition. Surely you've heard of Gracie?"

"Good lord, and is that what the British electors send to govern the remnants of a once decent Empire? No wonder things are going phut."

"And what's wrong with girls like Gracie?" Bob West turned quite hotly to face his friend. "They're a damned sight more intelligent than that lot we've been trying to smooth down. Old Commander Beltwhistle with his stock and his eyeglass. You'd imagine to hear him that America would declare war to-morrow because one decrepit millionaire went and shot himself where he shouldn't."

"No doubt Miss Gracie Richards would survey the floor of the House of Commons covered with dead millionaires without flinching. But sorry if I touched a sore place. Is it sore, I mean? I can't see you as a disinterested feminist, Bob."

West went red, but said nothing as he retrieved his coat and hat. The two men stood for a moment at the Members' entrance while the stalwart policeman's cry of "Tax-oi, tax-oi" rang across the yard. Big Ben towered solidly against the dark November sky. Palace Yard was silent. In it were parked a few cars of the Members who were still upstairs.

Policemen stood at every entrance. "It all seems so solid and so safe," said Don Shaw as the respectful constable opened the door of the taxi he had hailed for them and tucked them carefully into it.

"Safe? I should think it is. There's police and plainclothes detectives at every corner. The Home Office looks after M.P.s in this place as though they were the Crown Jewels. But, damn it all, the police can't be expected to search our dinner guests for firearms. And it's so much worse it being the Home Secretary. Did you hear old Beltwhistle, pompous ass—'If the political chief of Scotland Yard cannot look after his own guests——' The whole damned country will be doing a grin to-morrow."

Robert West lived in a very self-contained flat—a couple of rooms with a primitive bathroom-cum-kitchenette over some business premises in Soho. "It's like a conspiracy going up here," laughed Don, as West opened the street door and led him up the narrow dark stairs. West replied with a rather dry grunt, opened the flat door at the top of the stairs, picked up the letters lying on the mat, and tossed them on to a small table as he hung up his hat and coat. He lit the gas-fire, pulled a whisky bottle and a syphon out of the cupboard, found a couple of glasses, and then threw himself into a chair without speaking.

"No more whisky for me," said Don. "Got a kettle? Some good strong tea I want and I prescribe the same for you. No, don't you worry"—as Bob made an impatient move—"I'll find the doings."

While Don busied himself making the tea Bob moved restlessly round the flat, picking up a book and putting it down, lifting up the telephone receiver and putting it on its hook again without making a call, upsetting a loaded ash-tray and swearing viciously. Shaw took no notice of his fidgeting. His movements were almost old-maidish in their precision as he moved round the untidy, shabby little flat. He arranged the thick cups on the tea-tray quite daintily and carried it into the living-room. "It's no use wasting all that nervous energy tearing yourself to fiddlestrings," he said quietly. "Either now or, better still, when you've had a night's sleep, we'll go through the whole thing carefully. But it's not your fault in any way, and really, if it comes to that, it's not your Home Secretary's."

West dug his hands into his pockets. "I'm not an unfeeling brute, Don. But it's not Oissel I'm worrying about, or how he got himself made into a corpse. I can see us—the Government, I mean—being able to take his death quite philosophically if it had happened elsewhere, or even if we knew why it had happened here. But it may mean the most awful mess-up—America on her hindlegs, shares going to blazes on the Exchanges, the loan scuppered. And why? My God, Don, the most maddening thing in politics is just to be told enough about things to realize how much you're not allowed to know."

"Your Minister didn't seem so upset as all that," Shaw replied soothingly.

"That's because you don't know him. The Chief hasn't got where he is by his brains—every one knows that. He's the stupidest cuss in some ways. But he can be magnificent when a face has got to be put on things. A face-saver is the most useful member of any Cabinet, and that's why the Premier relies on him so."

"Well, he certainly kept a fine straight face this night of grace," said Don. "A general reading his own casualty lists couldn't have done it better. But what share has the Premier in all this?"

Before West could answer, the door-bell pealed loudly. Don moved to the door.

"Sancroft, I suppose?"

"Yes, don't go down. Sannie has a key. He often sleeps here on late nights at the House."

"Got anything to drink, you two?" called a cheerful voice

from the hall. "What a night for June! Pouring heavens hard now. Weeping for your millionaire, Bobbie, my lad, or perhaps the mess the Government will be in to-morrow because of this little flutter?" Sancroft strolled in and began to take his boots off by the gas-fire.

"What! That all the whisky left for three? Good thing you're eking it out with tea. Well, I've got a bit of news to provide some stimulus if the whisky don't. Guess what's happened to your friend Oissel now?"

"Happened to Oissel? Isn't he dead after all?" asked West.

"Dead enough, I'm afraid, but he's been burgled."

"Burgled—when? Since he committed suicide or when he was at dinner?"

Sancroft put on some ancient slippers of Bob's, and filled his pipe from a large tobacco jar. "Seems to have been taking place about the same time—no, a little later. The news was through on the tape as I was leaving the office after finishing my stuff."

"You've not been there, then?"

"Not me. Officially I'm not supposed to be interested in anything that doesn't happen in the House of Commons—a view I do my best to encourage. And anyway our crime squad is on a job like that. No, *no* tea, my dear Bobbie. Why do you allow wild men of the beyond to lure you into drinking the stuff? No wonder you up and murder your Chief's guests at the slightest provoc——"

A cushion caught him on the mouth. Sancroft tucked it behind his head and put his feet on the mantelpiece.

"And now, Bob, my son, you've got to give Uncle the inside dope about this pleasant little party in Room J. I've been looking up the record of Monsieur Georges Oissel and he seems to have been quite an interesting guest."

"What have you found out about him?"

"Director of the American Foreign Loans Corporation *and* President of the Eclair Texan Oil Corporation. In his spare time he seems to have directed one or two other useful enterprises. Now I can't see our Home Secretary concerned with Texan oil. He hasn't much money and what he has is in pretty dull securities, I think. But the A.F.L.C. is rather different. Was he just ghosting for our revered Premier, for I take it that the Treasury knew something of this happy occasion—or didn't they? Our P.M. is a devil for not letting departments in on their own jobs, if he can get 'em happily interested in some one else's."

West was twisting a wire toasting-fork into odd sorts of shapes. He put it down and began to walk up and down the room.

"Sannie, you know as much as I do. The Cabinet was keeping the loan negotiations pretty dark. They had to. You can't conduct business like that in the Albert Hall and charge for admission. But as far as I know both sides were doing a straight deal. The terms were pretty high, but, as far as I can gather, Oissel and the Home Secretary were engaged in a friendly attempt to strike a bargain and make a present of it to the Premier."

"Then why should Oissel have chosen such a moment to shoot himself without giving the Home Secretary even a hint?" asked Shaw.

"And is this burglary a pure coincidence? No, my lad, there's something fishy here," said Sancroft.

The three men, who had been pulling silently on their pipes after Sancroft's remarks, started as the door-bell pealed loudly again.

"Who can it be at this hour?" said Shaw, going to the

window and trying to peer into the street through the heavy rain. "Need we answer the door?"

"We'd better," said Sancroft. "Some one else may be in the soup by now. I'll go down, and if it's anyone without a brand-new bit of mystery I'll say you're not in, unless"—and he grinned—"you were expecting some one special to-night, Bob."

West managed an answering grin and returned to the twisting of his wire toasting-fork until Sancroft called out from the hall, "Bob, it's Inspector Blackitt."

West went out to greet his visitor, and Shaw heard a deep but pleasant voice saying: "I'm really sorry to intrude at this late hour, Mr West, but I had to see you."

"That's all right, Inspector. We aren't exactly feeling like bed just yet. Don, this is Inspector Blackitt, one of our crack men from Scotland Yard."

"I'm glad to meet one in real life," smiled Don. "Have a peg, Inspector?"

While he went through the whisky and soda ritual, Shaw got his impressions of the newcomer in his quiet absorbent way. A thickset man, Scandinavian in colouring, a humorous face, and a navy-blue lounge suit worn with that air partly of authority, partly of deference to the authority of others, which is so marked in the upper ranks of the British police service.

"Is this the gentleman who was dining with you?" asked the Inspector as he took the glass from Don.

"Yes, and Sancroft of course you know."

"Far too well," said the Inspector with a smile, "but he tells me he's here as your friend and not as a newspaper man, so we can get to business."

"Of course you've heard about the burglary at Oissel's flat to-night," said Sancroft, hoping that he hadn't.

"Just come from there. You got it on the tape, I suppose. Awful shame about poor Jenks, isn't it?"

"Jenks," gasped Bob. "What's happened to him?"

"He's dead too," said the Inspector gravely. "I thought you knew as you'd got news of the burglary. The thieves shot him."

"That wasn't in the first message I saw. Jenks gone west! The Home Secretary's own marvellous Jenks. My hat, your old man will think it's not his lucky day, Bob," said Sancroft.

"But who is, or was, Jenks?" asked Shaw.

"I told you at dinner. He was my Chief's own man. He saved the Chief's life when he was at the Foreign Office in the last Government but one, so the Chief took him on as his valet and confidential man, and he thought an awful lot of him. He really was the world's best, poor chap."

"It's mainly about Jenks that I've come to see you," said the Inspector. "He must have died very pluckily defending Oissel's property against the thieves, but I can't quite make out why he was there at all. Why wasn't Oissel under the ordinary protection of the Yard?"

"Because he simply would not be," replied West, pushing his tobacco jar towards Blackitt. "With all due respect to your fellows, Inspector, these personal bodyguards you supply to our distinguished visitors can be an infernal nuisance. Oissel has never had any guard except his own valet, a queer old Frenchman, Pierre Daubisq, who couldn't keep off a cockroach. A chap like Oissel has his good share of enemies, and it was pretty important to the Government that nothing should happen to him while he was here. When he sent your men packing it was a bit awkward, so after we'd thought of everything else the Home Chief had a brain-wave and offered the services of Jenks. And he and old Oissel got on together excellently."

"But what *did* happen at the flat, Blackitt?" asked Sancroft. "What were the thieves after?"

"We haven't got the full details yet. I've left a good man in charge down there. Oissel's man was found chloroformed. The hall-porter got suspicious when he saw the two men he'd taken up in the lift dash down the stairs, and he called the police. They found poor Jenks dead in the hall, and Daubisq chloroformed. Until we can get him coherent we can't find out what's happened."

"And you've no idea what they were after? Was it just ordinary robbery?"

"As far as one could judge it wasn't an ordinary burglary. There were plenty of things of value lying about which they might have taken if it had been that. Have *you* any idea what they might have been after, Mr West?"

"You must ask the Home Secretary that, Inspector."

The Inspector put down his glass, refused a refill, and leant over to Robert.

"Mr West," he said earnestly, "it's pretty important for the Government to have this thing cleared up, isn't it?"

"Very important, I should think."

"Then I want your help in getting certain information, and I don't think I can do much without it."

This was flattery indeed, as West's faint flush showed. But the young man was a politician of parts, and not given to rash confidences.

"You can have that, Inspector, but you know that a Parliamentary private secretary is never told anything, not even enough to know what he mustn't tell."

"I'm not after State secrets, Mr West. The message I got from the Home Secretary was that he was most concerned in having the whole affair cleared up so that at least the

Government should know what had happened, even though it might not be considered wise to let too much of Oissel's private affairs leak out to the public. My task will be impossible unless I have your friendly co-operation even to getting interviews with the Home Secretary when I want them. If you'll help I promise you that you won't be kept in the dark from my side."

"What an offer, Bob! Make that to me, Inspector, and I am your willing slave until Jenks' murderer is kicking the air," said Sancroft.

"You've helped me before, Mr Sancroft," smiled the Inspector, "but reporters aren't the birds wanted on this. As Mr West's friend we'll be glad to have what assistance you can give us, for I never met a better 'nose' than yours."

"An insignificant organ, but it has served," said Sancroft, stroking it.

"Am I to be left out of all the excitement?" Shaw added in his soft, slow voice.

"Rather not," said Bob. "You've put your foot right into the middle of it already, so it's got to stay there. Well, here we are at your disposal, Inspector. Now command us."

The Inspector smiled. "There shouldn't be any more difficulty now than is necessary to sharpen our appetites for the work," he smiled, "but I am afraid there will be. Anyway, there's nothing more that we can do now. You've given me what I wanted to know about Jenks. I have that appointment to meet the Home Secretary at twelve to-morrow at the Home Office—that is, if he doesn't have to call it off for a Cabinet meeting or something like that. It's then I'll need your assistance, Mr West."

"Right. I'll be in my room at the H.O. from half-past ten to-morrow. I can't promise to get you into the presence, but I'll carry messages."

The Inspector rose. "Then I think a sleep won't do us any harm, especially you, Mr West."

"I feel like nothing on earth," said West as he busied himself getting his guest's coat and hat. "You're not going, are you?" he added as he saw Sancroft putting on his boots again.

"Oh, I'll stroll along with the Inspector and chew over a theory or two. London seems to be a place where it's wise to walk about in twos after a night like this."

When Blackitt and Sancroft had left, West stood for a moment looking down at Shaw, who still lolled in the armchair.

"And London wasn't going to be exciting enough to keep you," he said.

"Done tolerably well for a beginning," replied Don with a yawn, "and I see the possibilities of a little more excitement when the rest of the picture gets filled in."

CHAPTER IV

Sir George Gleeson, the chief permanent official to the Home Office, was a man who expected people to be impressed with him—and they were. It was not difficult to see why. He was not a specially impressive figure—rather short, broad-shouldered, dark-haired, clean-shaven. At a casual glance he might have passed for any professional man of good standing. But once you had met his eyes you never could remember not having been impressed by the man. They were deep-set eyes, dark under heavy eyebrows—reflective eyes, eyes that seemed to take in all you had ever thought or felt and every lie you had ever told.

George Gleeson was a youngish man, barely fifty, with a sense of humour and a vanity that to some of his older colleagues seemed boyish at times. The higher ranks of the British Civil Service hold some remarkable men. All government is an elaborate game of bluff, and to the men who are on the inside of the pretence the bump of reverence is worn to a hollow. So there were a few of his colleagues, heads of other departments, who could play on George Gleeson's little weaknesses; and they were the ones who perhaps had the deepest respect for his brains, judgment, and his utter disinterestedness. George Gleeson, in fact, was the sort of civil servant whom Americans can never be persuaded to believe really exist.

In his department were centred not only all the police activities of Great Britain, but the administration of the immense Department of the Interior. Yet George Gleeson was one of the few men who always had some spare time. He needed that gift for clearing a space round himself this morning, for his big desk in the Home Office contained a mass of press-cuttings mounted on quarto sheets of plain paper relating to the Oissel murder. Here was the stuff which would form the mind of the public as to the strange happenings in Parliament the night before.

SUICIDE OF MINISTER'S GUEST
STRANGE DEATH OF MILLIONAIRE
AT HOME SECRETARY'S PRIVATE DINNER
AMERICA'S MYSTERY MAN DIES
IN COMMONS WHILE BURGLARS RAID FLAT

shouted up at him in streamer headlines.

If this had happened to any other Minister, Sir George Gleeson would not have been personally concerned with it. The police department ran its own affairs very largely, except when questions of policy had to be decided. But any happenings to his own political chief affected so efficient and loyal a civil servant as though they had happened to himself. Still—and George Gleeson shrugged his shoulders—if a mere politician, the chief of a fleeting hour, will go off on political adventures, instead of holding on like a good boy to the firm hand of his wise departmental nurse, what can be expected but trouble? And Sir George felt that he had had all the trouble he wanted from this Home Secretary, who was as outwardly dignified and inwardly stubborn as the great civil servant himself.

Sir George pressed one of the row of electric buttons on his desk, and a secretary glided in noiselessly from behind a screen.

"Who is handling this Commons case?"

"Inspector Blackitt, sir. They have rung up from the C.I.D. asking if he could see you as soon as possible."

"Is the Home Secretary here yet?"

"No, sir, they have telephoned from his house to say he won't be in till his appointment with Inspector Blackitt at midday."

"Better ring up and ask Blackitt to come to see me now."

"Yes, sir."

The phone bell rang. It was the Prime Minister's secretary. Had Sir George Gleeson seen the news, and the Premier's compliments and would Sir George give some special attention to the matter, as rather serious issues might conceivably arise?

"Does the Prime Minister wish to see me?" inquired the Home Office chief.

"Oh, no, he doesn't think it necessary to trouble you," drawled the voice on the phone in the most perfect Oxford accent. "He just wanted me to ask you——"

"Then please tell the Prime Minister that matters concerning my department will have my best attention, *as usual*." And the receiver clicked back into its rest.

Prime Ministers make mistakes when they rely too exclusively on the inhuman efficiency of the Service. A little personal flattery is a remarkable lubricant.

Sir George pressed a button for the appearance of Inspector Blackitt, who was duly wafted into his presence. Sir George did not make mistakes in dealing with subordinates. His manner to the Inspector was a subtle mixture of a deity receiving an archangel on perhaps the fourth rung of the hierarchy and one man of the world talking business to another. Nor did he ever keep a man waiting while he went on with his work. He plunged right into the business in hand.

"These facts are correct, I take it, Inspector. Have you any further details?"

Blackitt glanced at the pile of newspapers on the desk.

"You have the later editions, sir, with the news of the burglary at Mr Oissel's flat and the death of Jenks?"

"Yes. Poor Jenks! It really is a most extraordinary business. I never interfere in police cases, Blackitt, but as bigger issues than the deaths of these two unfortunate men may be involved, I have asked your Chief to let you keep in touch with me."

"Very good, sir." Inspector Blackitt felt a warm glow inside himself. Even to one of the crack detectives of Scotland Yard the chief permanent secretary is as a god in some far-away heaven. To be brought under his direct notice was a piece of good fortune that Blackitt appreciated at its true worth.

Sir George picked up the *Daily Deliverer.* "This seems to have the fullest report and will serve as a basis. I haven't seen the Home Secretary since this happened. The dinner with Mr Oissel was a purely private affair, I take it?"

"Yes, sir. Mr West arranged it for the Home Secretary."

"What had West to do with it?" inquired Sir George sharply. Like all civil servants of importance he detested these political private secretaryships, which carried no responsibility, but conferred such close personal access to the Minister.

"Mr West said that it was a personal matter, and had nothing to do with the Home Office."

"I see." It would have taken a three-volume treatise to expound all the criticism of such folly expressed in that remark.

"As far as I can gather, sir, Mr Oissel was unwilling to come at first. He never went out to social functions."

"Then why was this an exception?"

"That I don't know. Mr West said that I must ask the Home Secretary. Perhaps you had better do that, sir."

Sir George grunted impatiently. "But has anyone any idea why he should come to the House of Commons to dine and then commit suicide almost under his host's nose?"

"If he did commit suicide, sir!"

Sir George looked up startled. "*If* he did? What on earth do you mean? Is there any doubt about it? The papers all say that he committed suicide with a revolver that was found by his side."

"It may be convenient to let the Press go on saying so, until we see our way a bit clearer, but there are several features about the case that puzzle me."

"You and our experts have applied all the usual tests, of course?"

"Oh, yes, and that's the difficulty. The pieces don't fit the suicide theory."

"Doesn't the bullet fit the gun?"

"Same make, and the cartridge-case is in the revolver, which had certainly been fired. The muzzle was blackened."

"Well, then?"

"But when a man commits suicide, sir, he invariably holds the revolver close to his body, head, or heart, or mouth, or wherever he shoots himself. Then the clothes or the flesh against which the gun has been pressed show the mark of the scorch of the flash."

"Invariably?"

"May I show you, sir?" Blackitt took a matchbox from his pocket. "Now look, sir," he said as he struck a match down so that the tip touched the blotting-paper as it lit. "You see that mark of the flame, sir. However quickly you do that, you can't avoid leaving the mark on the blotting-paper. In the same way you can't avoid the scorch mark of the flash of a revolver if it is pressed against clothes or skin when it is fired."

Sir George tried the experiment himself. "Yes, I see," he said thoughtfully, "but need the revolver have been pressed against the body in this case? Could Mr Oissel not have held it away from himself when he fired?"

"It's just possible, though not likely, that there might be no scorch mark if a man was shooting himself through the mouth, as is usually done, but the heart is different. A man would want to feel where his heart was beating before he fired. He would have to press the gun against himself or it is very doubtful whether he would do the job properly. And that is another point, sir. Suicides don't shoot themselves in the body if they really mean to finish the job. It's too risky. The bullet may go anywhere, and they may just land themselves in hospital for a few weeks."

"And Mr Oissel was no stranger to a revolver, I should imagine."

"No, sir. From inquiries we have made he seems to have been a pretty tough lot in his younger days, and very handy with a gun. Though, of course, he has been a cripple since that time he was shot up so badly in Detroit."

"Would that affect his ability to shoot?"

"Oh, no, sir. As far as I can find out from his man, it was only in the legs that he was so badly crippled. He moved with very great difficulty."

"That would make it easier for some one else to shoot him, but who was there to do it?"

"That is the mystery, Sir George. Mr Oissel was alone in the room, Mr West says, when he and Mr Shaw and the waiter went in, the moment they heard the shot."

"Could anyone have got into the room between the time of the Home Secretary leaving and Mr West entering the room?"

"They could have got in easily enough, I should think. It was a busy night in the Harcourt room, lots of strangers about—any properly dressed person might have passed as a guest, but he couldn't have got out again without Mr West seeing him."

"Not by the windows?"

Inspector Blackitt smiled. "You know those windows on to the Terrace, sir. They're so narrow that it would be impossible for a man to squeeze through without attracting a great deal of attention. And it was fine at the time, and quite light. People were walking about on the Terrace. But in any case the windows were fastened on the inside, and you know what powerful hasps there are on them. No one could have got out that way and locked them after himself."

Sir George packed his pipe thoughtfully, and passed his pouch and a cigarette-box across to Blackitt, who took a cigarette. "Suppose some one went into the room after the Home Secretary had left, shot him, got away, and made a fake shot near by, so that that was the one that Mr West heard. Have you thought of that?" Inspector Blackitt was a well-trained man. He kept his face perfectly straight and even assumed a polite interest in so startling a theory.

"That ought to be considered as a possibility, sir. A quite ingenious theory, if I may say so, but there are one or two difficulties. No other shot was heard, and the sensation that this one made shows that it is unlikely another one could have passed unnoticed even at that crowded hour. I think there's no doubt that the shot Mr West heard was the shot that killed Mr Oissel."

"It was just a casual theory of mine. We all like to play at your job, Blackitt. But then who did fire the shot? The only person who was in the room and had a revolver—but, by the way, was it Mr Oissel's revolver?"

"Yes, sir. Daubisq has identified that. And it has Mr Oissel's initials engraved on it."

"Curious, that. And what about fingerprints?"

"The only ones are Mr Oissel's own and Mr West's."

"Mr West's?"

"He picked up the gun as it lay on the floor when he found the body. But his are very light fingermarks, not made with the pressure that would have been necessary to fire the gun. But of course gloves might have been worn by whoever fired it."

"But you don't believe it was suicide?"

"I do not, sir, not from the tests our experts have made."

"Then we can't leave it at that. The Government at any rate must know the truth or we should all be sitting on a mine that might go up at the most awkward moment. I trust to your experience and judgment in this matter, Blackitt. Now about the burglary at the flat. Jenks was lent to Mr Oissel as a personal bodyguard when he refused police protection. Why was he not with him at the House?"

"Mr Oissel seems to have been much more anxious about his papers than himself," said Blackitt, "and he disliked personal protection when away from home, even from Jenks. He went out very seldom, as far as I can find out, except on official business."

"Of course one can't say 'I told you so' to a dead man,

but——" and Sir George's tone conveyed his view of what he really thought about foreign visitors who wouldn't do as they were told by the perfect British police department and so got themselves into messes like this. Sir George remained silent for a while, leaning forward and tapping an inkwell with a pencil. Blackitt's eyes wandered round the big, sombre room. He had never seen this inner sanctum of High Authority before. Even to his professional eyes the room seemed gloomy. Huge books on the shelves proclaimed the majesty of the law in many thousands of pages. Sir George's desk seemed more like a monument than an article of furniture. The severely plain mantelpiece with its heavy slabs of white marble suggested the entry to a tomb rather than the appointed framework for a cheerful fire. But what interested him most was a printed form, with a black border, pasted on to cardboard, which was propped up on the mantelpiece.

In thick black type across the top was printed "Death Sentences." And there were seven names written on the lines beneath. Blackitt was professionally interested to see the other end of his work. He helped to track down criminals and hand them over to the law. The last stage but one of the process was the name of his captive neatly written on this card. It was one of the many duties of Sir George Gleeson to decide which of them should proceed to the last stage of all. With the pride of the good technician the Inspector began to wonder whether he would be able to add another one or perhaps two names to the list as a result of this case. Directly under Sir George, too. He was in luck.

Sir George ceased rapping with his pencil and turned to him.

"Well, I'm glad this matter is in your hands, Blackitt. Keep me informed at each stage. I'll see the Home Secretary, as

I said, and if he knows anything that is likely to help you I am sure he will be anxious to give you the facts."

"I had an appointment with the Home Secretary at twelve, sir."

"Oh, yes, you said so. I had forgotten. I had better relieve you of that. Perhaps he will see you later. When will the inquest be?"

"The day after to-morrow at twelve, sir."

"You will ask for an adjournment, of course?"

"Yes, sir. We shall only offer formal evidence then."

"Good, I'll see you before that. Probably later on to-day. Oh, by the way, you've got a guard on Room J?"

"I have given orders that it must not be left night or day, sir."

"Useful precaution. What are you going to do now?"

"If you are seeing the Home Secretary, sir, I think I will go to Mr Oissel's flat at Charlton Court for a short time. I haven't been able to go over the clues there yet, but I've put a good man in charge until I come."

"Very well, then. Good morning, and good luck."

"Thank you, sir." Inspector Blackitt's jaw set as he walked out into the corridor. The great Sir George had put the matter in his hands. He would show him. Promotion seemed very near to Inspector Blackitt just then.

CHAPTER V

Robert West walked sedately up the central staircase of the Home Office at ten-thirty on the morning after the crime, but in spirit he was bounding up three at a time, impatient to hear whether there was any further news. There seemed to be possibilities of a reasonably exciting time. All sorts of theories were jumbling together in his mind when he suddenly bumped into a man who was standing at the top of the staircase.

"I beg your pardon… oh, it's you, Kinnaird! Awfully sorry, I didn't see you. My mind was so full of last night."

"I don't wonder. I should apologize for waylaying you like this, but I was anxious to have a word with you before you went to your room."

"Of course." West leant against the stone balustrade. "Are you in on the great mystery, or have you called to assure us that no party capital is to be made out of the affair?"

"I'm hardly in a position to do that, am I?" smiled Kinnaird. "But what party capital can be made of it? Of course, it's most unfortunate, but every one will be very sympathetic to the Home Secretary."

"You're more of an optimist than a politician if you think that's all, Kinnaird. Anything you want me to do for you?"

"Well, I hope I shall be forgiven. I've taken a lady to your room."

"No more mysteries, Kinnaird, for heaven's sake! If *you* want to stage a murder or a suicide, plant it on the Ministry of Health. The poor old H.O. has had enough wished on it for one week."

"But the lady is Georges Oissel's granddaughter."

"Good Lord, Kinnaird, I can't stand a weeping woman on top of everything else! Besides, damn it all, why should I? I didn't murder the man, and I can't tell her who did."

Kinnaird looked at him quickly. "Murder? The papers all say it was suicide. Wasn't it?"

West could have kicked himself for the slip. "Of course it was suicide. Couldn't have been anything else. But by the time the police have finished with a fellow, he's nearly convinced that he did the deed himself. Why does the lady want to see me?"

"To be very frank, she doesn't. She wants to see the Home Secretary. She is a great friend of mine and I promised to help her in any way I could. You will see why when you meet her. But she isn't a tearful Madonna. You'd find her easier to deal with if she were."

With this not too hopeful description Kinnaird stood aside while West opened the door of his room, and then he said charmingly: "Annette, this is Mr Robert West."

West blinked his eyes as though some one had turned on an arc-light in his dingy little room. Women who could afford to spend £2000 a year on their clothes and pay a £300 salary to an expert dresser were not included among his acquaintances. Though dressed in black, Annette Oissel's elegance somehow gave the impression of brilliant colour. She did not rise at the introduction, but held out her hand. Bob bowed over it, and began rather nervously: "I offer my most sincere sympathy, Miss Oissel. I can't say how distressed we all are."

"Thank you, Mr West. I'm sure of it." Miss Oissel spoke with a French accent and a slightly American intonation. "A charming note from the Home Secretary was delivered to me this morning."

"Good. I'm glad the old boy thought of that," said West to himself, but privately he was a little annoyed that he had not had the pleasure of reminding his Chief of this duty. Aloud he said: "If there's anything I can do for you, please tell me."

"Thank you so much. I want to see the Home Secretary, alone if possible. Can you manage that for me? Mr Kinnaird says that it is very difficult to see a Minister just now."

"I'm sure the Home Secretary will be delighted." Robert took up the telephone receiver conscious that the best service that he could render his Chief was somehow to save him from this interview, but he did not see how that could be done. He got through to the Minister's personal secretary, and while waiting for a reply took the opportunity to study his visitor discreetly. No, she was not beautiful, as he had thought at first glance. Her face was too thin, her cheek-bones too high. But what *chic*! West did not know much about women's clothes, but he dimly realized the beauty and costliness of Annette Oissel's perfectly tailored black frock. She wore a cubist necklace of cut steel, of a design that was repeated in the clasp of her handbag and the buckles of her shoes. Her slim elegance from the tilt of her fashionably cocked hat to the tip of her unusual shoes made Robert wonder vaguely what one said to a woman like this.

The voice on the telephone called him. A rapid conversation, then Robert put down the receiver and turned to the lady. "The Home Secretary is in conference at the moment, but he will see you as soon as he can get away for a few minutes. You will understand the difficulty, I am sure, Miss Oissel."

"But of course. I am so grateful. A few minutes is all I want." She sat silent, looking down at her handbag.

West pulled himself together. If he were going to be useful to Blackitt he had better start now and take the opportunity of getting some first-hand information while he had before him the only person who could give it. He wished she had come alone. It might be awkward if one found out too much with Kinnaird sitting there. Curious that she should be so quiet. How had Oissel's death affected her? She would be the old man's heiress most probably. Was she upset by his death? Why did she not question him, the man who had first seen her grandfather dead. Of course she must know that. It had been in all the papers—photos of himself too. He must break the ice.

"Forgive my asking you, Miss Oissel," he began rather nervously. "You did not live with your grandfather?"

"Oh, no, I have a flat of my own in Clarges Street."

"I don't want to seem to butt in, Miss Oissel, between you and the Home Secretary, I mean—but as his Parliamentary secretary and as one of the chief witnesses I have rather a special interest."

"Of course, West, we realize that," Kinnaird interrupted.

West noted the 'we.' Annette said nothing; her attention remained fixed on the clasp of her handbag.

"Well, er, what I mean to say is this. You realize, Miss Oissel, as I know you do, Kinnaird, that Mr Oissel's death under such circumstances may cause the deuce of a mess all round."

Kinnaird murmured something sympathetic, but Annette remained silent.

"Confound the woman, she might help a fellow out," thought Robert. He determined on a direct question to her. "Will you help us to find out the truth?"

"About what do you want to know the truth?" Annette spoke at last although she did not raise her eyes.

West temporized. "Er, well, about the burglary at the flat for a beginning."

"The burglary at my grandfather's flat? How can I know anything about that? Surely your police are going to find the burglars?"

"Of course they will do their best, but we are all so in the dark about what I might call the background of the whole business. That is the most important thing at the moment. Can you throw any light on any reason your grandfather might have had for committing suicide last night?"

Then Annette looked up, and Robert realized why he had thought her beautiful. Her eyes, large, clear dark blue, were in startling contrast to the rather severe moulding of her oval face. They made her human, warm even. "My grandfather did not commit suicide, Mr West."

Robert was startled by the quiet assurance of her tone. Unless Blackitt had had his interview even the Home Secretary would not yet know that the police had any doubts about Oissel having killed himself. Yet Annette calmly stated it as a fact she knew, and about which there could be no argument.

"Then how did he die, Miss Oissel? I can assure you there was no one in the room when Mr Shaw and I dashed in."

"I don't know how he died," said Annette. "But I want to see the Home Secretary to tell him that it could not have been suicide, whatever the papers say, and he must find out who did it."

Then Annette looked up at him again with the odd power

of her dark blue eyes. "Do *you* honestly believe it was suicide, Mr West?"

Knowing what he did, Robert couldn't say yes. To say "No" might hamper the police and would certainly annoy Blackitt. Hesitation would give her at least room for doubt. He plunged. "Honestly I see no other solution, Miss Oissel, but the police must find out what they can, and you will help, won't you?"

"Certainly, if I can, but how?"

"Well, why are you so sure he did not commit suicide?"

"Because he had a love of life amounting to a mania, Mr West. He was attacked and badly wounded by gangsters at Detroit and nearly died. When he got better he was crippled for life. He spent thousands every year in keeping as fit as he could. He had endowed a research institution on rejuvenation and was going to start treatment in August. I was to go with him. He was terribly excited about it. I know he wouldn't take his life just now."

"But perhaps there were reasons you don't know, Miss Oissel. The crash of the markets has broken men nearly as big as he——"

"But the crash did not break him. He was right in the inside. I know he helped to bring about one of the breaks, and he made millions. I know more of his affairs than anyone. I say it is quite inconceivable that he should have taken his life himself. Quite impossible."

The girl did not raise her voice or hurry her words in excitement. She spoke so quietly and definitely that West realized that Kinnaird had spoken truly when he said they would have to deal with no weeping Madonna. Here was a determined young woman, trained in a business atmosphere and immensely self-assured. If she had inherited the whole of the Oissel fortune in addition, the British Government would have to reckon with a very formidable enemy if they did not please her.

A secretary arrived to conduct Annette to the Home Secretary's room. When the door closed behind her Kinnaird turned to West and said: "Well?"

Robert whistled. "I say, Kinnaird, what a handful if she's out to make trouble—" and he whistled again. Then checking himself he said: "But I forgot—you're a special friend of hers, aren't you?"

Kinnaird smiled. "I hope to be something more soon."

"Really! I say! You are in luck. The Oissel heiress—and in dollars! You won't need to form up in a bread queue even if the pound goes down to blazes."

"But I'd be in love with Annette even if she hadn't a sou."

"I'm sorry," said West, going rather red. "I'm the rudest blighter! I didn't mean——"

"Of course not, and I'm not going to deny that dollars are likely to be useful in Britain for a bit. Have a cigarette?"

The case was a lovely gold thing with a cubist design in enamel.

"Seems like Miss Oissel somehow."

"She gave it to me," replied Kinnaird.

As West smoked, he found himself wondering what it would be like to be the lover of Annette Oissel. She seemed so spiky, somehow, with her cubist ornaments, her thinness, and her elegance. Yet those deep blue eyes… they made her seem human, a woman who could be loved. But under those long lashes one didn't see much of Annette's eyes.

"Kinnaird," he said suddenly, "forgive my asking, but did old Oissel know you wanted to marry her? I mean, was he all right about it?"

Kinnaird flicked the ash from his cigarette. "He knew, of course. I had formally asked him, but he wanted her to marry a title, a French marquis—old family. He was very keen about it because his father had been a peasant on the estates of this family and you can imagine his desire for such a climax."

"And she didn't fall in with his plans?"

"Most emphatically she did not. She met the Marquis once and that was enough. A nasty little degenerate, and there was nothing doing."

"Oissel was angry, I suppose?"

"Yes and no. He was devoted to Annette and never more so than when she defied him. She knew how to do it the way he liked. I think he was getting used to the idea of having me for a son-in-law."

"Do you think Miss Oissel is right about the suicide?"

Kinnaird shrugged his shoulders. "Annette didn't know all there was to know about the old man, not by a long way. He dreaded her finding out about some of his less reputable side-lines. Oissel was a tough customer, West."

"So I've gathered. Good many enemies too, I should say?"

"Less than there might have been if so many hadn't died first," said Kinnaird grimly.

West remembered Shaw's remarks about the Regal Irak shares and whistled characteristically.

The door opened. It was Annette. The two men rose. West wondered what had happened at the interview with his Chief. But the girl was perfectly composed. Robert felt irritated. A woman with eyes like Annette's ought not to pose as a marble statue of a Madonna. Quite irrationally he wanted to shake her, to break through her defences, to assert in some way his sheer masculine superiority. Angry with himself, he yet found himself rapidly thinking of some way to impress her, to ruffle this cool indifference.

Besides, it was important not to lose touch. This girl could give information about Oissel that no one else could. It was all-important to have her as an ally.

"I mustn't keep you from your work, Mr West. Thank you very much for your help."

Robert held her proffered hand for a moment. "I want to be of a great deal more use in this matter, Miss Oissel. Believe me, we are as anxious to find the truth as you are. But if we are in difficulties about details, would you mind if I phoned you, perhaps later to-day?"

"Not at all. Please do. Any time."

Then she added: "So long as you understand that my grandfather did not commit suicide whatever the police may say."

"Then Blackitt hasn't seen the Chief yet," thought Robert as he bowed his visitors out of the room.

He returned to his desk and tried to think things out. Why was Annette so sure her grandfather had not committed suicide? Why was she so anxious to impress that on the Home Office. She had made this early visit with apparently no other object. Had she some inkling as to who the murderers might be, and was she afraid they might go unpunished if the police accepted the convenient suicide theory? Then suddenly Robert kicked himself for a fool. He had just mentioned the burglary at Mr Oissel's flat, but had not asked her one question about it. Damn those lovely dark blue eyes—they had flustered him completely. But obviously he must see her again and quickly. He ought to be able to get details from her about the atmosphere and the visitors at Charlton Court which she would not be willing to tell the police. Yes, decidedly he must see Annette very soon.

The telephone bell rang. "Could Mr West come to the Home Secretary's room immediately and accompany him to the House of Commons?"

"What's in the wind now?" said Robert to himself as he picked up his grey felt hat.

CHAPTER VI

It was nearly lunch-time before Sir George Gleeson was able to have a private talk with his political Chief. He was angry that the Minister should have agreed to see Annette Oissel alone, an unprecedented action. No Minister ever sees any visitor without an official nurse in attendance. It is recorded that a recent Home Secretary, after laying down office, remarked to his wife, "How nice to be able to talk to you, my dear, without having the minutes taken by a secretary."

When at last they were alone together the Minister and his chief civil servant settled down to their usual tug-of-war. The relations of Ministers with their civil heads in England follow one of two well-trodden paths. If the political chief has acquired an inferiority complex, as a result of years of explaining away his actions to a critical electorate and being anxiously amiable to his leaders lest he may be left off the list when posts are being considered, then he thankfully recognizes the domination of whatever variety of Sir George Gleeson is in charge of his department, and spends his ministerial time meekly repeating the lessons his chief civil servant carefully teaches him.

But if the Minister has won his place in the Cabinet by doing the dominating himself, he starts on his career with the determination to stand no nonsense from his civil servants. It takes his staff about six months—sometimes less—to reduce him to apologetic pulp. The Civil Service has its own ways of withdrawing an expected prop at unexpected moments.

But sometimes the Sir George Gleesons meet their match. Either they have a Minister with a mental equipment they can respect and work with, or they find, as our Sir George Gleeson was finding, a Minister whose immovable obstinacy positively frightens them. After all, the civil servant's main interest is the regard which is paid to his 'show' by the heads of other departments. With a Minister he cannot dominate, and who is not intelligent enough for skilled co-operation, yet is determined on playing the part he imagines a Cabinet Minister ought to play, and is thus likely to let down the department at any moment, the world is at its worst for a Civil Service chief. Sir George Gleeson had been discovering this painful fact for the last two years.

The Home Secretary, perfectly groomed as usual, received his chief permanent official with a grave air suitable to the occasion, but as a man properly concerned with the tragic death of an old friend rather than a politician worried by what might be a serious international affair. Indeed, he seemed much more concerned about the burglary and the death of Edward Jenks than about Georges Oissel.

"Let's leave the burglary for the moment," said Sir George impatiently. "The police have got that well in hand. Blackitt is down there, and I will let you have his report as soon as I get it. But we must face up to the death of Mr Oissel. I've sent a formal report and your regrets to the American Embassy, but we will have to follow that up with a full report, and there are some damned awkward questions sent in already as private notice questions."

A private notice question can cause more flutter in the Civil Service than any other of the few instruments of torture left in the hands of back-bench Members. Ordinary Parliamentary questions to a Minister have to be on the order paper in time to give the department at least forty-eight hours in which to concoct a reply. On a matter of urgency, with the Speaker's permission, the question can be sent in to the department only a few hours before it has to be answered. And answered it must be, or a very awkward Parliamentary situation arises, for the House and the Press naturally pay much more attention to private notice questions than to the routine variety.

The Minister made an impatient movement. Questions— of course there would be questions. There were always the insignificant fools who wanted to get their names in the papers, who would jump in at any occurrence that got into the Press. But the House of Commons as a whole was a sensible assembly. Obviously he couldn't help it if his guest committed suicide. Oissel's revolver was beside him as clear proof of what had happened.

Gleeson, who had kept the information for the purpose of puncturing the Minister's hide-bound self-confidence, said quietly:

"The police have very grave reasons to doubt the suicide theory."

The Home Secretary stared. "But what nonsense! There was the revolver—a shot had been fired from it, I suppose?"

"Oh, yes."

"Well, then, what's the difficulty?"

Sir George Gleeson repeated in great detail the reasons Blackitt had given him for doubting the suicide theory. He took particular pleasure in demonstrating the matchbox proof. Like all men who work entirely with their heads, Gleeson was immensely impressed with any little practical experiment.

The Home Secretary was impressed too. If the expert men at Scotland Yard had decided it was not suicide they were pretty certain to be right. "Damned awkward, Gleeson," he said.

"Very."

There was a certain directness about the Minister.

"If Oissel did not die by his own hand," he said, "then the means by which he died are in that room, if, as you say, it has never been left since West found him dead. Call West, and we'll go over and see the place for ourselves."

Robert West, in silence, accompanied the Minister and Sir George Gleeson across to the House. A group of reporters, who had kept watch on the door in the hope of catching West, as being softer game than his Minister, glanced with curiosity at the three set faces and followed at a discreet distance. Robert couldn't help admiring his Minister, whose whole demeanour gave no hint of undue worry. "There's nothing like having a presence at times like this," he thought irreverently. "It's all rot keeping down one's waistline, really. A politician is taken much more seriously if he has a substantial middle."

At the fateful Room J the policeman on guard saluted. Inside, another constable was seated. He sprang to attention and assured Sir George that under Inspector Blackitt's orders the room had never been left for an instant.

In the sunlight of a June morning the room looked oddly untidy. The flowers were wilting on the table. A half-peeled pear was still on the plate Oissel had been using. The windows were tightly shut, and the air of the room was hot and heavy.

"Rotten job a policeman has," thought Robert. "We just shove him into a hole like this and keep him there for hours on his own."

The Minister stood in the middle of the room, grimly surveying the table at which so recently he had been placidly talking business with Oissel. Then with determination he started on a tour of the room, asking questions of Sergeant Bourne, who had hurried to them on being told that the Minister and Sir George Gleeson had arrived, after first, with great presence of mind, telephoning for Inspector Blackitt.

Were there any secret panels? It was known that the place was riddled with strange holes due to the idiotic ventilation system. The sergeant assured him that every panel had been examined. The only two hollow ones were those that concealed certain lighting switches—a tiny box and a cupboard that held glassware. Bourne admitted that the police were a little hampered by the fact that it was not known just how Mr Oissel was sitting at the time, because the body had fallen to the floor after the shot. Robert repeated his story over and over again to impatient questions by the Minister and intelligent inquiries from Sir George. But it was hopeless. They searched every nook and cranny, but the facts would not fit together. If there was no one in the room when the shot was fired, and the last person to see Georges Oissel alive was the Home Secretary, and the police had grave reasons for doubting any theory of suicide, then what had happened in the ten minutes between the Home Secretary leaving for the division lobby and Robert West hearing the shot?

The Minister sat down heavily at the head of the table near the door, where he had sat that night opposite to his guest.

"You were right, Gleeson. This is going to be an extremely awkward business. I think we ought to see Blackitt while we are here."

"I took the liberty of telephoning for him when you arrived, sir," said the sergeant deferentially. "He should be here any minute."

Blackitt came while the Minister was still meditating over the untidy table.

"Of course we can't... er... keep to ourselves the fact that... er... well, the fact that suicide cannot be proved." The Minister's voice was reflective, almost hopeful.

"Well, sir, that was what I wanted to consult you and Sir George about," answered Blackitt. "We needn't say anything at the inquest about our doubts, especially as we are only going to give formal evidence and ask for an adjournment. Of course, if the police said nothing the verdict would be suicide, sure enough—but——" and the Inspector looked for guidance to Gleeson.

Sir George made an impatient gesture with his hand. "That's nonsense, Blackitt. The facts are bound to come out under cross-examination. First thing the Oissel solicitor would ask."

The Home Secretary was pulling the lobe of one ear, and it was obvious that he was thinking at that moment that the boasted incorruptibility of the British Civil Service could be a little overdone at times. "Of course, of course," he said, after a moment's interval, "we couldn't think of such a thing."

"All the same, we'd better give the police a breathing-space," said Sir George, "and as the inquest will be adjourned—it's to-morrow at twelve, you said, Blackitt?—the more non-committal the answers in the House this afternoon the better."

"They will be hot on the loan negotiations, I expect," said the Minister.

"Loans are safer Parliamentary fodder than murders,"

smiled Sir George. "Then you've no further news from Charlton Court, Blackitt?"

"Nothing much yet, sir. When Daubisq came round after the doping he'd had he couldn't add much. Jenks had gone out to get the late sporting editions. There had been a ring at the door. Daubisq assumed that Jenks had forgotten his keys and went to open it. He isn't quite sure whether there were two or three men there. Anyway they threw something over his head, and when he came round Jenks was dead, as we know, and our men were in charge of the flat."

"Were any papers found on Jenks?"

"Just private papers, letters, some photographs, a wallet, a diary, just oddments like that, and some money. I suppose it would be best to keep the papers for the time being, but we might send the money to his wife, sir?" Blackitt glanced at Sir George.

"Jenks wasn't married. Send it to his mother. I am sending her some money also," said the Minister. "The papers are all listed, Blackitt?"

"Yes, sir."

"A great pity about Jenks. I thought a great deal of him, Gleeson."

"I know you did. It's a shame he should have been shot like that. Thanks, Blackitt, we needn't keep you and Bourne any longer just now."

When the two officers had left the room the Minister said gloomily: "He was a first-rate man, and not easily replaceable. I wish I'd insisted on Oissel having the ordinary Yard detectives, but he made such a fuss about them that I thought I was doing the best thing in easing the negotiations by pleasing him. And he certainly took to Jenks. They became great friends."

Sir George felt the Minister's emotion and bit his lip to prevent him saying: "This is the sort of thing that happens when you *will* go outside official regulations." The Minister had consulted him about Jenks going to Oissel in the first place, so it was difficult to say "I told you so" now. But he wanted to find out more about the negotiations that had preceded Oissel's death.

The Minister had been like an oyster about them all through. Of course, it was Treasury business, but when trouble comes to the Home Secretary the Home Office has to clean it up.

The Minister rose.

"That seems all we can do for the moment, then. Send me the answers to the private notice questions as soon as they are ready. I'll have lunch in my room."

"Very well. And I'll send your boxes over too, shall I?"

These red dispatch-boxes full of papers to be read and minutes to be initialled follow a Minister every hour of his day, almost into his bathroom. "Please." Then he turned to West, who had stood silent all this time. "Come up to my room, Robert, will you? I'd like to have a talk with you."

West followed his Minister from the room.

Gleeson was annoyed. "Damn these Parliamentary private secretaries," he said to himself. "The Minister will tell all he knows under pledge of confidence to that lad, instead of trusting me, and God knows when we shall be blown out of the water by some unexpected move. Heaven send me a Minister who has sense to trust his officials." Gleeson then suddenly realized that he was glowering fiercely at an innocent constable who was uncomfortably standing against the wall. The haughty civil servant managed a reassuring smile and said: "You will be sure that no person enters here under any pretext whatever, except Inspector Blackitt and myself."

Sergeant Bourne hurried forward as Sir George walked into the corridor and Gleeson repeated his orders to him.

"Certainly, sir," said the sergeant.

No, that really wouldn't do. Gleeson realized he couldn't checkmate West as obviously as that.

"Except of course the Minister and—er, Mr West."

"Yes, sir."

"But if Mr West comes alone, see that I am apprised of that fact by telephone."

"Very good, sir."

"Whatever orders you are given by anyone—you understand, *anyone* except Inspector Blackitt and myself—this room is not to be left without a police guard."

"Very good, sir." The sergeant saluted very respectfully as a man who knows who is the real power in the land.

CHAPTER VII

The lobbies of the House of Commons were buzzing with excitement when Robert West came down from the Home Secretary's room at half-past two. The quarter of an hour between two-thirty and two-forty-five when the House meets is always interesting even on the quietest days. Visitors are allowed into the square hall called the Members' Lobby, and there they form two sides of a square to watch the Speaker's procession. The cry "Speaker. Hats off, strangers!" echoes along the corridors, and down the main lobby comes a little procession inspiring awe in the stranger by its simple dignity. A small affair—the Sergeant-at-Arms with the enormous gilt (but hollow) mace over his shoulder; the Speaker, tall, dignified in a grey wig and a long black gown with its train held up by a little man in black Court uniform; a secretary, the chaplain, two stalwart messengers, and that is all.

But it is sufficient to bring home to the watching public and even to blasé M.P.s themselves that the Speaker is the symbol of the power of the Commons, and that a glance from the Speaker's eye secures the rights of Members to hear and be heard.

To-day the crowd was much larger than usual. The newspaper headlines had caused a great sensation. Even a Member dropping dead in the House of Commons, as has happened several times, is a considerable news item, but a suicide—and of such a man—in the centre of critical negotiations was nearly enough to please even a news editor.

Already some papers were beginning to question the suicide theory. Annette Oissel had been interviewed for the lunch-hour editions. Characteristically she had said nothing to the reporters except "My grandfather did not commit suicide," but that was sufficient for a Press sensation.

The reputed size of the fortune to which she was the presumed heiress and her refusal to make any other remark only added salt to her words.

In the division lobbies at either side of the debating chamber M.P.s in groups were discussing the situation. As they surrounded him, West almost regretted his decision to come down. But one of the most important duties of a P.P.S. is to 'sense the atmosphere' of the House for his Chief, and it was specially important for the Government at this moment to know what was being said. West felt that the decision to hold back, however temporarily, the evidence against the death being by suicide was a profound mistake. Why did Governments and the Civil Service invariably lay up unnecessary trouble for themselves by this determined secrecy about everything?

The evidence was bound to come out. Why not anticipate gossip and avoid misunderstanding by saying all they knew quite frankly? But he had been warned he must say nothing about it, and so as he entered the division lobby he felt like an unarmed Christian being thrown to some gorgeously hungry lions.

Questions poured upon him:

"What's your Chief been up to?"

"Why was he in the loan negotiations?"

"What did he say to Oissel to make him commit suicide?"

"What will America say?"

"Is it suicide?"

"Annette Oissel says it isn't."

Robert tried to parry all these questions by the method of starting to answer one, then turning on to another before he had committed himself. The man he dreaded was Michael Houldsworth, a young Socialist from Lancashire with eyes as keen as a hawk's. He was standing by West's side waiting for the hubbub to fall a little. When it did, he said in clear tones:

"It wasn't suicide, West, and you know it." There was silence. West hated Houldsworth at that moment. The crowd of M.P.s waited. He couldn't ride away now in the general excitement, and Houldsworth knew that.

West's temper rose. "If it wasn't suicide," he said hotly, "it was an act of God, for there seem to be no other means by which he could have died."

Houldsworth smiled grimly.

"Is your Chief going to invoke the Deity when he answers my private notice question?"

West was saved from a further retort by the cry of "Speaker at prayers" which rang through the corridors in the deep musical voices of the House messengers.

Just for three minutes' peace Bob slipped into prayers, at which he was a very infrequent attendant.

A hush was on the House. All the galleries except the Ladies' Gallery far away in the roof are kept empty for the simple daily ritual. M.P.s stand at their benches, and the quiet voice of the chaplain intones the service. At the prayers the Members turn their faces to the wall. "Prevent us, O Lord, by Thy mighty power… that we, putting aside all private interests, prejudices, and partial affections…"

West usually smiled to think how much that petition was needed in such an assembly, but this afternoon he was thinking of Annette.

Prayers were over. Members who had remained outside the doors of the chamber until they were informed of that fact crowded into their seats. Questions began.

As always, they ranged over a bewildering variety of subjects. Why had some natives been shot in the Andaman Islands? Why had a pension been refused Mrs Smith? Why were the lockers in H.M.S. *Rochester* no longer heated?

Gracie Richards had a private little battle with the Home Secretary about a woman whom she considered had been wrongfully imprisoned as a prostitute. At any other time, West would have been keenly on her side. Her heavy dark straight hair, framing a warm, almost Southern olive complexion, and her bright black eyes made a picture well worth looking at in such a depressingly male assembly.

Robert usually got considerable amusement out of the fact that he was secretly on friendly terms with this young rebel, though to the world outside the House he appeared as her relentless critic in a neighbouring constituency. But to-day Gracie failed to excite him. He had an appointment with Annette when questions were over.

He had telephoned to ask her to tea on the Terrace to talk things over. It was daring under the circumstances, but the conventions of mourning did not seem to trouble Annette. She had agreed at once.

The private notice questions were coming on. He wanted to get them over. Impatiently, and for the first time, he wished Gracie were less aggressive. Why couldn't she let the matter rest? Why worry at it like a terrier with a rat? Why worry anyway about this imprisoned trollop when women like Annette——? Here Bob pulled himself up, told himself he was a fool, and tried to take some interest in what was being said.

Miss Richards was silenced but not appeased when the clock showed a quarter to four. At this time the questions on the order paper end, however few or many are left to be answered. The private notice questions, if there are any, begin. They always provide a thrill, because this method of asking questions can only be used for really grave and urgent matters. Members settle themselves for the choice bit of the day.

Michael Houldsworth stood up in his place high on the fourth bench, and his Lancashire accent emphasized the prescribed formula. "May I ask the Home Secretary a question of which I have given him private notice? Can he make any statement to the House about the death of Mr Georges Oissel in this House last evening?"

The House went deadly quiet. The Home Secretary rose. In firm but colourless tones he read the answer Sir George Gleeson had supplied. "I regret to have to inform the House that Mr Georges Oissel, with whom, as is well known, the Government were conducting important negotiations, and who was with me last night at a friendly and informal dinner, was found dead by a Member of this House some minutes after I had left him to vote in the division on the finance bill. The police are investigating the matter. His Majesty's Government wish to place on record their profound sorrow at the occurrence and their deep sympathy with the relatives, which I have already had the honour to communicate to them."

The official voice ceased. A murmur went round the House. The Home Secretary took off his glasses. "I may perhaps be permitted a personal word. Mr Georges Oissel was an old friend of mine. His death, so unexpected, in the middle of a friendly discussion has come to me as a profound shock. I would like to add an expression of my personal sorrow to the words I have just read."

This time the murmuring was definitely sympathetic. The House loves a personal touch. It will forgive almost anything if such an explanation is tactfully made. Michael Houldsworth was not impressed. Both Front Benches dreaded to see him on the warpath, just because he remained completely unmoved by the considerations which usually influence that rather sentimental assembly. Gracie moved to the seat next to Houldsworth and was apparently encouraging him.

"Has the Home Secretary seen the statement by Miss Oissel that she is convinced her grandfather did not commit suicide, and has he any reason to doubt the official police theory that it was suicide?"

It was a cleverly phrased question, not so direct in attack as to rouse sympathy for the Minister, but enough to put doubt in the public mind.

"I have seen Miss Oissel's statement. I may say I have seen Miss Oissel herself. I can only assure the House that every theory will be carefully examined, and that the most skilled attention of Scotland Yard is being concentrated both on the death of Mr Oissel and the burglary at his flat which seems to have taken place at approximately the same time." A chorus of "Hear, hears" from the Government benches greeted this remark. To West's relief Houldsworth did not rise to put any further questions. He was obviously going to make trouble, but they were over the first hurdle. Now for Annette.

So intent was he in pushing his way out through the crowd of Members also moving tea-ward, leaving a very thinly attended House behind them, that he did not notice Grace Richards put out her hand to attract his attention.

But Houldsworth noticed. "Have some tea with me, Gracie, and let's chew the mystery," he said.

"Yes, let's. I'd love to," said Grace Richards with an annoyed glance at Robert's back. She was accustomed to find Robert eagerly seeking her at the tea-hour.

West was not in the mood to be deterred by any more M.P.s wanting news. The worst was over for the moment. He went down the corridor where only last night he had looked for Don Shaw. This time his quest was for Annette. As befitted her importance she was not out in the crowd in the Strangers' Lobby, but sitting on one of the benches in the corridor, a privilege only allowed by the attendants to those known to be 'somebody.'

Seated there under the glances of the curious (for any person of special interest is always pointed out to visitors by the all-knowing policeman) Annette certainly looked 'somebody.' The smart black woollen dress of the morning had been changed for one of rich dull satin that moulded the angular lines of her lanky limbs. Robert, quite aware of the sensation they were causing, led her to a table on the Terrace he had booked for the two of them.

The Terrace of the House of Commons on a warm June afternoon is one of the liveliest sights in London. Groups of earnest and self-conscious constituents are given tea by their equally earnest Members. Less conscientious M.P.s decorate their tables with a pretty girl or two. The very dutiful sit surrounded by relatives and try to look impressive. Up and down walk the political bigwigs at exercise. No one could deduce from their noble aloofness that they are aware of every nudge, every whispered "That's Mr So-and-so." A politician has to reach very great eminence and the fullness of many years before he really avoids the Terrace in the height of the season. Robert was quite aware of the whispers that followed his dignified progress with Annette Oissel, but he was annoyed to find Grace Richards, his usual tea companion, in earnest conversation with Michael Houldsworth. She smiled up at him as he passed. He hesitated for a second and then did not introduce Annette.

After all, he could tell Gracie afterwards that Miss Oissel had come to talk business, and her mourning obviously excused the ordinary politenesses. But he knew that he did not want the two girls to meet. His bringing Annette to the Terrace at all was a gesture of political bravado, and now she was here he hardly knew what to say. He was tempted to tell her about the police evidence—tempted because he wanted somehow to raise interest in himself, but Annette, alone, was fortunately much more approachable than when she had met him earlier in the morning accompanied by Kinnaird.

"I have seen the lawyers, and we have been through my grandfather's papers," she said after they had talked generalities for a time. She accepted the tea he poured out, having neglected to do anything about it for herself. "Anything much missing?" asked Robert, struggling with the hot handle.

"Well, it's difficult to say. I don't know all that he had, of course. One thing worries me—the loss of a notebook he always carried when he was conducting business negotiations."

"You've told the police about that, of course."

Annette made an impatient gesture. "I tell the police as little as possible. I trust them as little as my grandfather did."

"This is not America, you know." Robert smiled as he passed the bread-and-butter.

"I care not. Police are police the world over. I came to you. You are a politician. You are discreet."

Robert bowed. "I'm glad I've earned that favourable opinion so soon." He loved watching Annette—so quiet and still, yet so exquisite were her hands. He wanted her to put lots of sugar into his tea so that he might watch the curl of her small white fingers over the sugar-tongs, but instead he had himself to ladle it in.

Annette was silent again. Then she said quietly: "I want you to help me to find that notebook without telling the police either of its loss or of its importance."

"But really, Miss Oissel," Robert protested, "the police can't work in the dark. Why not tell them?"

"Because if the book has gone it has gone, and it is better that whoever has it should not know that we attach any special importance to it."

"If you feel like that, then I will help. Can you tell me what it was like?"

"Quite small, quite shabby—a black leather book. The entries are in cipher. If the thieves can find the key to the cipher it will be very serious. If not—then the less said, I think, the better."

"But that might be a very important clue," said West. "If we could find out the people who might know the cipher…"

"No one knew the cipher. Grandpère once told me that he and a friend had made it up together many years ago."

"Then that friend… do you know who he was?"

"No, probably he isn't alive now. I never asked my grandfather any questions. That is why I was the only person he could endure to have near him for long, except Pierre of course. I never showed the faintest interest in his affairs, or felt any."

"Could anything interest you?" asked Robert. He badly wanted to bring the conversation round to something more personal than the affairs of Georges Oissel.

"I suppose I should not show it if anything did," Annette answered with her slow smile. "I have lived for twenty years with my grandfather, Mr West. That is good training, believe me."

She rose, and West collected her gloves and handbag for her. Training, yes, but for what? Why were the Oissels so secretive? Had they had things to hide even from each other? Was Annette hiding something now, or was she trying in some oblique way to give him hints—she who had been so determined that the police should not conclude that her grandfather died by his own hand? As he piloted her through the lane between the crowded tables Robert felt more interest in this woman than in any human being he had ever met. So absorbed in her was he that he did not even remember to smile at Grace Richards as they passed her table.

CHAPTER VIII

The Members' cloakroom is one of those quiet places for intimate gossip in the House of Commons where a whispered word may sometimes have more effect than an hour's speech thundered in the debating chamber. Coat and hat pegs line one side of an L-shaped corridor in the oldest part of the building. At one end is a small room without a door. It is the place where the death-warrant of Charles the First was signed. A good few invisible signatures ending other reputations have been affixed by the gossip in the cloakroom. Its genie is a tubby man who sells matches, cigarettes, Parliamentary gazettes, and other little things which help to make M.P.s happy.

Colonel Stuart-Orford was coming out of the cloakroom as Robert passed on his way back to the Members' Lobby after seeing Annette to her car.

"Could I have a word with you, Robert?"

With an irritated mental shrug, but an outwardly polite "Certainly," Robert followed the Colonel back into the cloakroom, and propped himself against the antique weighing-machine that has told the sad truth to generations of increasing statesmen. Colonel Stuart-Orford was the representative of too much that was typical of his party for a Parliamentary private secretary to ignore him.

Stuart-Orford was county and country, the Army and the Great British Tradition.

"I am concerned about the *affaire* Oissel, Robert."

"So are we all, Colonel, I can assure you. The Minister more than any of us."

"I am not particularly concerned about the death of this man. It might be a useful sanitary measure if a few of his kind were put against a wall. But it seems to me as though the Government has actually put itself in the power of men like that. I don't like it, Robert. I do not like it. Imagine what Palmerston or Disraeli would have said at the idea of Britain going cap in hand to such a creature for money... the British Government... damn it, Robert, was this why we fought the War?"

"I was at school when you were fighting that war, Colonel, and I supposed that you all knew what you were doing, but it's left a pretty mess to be cleared up. And the England it has left is not the England of Palmerston and Victoria. We've got to deal with the facts, and American dollars are about the biggest of those facts. We've got to have them, so it's no use getting high and mighty about it."

"Let the Socialists talk like that," said Stuart-Orford furiously, his white moustaches standing out against a face gone suddenly red. "I tell you our party ought to have been prepared to ask every Briton, yes, every Briton from Court to slum, to give the shirt off his back rather than be beholden to such a creature."

West felt sorry for the old man, his fierce pride, and his patriotism that could only see a little island leading the world. The new age was hard for the Stuart-Orfords. He tried to be comforting.

"Americans are God's creatures, you know," he said flippantly, "even if you do think the Almighty might have been better employed than in making such a continent. And we've got to live with them. The whole world is about as small as Britain was in Palmerston's time. Communications, I mean, getting together. Of course America's got most of the gold there is, more or less, and will soon have the rest, but after all, Colonel, it's not the first time men like you have had to deal with the City chap who has bought the old park next to yours. You rope him in somehow, and that is what we have had to do with Oissel and his crowd."

West left the old man muttering that even the Conservative youth was Socialist nowadays. It was useless to argue. Robert knew he spoke a different language from the Stuart-Orfords. The New York of jazz and dollars was, he felt, much nearer to him than Victorian sofa-cushions. But why would these old men whine like ladies in reduced circumstances, like genteel governesses always talking about the glories of the old families, and refuse to face the facts of the world they were living in? They hung on to the rope, jealous that the ship should sail on new adventures.

As he pushed through the swing door into the buzz and light of the central lobby, Sancroft, who had been talking with a group of fellow-journalists, hailed him. "Blackitt is wanting you. He's out in the Strangers' Lobby. I said I'd tell you."

"I'll see him at once."

"Let me come too. If it's all too private I'll take the hint, but you promised I should be in on this, you know."

"It depends on Blackitt, of course. I'd like to have you there. We must get some sort of a move on, or there's going to be trouble. Houldsworth is getting his teeth in."

"I know… and don't neglect Madam Gracie too ostentatiously," warned Sancroft, who had been on the Terrace earlier in the afternoon.

West collected Blackitt, and the three men went downstairs to the smoking-room, that large drab room with its tiled walls and leather benches that might have served as the model for the first-class railway waiting-room in any large British station. Crowded, full of smoke, it represented a familiar and snug haven to many M.P.s rather bewildered by the strange place to which their electors had sent them.

"It's the best I can offer for a talk, Blackitt," said West apologetically as he ordered drinks. "The Home Secretary is in his room, so we can't talk there, and in this whole place there isn't a quiet corner for a chat."

But they were left alone in their corner by the window. Crowded on each other as they are, with no proper facilities for work or consultation, M.P.s out of desperation have evolved a certain technique of solitude. An earnestly talking group is usually left to itself.

Blackitt pulled at his pipe. Amid all this coming and going he found it hard to concentrate as easily as West and Sancroft, to whom it was the *milieu* in which all their work had to be done.

"We got over the first hurdle in the House to-day all right," said West, "but the possibilities of trouble are there, and they may come from our own side as much as from the Opposition. Have you got any clues as to the burglars yet which will throw any light on Oissel's death?"

"I've got bits, just bits and pieces, as I'll tell you, Mr West. But they don't fit together. I haven't got the picture. And that's where I want you to help me. I can't go direct to the Home Secretary yet, but if you will give me something to go on I may be able to fit together enough to be worth taking to him. You know that anything you tell me will be safe enough, if it has to be dropped later."

"I know that, so fire away."

"Well, sir, we've got to get back to this dinner and the reasons behind it. The Home Secretary insists that it was just a personal affair, a little courtesy that would always be offered when negotiations of this kind were in progress—and that's all right, of course, if it wasn't that Oissel has never accepted a social engagement of any kind for the last ten years, his man tells me. Well, you must admit that it's a bit of a coincidence that the very first time he breaks that rule he gets shot and his flat is burgled."

"I can put you right as far as the Home Secretary is concerned. I had a talk with him this morning. The negotiations were at a very delicate stage. The Government wanted the loan rather more urgently than they are prepared to admit publicly. The terms were stiff, and included several objectionable provisos. I don't know what those were. The Minister wouldn't tell me, and of course I couldn't have told you in any case. The Prime Minister was not certain whether Oissel himself really cared about these provisos or whether he was using them to force higher interest terms. The Home Secretary, who was only in the affair at all because he was an old friend of Oissel's, took the chance of finding out what he could by a direct personal talk."

"For the sake of his beautiful eyes, or for a bribe to be arranged?" asked Sancroft.

"You don't expect he'd tell me that, do you?" asked West shortly. "And I can tell both of you this for a beginning. I've known the Home Secretary as intimately as anyone—probably know more about him than his own family. He can be as stupid as a mule, but he's not the man to tackle any intricate dirty work. He's as straight a man as there is in politics."

"I'm always touched by the confidence in each other

that politicians of the same party insist on displaying on State occasions, Bob," said Sancroft teasingly, "but surely an appropriate application of whatever type of palm-oil Oissel preferred might be a positively patriotic duty in such circumstances."

West shrugged his shoulders. "The Home Secretary is not likely to tell me what terms he was empowered to offer, and anyway I don't see what that's got to do with the mystery. I think we're tackling this problem from the wrong end if we concentrate on what happened in Room J. I believe we've got to work from the flat."

"Did Oissel have many visitors?" asked Sancroft.

"I've put a special man on to that. Very few and all well-known people—Lord Finsburgh of the Central Bank, Fishwick of the Treasury, Kinnaird, and one or two other big City men."

"Perhaps Annette could help you there, Bob?"

West flushed. He did not like Sancroft's teasing tone, nor was he particularly anxious for Blackitt to suspect any collaboration with Oissel's granddaughter.

To turn the conversation he said to Blackitt: "But can't Daubisq tell you anything? He has been with Mr Oissel for years."

"He either cannot or will not. I can't get much out of him. Mr Oissel couldn't have chosen him for his intelligence."

"Perhaps discretion was a more important quality," said Sancroft with a grin. West remembered Annette's attitude at tea. Oissel seemed to have infected every one round him with a rooted objection to telling anything to the police.

"Daubisq sticks to it, and there seems no reason to doubt his story, that he was chloroformed by the burglars as soon as he opened the door to them. We can get nothing more out of him than that, and the fact of Jenks having gone out to buy the sporting special to get the results of the Kid Oakley fight."

"And the hall-porter, didn't he suspect anything?"

"He didn't know Oissel was out. Took up two well-dressed men in the lift. Didn't suspect anything even when he heard what must have been the shot that killed Jenks. Thought it was a motor backfire. He got suspicious when the men came out in a great hurry without ringing for the lift, and so he fetched the police."

"Of course, we musn't rule out pure coincidence," said West. "We kept the fact of the dinner out of the papers beforehand, but nothing that happens in this House can really be kept a secret. Ordinary thieves may have got the tip and have been out for money and valuables, so that the robbery would have nothing to do with the murder."

"That won't hold water for a moment, Mr West," said Blackitt. "In one of the drawers that had been opened was a valuable diamond watch bracelet that Mr Oissel had bought as a gift for his granddaughter. The case had been opened, but the watch hadn't been touched. There is no doubt, I think, that they were after papers of some kind, and that that is what they took. Both Daubisq and Miss Oissel agree that he never kept any kind of valuables or money in his rooms. They were always kept in the strong-room at the bank."

"It's a thousand pities those swine killed Jenks," said Robert reflectively. "He was an exceptionally intelligent man, and must have got to know quite a lot about Oissel's affairs. I know Oissel told the Minister that he'd been trying to persuade Jenks to go back with him to America. He might have formed some conclusions—about visitors, for example. You said that nothing was found on Jenks, no diary or anything that could help us, Blackitt?"

"Come over and have a look at what there is. Nothing that I can see—all personal stuff about boxing, date cards, and things like that... unless of course the figures in his notebook mean anything."

"Notebook, Blackitt?" said Robert, looking up sharply. "Was there a notebook? You didn't tell us that."

Then, remembering his promise to Annette, he said more casually: "I'll come over with you now and look at Jenks' stuff."

CHAPTER IX

As West walked across Palace Yard, and round to Scotland Yard, talking apparently casually to Inspector Blackitt, he had a feeling as though a mine were about to explode under his feet. He looked up for comfort to Big Ben, standing like a gigantic Guardsman against the clear blue sky. The clock-face looked so benevolently familiar that West tried to shake off the thought that so often came into his mind in these days—that this was all a façade, that the reality of Parliament was something quite different, that the real seat of Government had gone elsewhere, to Lombard Street or perhaps even across the Atlantic Ocean.

He said whimsically to Blackitt: "I find myself thinking of poor dead Oissel as a symbol—a jackal killed by a flick of the dying lion's paw."

Blackitt looked astonished. "A dying lion, sir?"

West laughed. "Only a fancy. I'm not offering you a new theory as to the murderer."

Blackitt unlocked a cupboard in his bleak little room at the Yard, and put on the table one by one the articles that comprised what he called "the Jenks exhibit." Pathetic, these odds and ends we leave behind us. West, who had many little acts of kindly thoughtfulness for which to thank the dead man, felt rather ashamed as he glanced at the well-worn wallet, a little packet of letters, some photographs and cards relating to sports events.

Finally Blackitt placed on the table a small black note-book, with a worn leather cover.

West felt his heart miss a beat. He picked up the book. Inside there were figures jotted down apparently haphazardly, some words that seemed like code words in black letters, and odd hieroglyphics. It corresponded in every detail with Annette's careful description of the notebook which she had declared was the real object of the burglary.

Then what was it doing in the pocket of Edward Jenks, the man specially sent by the Home Secretary to be guardian angel to Oissel and everything he owned?

Could the Home Secretary conceivably have had any-thing to do with it? The room seemed to turn round him. Robert kept his eyes fixed on a page of the book to hide his utter bewilderment. Of course the Home Secretary could know nothing… but what did it mean? Robert was glad he had checked his exclamation of surprise, which would have roused the suspicions of Blackitt. He must see his way clearer through this mystery before he could trust even the Inspector, who, after all, was the servant of Scotland Yard and not of the Ministry.

Annette must see the book to identify it positively. But how could he manage to get possession of it in order to show it to her, without explaining its importance to Blackitt, who would certainly not allow it to be taken from his room without very good reason.

"If we could puzzle this out, Blackitt, it might tell us something of what we want to know," Robert said slowly, feeling his ground.

Blackitt took the book and turned over the pages. "Do you think so? It looks to me as though Jenks had jotted down notes of his bets, and perhaps notes on form, in some code of his own."

"But it might be more important than that. Jenks might have been making notes of his experiences with Oissel. You know what a chap he was for telling good yarns. I'd often told him he ought to write his reminiscences some day."

West invented this story on the spot, but it seemed to interest Blackitt. After all, West knew Jenks much better than he did.

"There may be something in that, sir. I'll put our cipher men on to it at once. They can puzzle out anything that's got any meaning to it at all."

This was the very last thing West wanted.

"Yes, of course," he said slowly, "that would be a good thing to do. But… er… you know, Blackitt, there are so many delicate issues involved. Look here, I used to be a whale at deciphering codes. It was the only thing I ever worked at in school." West began to fancy himself as a ready liar. "Let me have this book for a night. I might be able to do something with it, and it would be wiser not to bring in any official, however trustworthy, at the moment."

Blackitt hesitated. It was against all rules, and all his training, to let documents out of his hands or from under lock and key for a moment. On the other hand, West was, in a way, a more responsible person in this business than himself, from the Government's point of view, and he had to think of Sir George Gleeson. He must keep in with West if he was to do anything towards untangling a knot in the strands of which he could see neither the beginning nor the end.

"It's absolutely against all rules, sir," he said.

West was too wily to argue that point.

"We must trust each other, Blackitt," he said simply. He felt rather uncomfortable at the effect produced, for he was not trusting Blackitt, but the Inspector said: "Very well, sir. Anyway it won't be wanted before morning. You will be sure to let me have it back first thing. It may have to be produced at the inquest."

With the precious book in his pocket West went along to his room at the Home Office and phoned Annette. She would see him at once. The taxi seemed to take an incredible time finding its way through the traffic to Clarges Street.

Annette's flat was stamped with her curiously reserved personality. The walls and ceiling, the carpets and hangings, were of the same shade of old parchment. The modern furniture was of black wood. The only notes of colour were a magnificent Gauguin painting and Annette herself in a trailing dress of orange velvet. Mourning was evidently a duty which sat lightly upon her shoulders.

Characteristically her only greeting was a smile. Robert felt that he must be equally dramatic. Annette had to be lived up to. He produced the little notebook from his pocket and held it out to her.

"Is this it?" he asked.

"Yes," and her fingers closed over it.

West caught his breath in a moment of sheer fright. It had been a good entrance, but suppose she would not give up the book? He felt horridly *gauche* and embarrassed beside this elegant woman; he did not understand what she was after, but he must keep control of the situation.

"It has been very difficult to get it," he said. "And I have it on loan from the police department for only a few hours. I must take it back with me to-night."

"But it is my property. My grandfather has left me everything that belonged to him."

"My congratulations. But this is more than property. It may be the most important link in the whole chain of evidence, and you must help me to use it to find who killed your grandfather."

Annette looked up at him with her deep, untelling eyes. "But of course. You are so good to take so much trouble. I will do exactly as you wish."

Bob felt this was almost equally embarrassing. "You are sure that this is what the burglars were after?" he asked.

"I think so. It is the code-book in which he kept notes of all his financial transactions. It is certainly the most important document that was in the flat that night as far as I can tell. But where did you find it?"

"In the pocket of Jenks."

"But why? What was he doing with it?" asked Annette. "Do you think he was trying to steal it?"

"Well, it's most unlike anything I have ever heard about Jenks if he was," said Robert in a worried tone. "And what could he do with it anyway? Perhaps he had wrested it from the burglars before they shot him?"

"Would they be likely to leave it with him, then?"

"No, I suppose not, but of course there is the further possibility that your grandfather might have handed the book to him for safe-keeping. That really fits in best with what I know of Jenks. Mr Oissel was breaking his rule in being away from his rooms at night. We know that he thought a lot about Jenks. Surely the simplest thing to do would be to give him the book to look after."

Annette smiled her slow smile. "You did not know Grandpère well, or you would know that he would never do that. He never trusted any living person, not even those he liked, not even me. He had no faith in any human being except himself. Awful, isn't it, but it's true."

They were silent. Robert wondered what was the real history of this strange pair that fate had thrust into his life. Annette was so unlike the other women he knew. He had no key to her mood. He would have liked to have her painted just as she sat, with the colour of her orange velvet dress repeating the rich tones of the Gauguin picture, vivid against the parchment of her walls.

Her white arm rested on the plain black wooden arm of her chair, and the wood seemed no shinier or blacker than her hair. And so still. She talked almost without moving, but Robert was not conscious of peace, rather of a hidden power rigidly controlled.

It was no use trying to get Annette to talk at large. Her handling of the Press had shown that. The problem he could not decide was whether she wanted to be helpful, whether this self-control was a screen behind which she had something to hide, or whether this was her usual attitude.

To break the silence he said gloomily: "Then you are inclined to think that things look black against poor Jenks."

Annette considered this for a while, then she said evenly: "But if he were trying to steal information, how did he know that this book was the key document to steal? Grandpère would certainly not have let him know that. No one would know who had not been in actual negotiations with him."

"Then you mean that Jenks was trying to get this book for some one who knew its importance?"

"That seems the most obvious explanation."

"Could it be for one of your grandfather's friends. Did you know them?"

"Yes, I think I knew all the men he received as guests. The only duty Grandpère ever required of me, in return for his immense generosity, was that I should act as hostess at the small business dinners he gave. I was the only woman, of course, and I left at the end of the meal. I never joined them after coffee. It was such a trifling duty when he was so good to me."

West repeated the names Blackitt had mentioned. "Forgive me if I seem to have pried already into your affairs. Were there any others?"

"No," she smiled. "Your information seems to be quite complete."

He wanted to bring in Philip Kinnaird's name and watch her reaction, but it's a little difficult to ask a woman if her lover is a thief.

"I know all these men so well, except Kinnaird, whom I just meet casually at the House," he said tactfully. "You don't think he had fixed things up with Jenks? I mean... er... I don't want to accuse him, of course..."

West expected to be annihilated, but Annette remained calm as ever. "Jenks disliked Philip too much to do anything for him. You know Philip's way with servants? He is not tactful, and Jenks was not quite a servant."

"Then the only suggestion that I can make is that some rival group to your grandfather was operating. But killing a man and burgling his flat, however much the mode in Chicago, seems a somewhat drastic method of managing business relations in London. Besides, they could hardly ring up the Prime Minister on the phone and offer to take over the interrupted business where Mr Oissel had left it."

Annette smiled her slow, non-committal smile. West felt that he could get no farther with her now. He had established the identity of the book. That, while it seemed to complicate things even more at the moment, must be a valuable clue, but Annette had withdrawn into herself again. She was the silent, defensive woman of the morning's interview.

West tried in various ways to draw her out of herself. He felt that something had happened even in the few hours that had elapsed since they had talked on the Terrace. At tea she had been friendly, almost confidential. Now she seemed to have withdrawn behind a sheet of glass. She would not even help when Robert, determined to keep the interview going as long as possible, tried to turn her mind from the grim facts of the tragedy by talking at large. Yet she did not seem to want him to go. He wondered whether she was just lonely in spite of her wealth, or whether she was frightened of something or some one.

He leant forward and put his hand over the hand that rested on the arm of her chair.

"Miss Oissel, I do want to help. Is anything worrying you? I don't expect you'll feel like trusting me. You feel I'm a British Government man and all that, and of course I've got to be, but if there's anything on earth I could do for you…" He paused, embarrassed. He wanted to say: "Oh, hang the Government, take me as your ally, I want to serve *you*," but obviously he couldn't do that, and she wouldn't believe him if he did.

He found himself staring at his own hand that was pressing on hers, and forced himself to look up at her. Her dark blue eyes glistened a little. She seemed for the moment near to tears.

"I'm sorry… I…" he stammered.

She rose, and he stood beside her, but not looking at her. "I can't do anything?"

"No," she said. "I wish…" She pulled herself together. "It's the notebook that's important. Terribly important. If you could find out who was after that I am sure you would have the key to the whole affair."

He put the little notebook back into his inner pocket, as though it were a personal gift from her. "You can rely on me," he said. "I'll find the blighters."

She smiled and held out her hand. He bent and kissed it, and then, to hide an Englishman's slight embarrassment at this courtesy, he said lightly: "I feel as though you were sending me off to the Crusades."

"Perhaps I am. Goodbye, Mr West. Come and see me again soon."

Robert, whose mind was filled with memories of an orange velvet dress as he drove back to the House of Commons in a taxi, was jolted into consciousness by a crowd in Parliament Square. He was startled to see a posse of mounted police ride by his window and into the crowd. Putting his head out he hailed a near-by constable, who recognized him.

"What's the matter, officer?"

"Unemployed demonstration, sir. They're having a deputation about the price of bread. But you will be through in a moment, sir. The mounted police are clearing the square."

Robert watched the well-trained horses chivvying the crowd before them. A woman with a baby slipped. Robert opened the door to drag her for safety into his cab, but a policeman helped her to her feet, and the crowd swept her with them.

The price of bread. The costliness of Annette. But a bread-march was not like England. Robert suddenly realized that he had never seen a bread-march in his life before. He had read of the demonstrations of the eighties and nineties, the long parades of unemployed in 1911. But the unemployment benefit had settled all that. Now it had been cut to the bone, and so...

The taxi moved slowly into the peace of Palace Yard. Constables were massed at the entrance, instead of the usual couple of amiable bobbies. When he had paid off his taxi, West stood for a moment at the entrance looking across the silent Yard framed by the dark surging crowd outside.

The House with its lighted windows seemed the quiet centre of the whirlpool that was London. A harassed Cabinet Minister negotiated with an American financier inside, and outside the raw material of their transactions, the people who elected the Minister and would have to pay interest on the loan, surged and demonstrated. They wanted bread. It wasn't like England—Stuart-Orford was right about that. But it was the new England, and what was to be done about it?

The division bell rang for the last vote of the day. West ran up the stairs to vote. He hadn't the least idea what about. But that is the comfort of the House of Commons. It gives everybody such a comforting feeling that 'something has been done about it.' But what, and how, and why, even the men who were doing the 'something' had very little idea beyond the immediate details of the day.

CHAPTER X

When Donald Shaw called at West's flat the next day to accompany him to the inquest he was surprised to find his friend looking so worried. It was obvious that he had not slept much the previous night.

"Buck up, Bob," said Shaw. "If you go into the witness-box looking like that, they'll convict you of the murder without troubling to call witnesses."

"I'm worried, Don. Damnably worried. There are too many side-issues coming into this affair. Every one connected with it seems to have something to hide. No one is telling all they know… and can't—that's the devil of it."

"You haven't been noticeably frank yourself, Bob," replied Shaw, who felt that he had not been in things very much since the conversation with Sancroft and Blackitt on the night of the double crime.

"I know, Don, and I'm sorry. About you, I mean. But I can't tell you everything, and I expect the others are in the same boat. I tell you I am dreading the inquest. The show is taking place on a barrel of international gunpowder, and the coroner may chuck a fuse into it without knowing what he's doing."

"And what will go up if he does?"

"The whole bally Government as likely as not," answered Bob gloomily, as their taxi stopped at the door of the coroner's court. "But what worries me most is that the Chief and Gleeson are at outs as to police evidence, so anything may happen if Oissel's solicitor wants trouble."

There was no doubt as to the immense public interest in the inquest. The gallery had been restricted to ticket-holders, but even so there were many M.P.s and other important people who were unable to gain admission.

West noted gloomily that Michael Houldsworth was in the front row. Of course, he would be. West had seen something of this Lancashire man's quiet determination when he was following a trail. He had admired it then, but he was not feeling too pleased at the prospect of having to deal with it himself.

The evidence of West, Shaw, and Dr Reading was taken first and disposed of very rapidly. Everything they could say had already been reported and written about from every angle in the Press. Dr Reading considered that the wound might have been self-inflicted, but he refused to commit himself further, and was not pressed beyond that.

Then the waiter was called. West noticed that the Oissel solicitor, who had asked questions in a very perfunctory fashion so far, began to take considerably more interest.

No amount of cross-examination, however, could shake the simple story of the waiter. He had changed the plates after the Home Secretary had left the room. Mr Oissel had told him not to bring coffee until the Minister had returned. He had not noticed anything unusual about Mr Oissel. The waiter was quite sure that there had been no quarrel during the meal. The Home Secretary and Mr Oissel had been talking quite cheerfully whenever he was in the room.

"Did you see the revolver on the table when you changed the plates the last time?" asked the solicitor.

"No, sir."

"Nor in Mr Oissel's hand?"

"No, sir."

"What did you do when you left the room after changing the plates?"

"I went to the end of the corridor to tell the still-room maid I shouldn't need the coffee just yet. It is always made fresh for each dinner, sir."

"And where is the still-room?"

"Right at the other end of the corridor."

"So some one could have entered that room between your leaving it and your getting back to the door, without your seeing them?"

"Oh, yes, sir," said the waiter with conviction. "It would have been quite easy. There was a crowd of people up and down the corridor all the time. No one would have noticed anyone going into one of the private rooms, sir."

"But could they have got out again after you heard the shot?"

"No, sir, I was standing just at the door when the revolver went off, and Mr West was there too, sir."

"Why were you at the door just then?"

"The division bell was just ringing, sir, so I knew the Home Secretary could not be long. I was going in to remove the dessert-plates and get all ready to bring in the coffee when the Minister returned, as I had been ordered, sir."

"So in another few seconds you would have been inside the room?"

"Yes, sir."

"And seen how Mr Oissel died?"

"I suppose so, sir."

"It might have saved us a lot of trouble," commented the coroner.

There was a faint ripple of laughter in the court.

The summoning of Annette Oissel into the witness-box caused much craning of necks.

"Queer the effect she gives of brilliant colour even in jet black," thought Bob as he watched her go through the preliminaries with perfect self-possession, utterly indifferent to the curious glances from the public gallery.

Annette identified the revolver as belonging to her grandfather. "Was it not unusual that he should take a revolver with him to a friendly dinner at the House of Commons?" asked the coroner.

"My grandfather never went out unarmed," she replied.

"Had he any special reason to anticipate any attack upon his life?"

"Not more than usual, not at all really, but that would not make any difference. He was shot and very badly injured once when he was unarmed. He never again was without a revolver when he was alone, not even at home."

"Once bitten, twice shy," commented the coroner, and again audible laughter came from the crowd. Robert, watching Annette's every movement, sympathized with her silent contempt at this flippancy.

"But how do you account for the waiter not having seen the revolver when he was in the room and clearing the table?"

"That I don't know. I am only positive from my knowledge of my grandfather that the waiter would be covered all the time he was in the room while Mr Oissel was alone."

"Without his seeing the revolver?"

"My grandfather was a trick shooter. He could shoot from

anywhere. Normally he kept his revolver in the pocket of his coat."

"But would that be possible, as he was in evening dress and wearing a tail-coat?" asked the coroner.

"No, but I have seen him keep his revolver hidden between his legs and the man he was talking to quite unconscious of the fact."

"If that were so in this case, the revolver might have fallen to the floor when he was shot?"

"That is possible," said Annette.

"But surely, Miss Oissel," said the coroner, "a simpler explanation is that Mr Oissel shot himself, and the revolver fell from his hand as he fell from his chair."

"I do not believe that my grandfather committed suicide. His hold on life was quite extraordinary."

The polite gesture of the coroner conveyed the impression that that was of course what a dutiful granddaughter would be expected to say, however overwhelming the evidence against her view. The crowd was obviously disappointed when Annette's evidence was finished and her elegance was replaced in the box by the stolid, unexciting figure of Inspector Blackitt.

The Inspector's evidence followed the familiar lines as the coroner took him through the story again. Then the Oissel solicitor took charge.

"You examined the revolver when you took over from Sergeant Bourne?"

"Yes, sir. He, of course, left everything as it was until I came."

"How many shots had been fired from the revolver?"

"One, sir."

"And do you consider that the bullet that killed Mr Oissel had been fired from that revolver?"

"It could have been, sir. It was of the same make and size."

"Could have been? Does that mean that you are not quite sure that it had been?"

There was dead silence in the court. Blackitt in his slow way said quietly: "I am not convinced of that, sir."

West groaned inwardly as the sensation of this swept through the crowded court. It was the first intimation that the police in any way doubted the theory of suicide.

"Have you any reason to doubt that Mr Oissel committed suicide."

Quite calmly and undramatically the Inspector detailed the reasons that had already convinced Sir George Gleeson— the absence of scorch, the impossibility of a man shooting himself in such a place without holding the gun so close to himself that a scorch mark would be inevitable.

Press and public hung on his words. The suicide theory was definitely smashed in the public mind.

"Did you know that?" whispered Don.

"Yes, but I was pledged not to tell a soul till this inquest. Damned silly to let it come out like this. Looks as though the Government had been trying to keep it dark for a time because they had something to hide."

"It would be a very strange Government if it hadn't," said Don with a smile.

"I know, but this is worse than sending the bellman round to call attention to the fact."

The Oissel solicitor, having got what he wanted, seemed as anxious as anyone to dissipate the sensational atmosphere caused by the police inspector's evidence. The remainder of his questions to Blackitt were concerned with technical details.

The coroner then adjourned the case for a week, and the proceedings ended.

As he rose to leave the court with Don, Robert caught the eyes of Michael Houldsworth, who was looking down from the gallery. Houldsworth smiled.

"Now we've got to reckon with that lad," thought Robert, "and official excuses will make precious little impression on him. Let's go and have a beer and some Stilton at Barney's," he said, turning to Don.

"Good enough for me," replied the other. "Hello, here's a messenger for you."

A young constable handed Bob a message. It had been telephoned from the House of Commons. Would Mr West see the Home Secretary in his room at the House as soon as the inquest was over?

On his way back to the House of Commons Robert determined to lose no more time before telling the Minister what had been found in Jenks' pocket and consulting him as to what could be the possible explanation. The inquest stood adjourned for only a week, and Robert was convinced that there ought to be no more sensations at the next one. The inquest on Jenks was being held to-morrow, and something might come out then, though Annette would see to it that her solicitor asked no questions about the notebook, if, indeed, she had told him anything about it. She seemed as anxious as Robert himself was to avoid publicity about that.

West was therefore annoyed to find Sir George Gleeson with the Minister, and to judge from the mass of papers before them he was not paying any fleeting call. The Minister's glance when Bob greeted him showed that he had not expected Sir George when he sent the message to his P.P.S. It was, of course, impossible to discuss anything about Jenks with the chief permanent secretary present.

The Minister asked questions about the inquest, and

Robert told him about Blackitt's evidence. He made no comment, and neither did the Minister, but a glance passed between him and Sir George which Robert could not interpret.

"And are you enjoying your new *rôle* as amateur detective?" asked the Home Secretary with a smile, as Robert finished his report.

"You haven't found out anything very startling yet, have you?" added Sir George with a slight sneer.

Robert met his eyes quite calmly. It is easy to stand sarcasm with the card that may prove the ace of trumps in one's hand. Robert smiled inwardly at the effect he could produce at that moment, if he wished to, but he was not ready yet. He must see the Home Secretary alone first.

"Could I see you later, sir?" he asked. "On another matter," he added as Sir George looked up.

"Let me see. I have a Cabinet meeting at four o'clock. It should be over by six. Will that do?"

"Perfectly. Then I think I'll go and get some lunch, if you don't want me any more now."

"Just a moment. Can you do anything about this? Houldsworth has given notice to raise the matter on the adjournment. The Government definitely do not want a debate until the police have formed some conclusions. It makes things awkward with the American Embassy. Couldn't you see him this afternoon and soothe him? Of course we can't refuse some statement if he persists, but it would be unfortunate if we had to face the House on the matter just now."

One of the privileges most prized by private Members and most dreaded by Ministers in an awkward corner is the right of any M.P. to raise any subject of public interest, after proper notice to the Speaker, on the final motion of the day, "That this House do now adjourn." The debate must come to an end at eleven-thirty, but if the other business of the day has finished early a quite insignificant Member may find himself with time to initiate a first-class debate on some matter well in the public eye. Michael Houldsworth could be trusted to stage his motion on the best possible day.

A P.P.S. who can turn the wrath of back-benchers into safer channels when they are out for a scoop is a treasure. Robert was anxious to live up to the traditions of his post. He suddenly realized that Gracie might be of use in this.

"Leave Houldsworth to me, sir," he said with a confident air that was intended to impress Sir George.

"Really, Robert, you are a great help to me," and the Minister turned to his Civil Service head as though asking that his commendations should be added.

"I wish you joy of tackling Houldsworth," said Sir George.

Robert felt that it was just about time to indicate to the magnificent Gleeson that though he might at the moment be only a Parliamentary private secretary (unpaid) he was also a Member of Parliament.

"There are ways of dealing with him if you know the right way to go about it," he said grandly. "Well, if you don't need me any more at the moment," he added to his own Chief, "I'll get a spot of lunch and then see what I can do with Houldsworth. Afternoon, Gleeson."

Robert felt that was quite a good exit. But he had got to live up to it. Houldsworth had to be squared somehow, and he saw no hope of doing that without the help of Grace Richards.

The attitude of Robert West to the modern young woman was typical of that of a very young man. He preferred the intelligent woman. He liked to be seen about with one who was making a name for herself. But while he was interested in her he expected her to put her own affairs into the background, and devote herself to his. When she was no longer needed she might be permitted to pick up her own threads again, but she must not trouble him. This he called allowing a woman to live her own life.

While they had been in the House together—for Grace, a Cockney of the Cockneys, had won a constituency at a by-election about a year after West had won his seat—he had managed to see a lot of her in a circumspect way. They had fought hard over politics. 'Yes-women' bored Robert, and he was coming round to Grace's point of view more quickly than he was prepared to admit. He saw no other way out of the muddle. But what Grace thought of their unusual friendship Robert had no idea, a fact which added to his interest in her. Grace had not been bred in drawing-rooms, but in the factory and in the London streets. She was not the sort of girl to give herself away. Though as outwardly frank as Annette Oissel was reserved, she had her own defence mechanism, as West had already discovered. Still, she always seemed ready to put her own affairs on one side when he wanted to talk to her.

West walked round the corridors looking for Gracie, who would have finished her morning committee by now. She was not in the dining-room, but he caught sight of her signing for some papers at the vote office, that convenient little window in the corner of the central lobby whence M.P.s can secure their Government publications free of charge.

He knew better than to apologize for his recent neglect. The brisk one-busy-politician-to-another was the line to take with Gracie, who though in the bloom of her twenties, and very young and lovable, was determined to live up to her chosen *rôle* as a grim and sexless legislator.

It seemed a little comic at times to the older men who watched her, but it was a gallant effort.

Robert went behind her and said hurriedly: "I've just come from the inquest. I'd like to talk to you. It's rather important. Have you lunched?"

"No. I had rather promised I would join Michael, but if you like…"

"Good. Then let's lunch together. Let's find a quiet table where we can talk." Robert felt some satisfaction that he had taken the girl away from the determined Houldsworth.

He told Gracie the story of the inquest as they lunched.

"Why are you all being so secretive about the affair?" she asked impatiently. "The public will get the impression soon that you know who did it, and are trying to keep it dark."

This gave Robert the opening he was looking for.

"If we knew who did it, or had the remotest idea why Oissel was killed, if he didn't kill himself—which, after all, isn't absolutely certain—or even if we knew why his flat was burgled, then we could be perfectly frank about all these details. But we have to go carefully, because we don't know, and we may spring a mine any minute."

Gracie tossed back the thick mass of her straight black hair. "I can't see why. Two men have been killed. Your crowd seem only concerned about Mr Oissel, but I consider him of no more importance than Mr Jenks." (She emphasized the "*Mister* Jenks.") "The police must find out who did it, and they must be punished whoever they are."

"I wish it were as simple as that. I hope whoever did it will be punished, and the full penalty at that. I liked Jenks, and am not in the least disturbed about Oissel as a man. But there has been a further slump in British securities. The Americans are furious—all sorts of rumours are flying about.

We are working like hell in tracking the murderer. I was on the job all last night."

Robert received such a sympathetic and even horrified glance as he said this that he felt it hardly necessary to explain that 'being on the job last night' had consisted in walking up and down his bedroom trying to think what Jenks could have been up to. But it sounded well, and was as true as most politicians' statements, he felt.

"I didn't know you were in it like that," said Grace.

"I'm not only in it, but I think I'm on the track," said Robert with pride. "I wish I could tell you, but I'm sworn to secrecy."

"I say, how thrilling!" Grace was as excited as a schoolgirl.

"I want you to help me." Robert's confidential tone would have received applause on the Lyceum stage. He was enjoying himself.

"Of course. I'd love to, but how?"

"Can you persuade Houldsworth not to raise the question on the adjournment to-night?"

"Will it upset things as much as that? Or"—and Gracie suddenly became the suspicious political opponent again—"are you just trying to get your Minister out of a fix? Because I'm not going to help that old stupid."

"My dear girl, your bump of reverence needs development. My Chief is not as stupid as he likes to be thought. But anyway you are not helping him if you do this. You will help me."

"And why should I help you?"

Robert was positively shocked. Why should she help him! What did she think women were in politics for if not to be helpful? He came of an old political family. Had one of the women of his family ever asked why she should help? He had always approved of women getting the vote just because he felt it was good to have women about. They were always willing to be helpful—at least, those one liked. And here was Grace, on whom he had bestowed certain attentions, actually wanting to know the why and wherefore before she would help in a most important political matter.

"Of course, if you feel like that, there is nothing more to be said," he replied huffily.

Grace chuckled—that odd little Cockney chuckle that always reduced the high-and-mighty Robert West.

"Oh, come off it," she said. "There's lots to be said, but it's no use your thinking that I can call off our people if I haven't the least idea why. Besides, I am not going to try. You either trust me, or do the job yourself."

Robert was in a quandary. He could not do a thing with the suspicious Houldsworth without Grace's help. And he could see Gleeson's smile if he failed. Besides, his prestige with the Home Secretary was all-important just now. "Oh, damn these modern women," he thought desperately. If only they would be either modern or just women, but the combination of the two was really unfair on a fellow who had to deal with them!

Robert looked at his companion with a smile that usually worked wonders. "Now if I were a woman, and you were a man M.P. in a fix, this is where I should begin to use S.A. What is the equivalent for me? There isn't one. It's not fair."

Grace's glance was enigmatic. "You could tell the truth, of course. Unusual, perhaps… but often helpful."

"Gracie, I can't. Honestly, I'm not asking you to do anything against your party. If I can only have this week-end clear on the job I believe I really can get on the track of these people. If there's a debate now, and the Minister has to admit certain things, it gives them warning, and all my clues are covered up. Won't you trust me? Houldsworth, or you, if you like, can have your debate next week. Won't you help?"

"I shouldn't worry about the missing S.A., Robert. You're doing quite well."

"Damn it, Gracie, are you going to help me?"

"Yes, of course I am. Now I'll go and find Michael."

Robert made a movement as she rose and signed her own bill. What was one to do with a woman like that? As he went back to the central lobby he found himself meditating on what sort of a woman he would like to marry. He had managed a combination of Grace and Annette before he was roused from his reverie by a couple of journalists wanting to know the latest news of the murder.

CHAPTER XI

Inspector Blackitt returned to Scotland Yard after the inquest in a state as near to bad temper as his usually calm disposition allowed. He felt that he was not being quite fairly treated. The evidence which he had given at the inquest had been determined by his official superiors. Still more annoying were the invisible but unscalable barriers that seemed to arise whenever he was pursuing a hopeful line of investigation. He had a feeling that he was being checkmated from above, and that even Sir George Gleeson seemed more anxious to keep his investigations within prescribed limits than concerned in finding the murderers.

Blackitt sat down at his desk and pulled some sheets of foolscap towards him. It was his habit when thinking out a problem to make little drawings of the things that puzzled him. He had a gift for delicate and accurate sketching that had come in very useful in his previous cases. This time he drew a sketch of the revolver that had been found by Mr Oissel's side.

Three things had to be decided about that. Had the bullet found in Mr Oissel's body been fired from that revolver? If so, what hand had fired it? If not, from whence had the shot come?

The expert's evidence on the bullet was not absolutely conclusive. He glanced at the report that had been sent in. The bullet could have been fired from that revolver. It was of the same pattern and make, but for a standard make of revolver that did not tell him much. As no other weapon had been found in the room, whose doors and windows were closed, he might assume for the moment that the shot had been fired from the revolver found beside the body.

Then whose was the hand that held it? Could the waiter have had his hand round the door? But that theory would not hold water. West had seen the waiter outside the closed door as he heard the shot. Suicide was the only theory that fitted all the facts, except the state of the body itself.

By his expert knowledge Blackitt had convinced his superiors that the old man could not have committed suicide, so now he felt that if, after demolishing a theory so obviously convenient to the Government, he failed to produce the murderer he might have been better advised to let well alone.

His meditations were interrupted by the arrival of a messenger with a card, and an intimation that the Chief had given orders that Inspector Blackitt should see this visitor when he came back after the inquest. The card was a professional one of good quality on which was engraved "John Bowes, Photographer." The address given was Duke Street, St James's.

The Inspector glanced with no special interest at the little man who was shown into the room. He was very thin. His clothes were carelessly worn but of good quality. His head was the head of a scholar, bald and with a fine forehead.

"Good morning, Mr Bowes. You wanted to see me?"

"No, not you particularly. I asked to see the official in charge of the Oissel murder case, and I was told to wait for you."

Inspector Blackitt's face took on a keener expression. "I am very glad you did, if you have anything to tell me. The case has been put in my hands. You are a photographer, I see from your card, Mr Bowes."

"That is so," replied the other in a strong Scots accent. "That is to say, I do not take photographs of people—mine is specialist work, mostly connected with museums. I photograph old documents. I have photographed a document recently that may be of interest to you."

"Indeed, Mr Bowes." Blackitt kept his 'poker face,' but his interest increased considerably.

"Do you recognize these?" John Bowes put on the table about a dozen large-size photographs.

Blackitt looked at these carefully. "Yes, I think I do. Where did you get them?" he asked in surprise.

The little man smiled. "So you have got as far as that?"

"Oh, yes, we have got that far. Now will you tell me how you came by these. You did the photographic copy, I suppose?"

"Yes. I took the photographs myself."

"And whom did you photograph them for?"

"That is what I have come to see. Last week a man came to see me to ask me if I could photograph certain documents in a hurry. He arranged to come with them on Monday night at eight-thirty. He could only stay half an hour, he said. They must be done in that time."

"Didn't you suspect there was something wrong about that? It must have seemed a little unusual."

Mr Bowes shrugged his shoulders. "Many things happen in London which are somewhat unusual. That was not my affair."

"And he came as arranged?"

"He came, and I took the photographs. He paid me in advance, and promised to call for the proofs the next day."

"And did he call?" There was an eager edge to Blackitt's voice.

"He has never called, Inspector."

"You could describe him to me?"

"There is no need. This is the man," and John Bowes placed on the table a cutting of a photograph from a daily paper. It was the picture of Edward Jenks!

"To-day is Thursday, Mr Bowes. You have taken rather a long time in bringing this to our notice. Of course, we are very grateful, but may I ask why you did not come to the police on Tuesday?"

"I am a busy man, Inspector. I do not read the daily papers. I am not interested. It is purely by accident that I saw this photograph."

"Just one more question. This document, as you call it—could you describe it?"

"It was just a plain ring-leaved notebook, bound in black leather. It seemed to have been much used. It was rather worn."

"You couldn't have photographed all the pages in it in that time."

"I photographed all the pages on which anything was written."

"Did Mr Jenks say anything to you about the book? Did he make any explanation of his somewhat strange request?"

"No, and I did not ask him. It was not my affair."

"But, really, Mr Bowes," protested the police officer, somewhat scandalized, "surely you must have realized that you were being asked to do something which might possibly be part of criminal proceedings. In fact, that is quite likely what you were doing." The Inspector's voice was stern.

The little Scotsman remained quite unimpressed. "It is no part of my duty to ask questions of my clients. He asked for a perfectly feasible job to be done in a hurry. I did it. He paid me. There the matter ends as far as I am concerned."

"But it does not end there, Mr Bowes, if respectable citizens will not realize their duty to the police in such matters..."

Mr Bowes rose and smiled a broad Scots smile. "The police have had no reason yet to complain of my conduct. I need not have come to see you at all. I could have put the prints in the fire, and that would have ended my part in the affair."

Blackitt began to feel that he was being tactless. In the rather elephantine manner of the British police force he tried to be amiable as he handed his visitor over to a messenger to be conveyed to the front door, but a whole leading article in the *Weekly Scotsman* on English police methods was expressed by the set of John Bowes' shoulders as he solemnly took his leave.

After his visitor had gone Blackitt sat for some time at his desk looking at the photographs. He compared them carefully with the pages of the notebook. There was no doubt these were the originals. What was the explanation? Why should Jenks take his own notebook to be photographed? Was he anticipating trouble and so in need of evidence of some kind? Blackitt had not been told of the information given to West by Annette. He did not know that the book belonged to Oissel. But he felt that West had realized its importance and probably knew something about it. Had West managed to decipher any of the coded words? He had simply returned the book that morning with a scribbled note: "See you about this later." Obviously, therefore, Blackitt thought to himself, he could do nothing further until he had seen West and found out what he knew about the book.

He strolled over to the House of Commons hoping that he would not have to wait an hour while his card travelled round the building in search of West. He found poor Robert soon enough, for the unfortunate youth was in the centre of the Strangers' Lobby surrounded by massive and determined-looking ladies. The policeman on duty at the door, an old friend of Blackitt's, explained with a grin that the Home Secretary's League of Women Voters had arrived *en masse* to be shown round and given tea. The Minister had escaped after assuring them how glad he was to see them, how delighted Mr West would be to show them everything, and how terribly disappointed he was that a Cabinet meeting prevented him from having that great joy himself.

West looked desperately at Blackitt from a heaving sea of printed voiles. He escaped for a second to explain.

"Let me tell 'em you're wanted for murder," suggested Blackitt helpfully and with a broad grin.

"If you were the hangman himself, they would insist on being shown round first. They've saved up for this trip, Blackitt, and they will have their money's worth."

"How long?" asked Blackitt.

"Can't do 'em under two hours, and I have to see the Minister at six."

"I must see you before you see him. I must see you now. Can't you get anyone else to do this job?"

"Is it likely? Every M.P. has his own troubles. I'll manage five o'clock somehow. Meet you in the upstairs bar.—Yes, ladies, this is called the Strangers' Lobby, but of course you are not strangers now, you are voters… When the suffragettes…"

Blackitt fled from the old, old story and took refuge in that quiet bar where those who have to be in the House but not of it can secure peace from the restless crowds of the lobbies.

"Hope you haven't pushed them in the river," said Blackitt when West joined him punctually at five.

"Told them an horrific tale about a crisis, and left them having tea in charge of all the waiters in sight. I have told the head waiter to give 'em all they want and send the bill to the Home Secretary. Serve him right. Now, what's new?"

Blackitt told the story of John Bowes. West felt very glad that he had not committed himself more in the note with which he had returned the notebook that morning. He could now confide in Blackitt without appearing to have been holding anything back from him. He told Blackitt frankly that he had shown the book to Miss Oissel, and that she had identified it as the key document for which the unknown burglars were undoubtedly searching.

The two men looked at each other. "Then what was Ted Jenks doing with it?" asked the Inspector.

West lit a cigarette, and watched the match slowly burn away. "I think, Blackitt," he said, "that we have given Jenks the benefit of our friendly doubts long enough. He is found dead with the notebook in his possession. We tried to explain that away. He might conceivably have been trying to hide it from the thieves and died in defence of it, though we could not see how. Now we know he left Oissel's flat and had some pages of the book secretly photographed. Well, that information, even if he could have decoded it, is of no use to him. Was he getting hold of it for some one else? It looks like it. Now we have to consider who."

Blackitt scraped out his pipe. "I suppose we can rule out the possibility that he was having the pages photographed for Mr Oissel, and by his instructions."

"I suggested to Miss Oissel that her grandfather might have given Jenks the book for safe-keeping, but she squashed that idea emphatically. It's even less likely that Oissel would have gone to all that trouble to have his own property photographed, and anyway why should that be done on the one evening when he breaks his usual rule and leaves his rooms for dinner?"

"Then we've got to consider who wanted the information. It must be a limited list. Don't you think the Home Secretary could help us there? He was in the midst of negotiations. He would know if there was anyone else operating on the job, who could be considered the rival of the Oissel group."

West glanced at his wrist-watch. "I've an appointment with him at six, and I'd already decided to tell him what we suspect about Jenks. It will be a blow to him, you know, because it will look as though he'd not been playing straight when he sent Jenks to Oissel. Of course, anyone who knows the circumstances would see that was out of the question. Jenks went with the full knowledge of Sir George Gleeson. Still, it might look a bit awkward in Parliament if that comes out."

"As come out it will."

"Of course, but everything depends on how it's done. Nothing gives the other side such a chance in politics as looking as though you were having facts dragged out of you. The best way to keep a political secret is to take a large hall and call a meeting to make a speech about it. Then no one takes any notice."

Blackitt grinned. "I've never wanted to be a politician, Mr West, but after my experience this week I'd rather be sentenced to penal servitude than to Westminster."

"Oh, come," said West, looking round the oak-panelled bar. "You must admit we do ourselves pretty comfortably. Besides which we see to it that the restrictions that apply to every other pub don't apply here. It all helps to make life bearable, you know."

"Oh, the quarters are comfortable enough, but what I can't understand about M.P.s is why, when they have gone to such a lot of trouble to get themselves elected to such a good club, they can't settle down and enjoy it. They no sooner get here than they try to upset everything in order that they may have the trouble of an election again, when all that ordinary folk want to do is to settle down to their own business and leave the politicians to mind theirs. Silly, I call it."

"Perhaps you're right, Blackitt. But that's politics."

As it was not quite six when West left the Inspector, he thought he would glance in at the debate in the House and see what was on. Few rising politicians care to be seen much in the debating chamber except during the high spots of a full-dress debate, or when they are themselves trying to catch the Speaker's eye. There is an assumption that men who are in the chamber merely to listen to arguments are there because they have nothing better to do.

Robert stood for a few moments at the Bar of the House, that narrow piece of leather sewn across the green matting on the floor which separates the 'precincts of the House'—that part where a Member is under the Speaker's eye, and may rise to speak, or otherwise must sit down and be reasonably quiet—from that part where Members, although actually in the debating chamber, can stand about and talk in audible voices, and generally act as though there were no debate in progress at all.

This debate was very sparsely attended. One of those hardy annuals, a land drainage bill, was dragging its way wearily through a desultory second reading discussion. Robert was just turning to leave the chamber when he was joined by Michael Houldsworth.

"So you've put Grace Richards on to call me off."

"Did she tell you so?"

"Is it likely?"

"I congratulate you on your acumen, then."

"Hardly needed, are they—the congratulations, I mean?"

"And you've promised her?"

"Naturally. But what are you trying to hide, West? Don't you, or, rather, doesn't your Minister see that things are drifting to a crisis over this Oissel affair? I sometimes wonder whether British Cabinet Ministers ever trouble to read the financial columns of a daily paper. If they do, they act as though anything but the leader page was beneath their august notice."

"Well, in the light of the financial columns do you suggest that your adjournment debate would have done any good at the present time?"

Houldsworth slightly elevated one shoulder as a reply. "Grace can call *me* off, but she has no influence with the Scots. They have taken over the job for Monday. You had better get your Minister primed with some yarn by then that will hang together. Are you really on the track of a solution? Grace hinted that you were, but I assumed that had been provided as a little bit of sugar for the bird."

West glanced at the lined face of the man beside him. Young though he was, Houldsworth was not new to the Parliamentary game. He knew every move. West would have liked to talk over the problem with him, but of course that was impossible. Houldsworth was not even an orthodox member of his own party, but was running a semi-Communist show of his own. It was his lack of allegiance to any party that made him so dangerous a foe. All parties in the British House of Commons are more or less pledged to keep the show running

somehow. There is always a bond of union somewhere at
the bottom which gets the Mother of Parliaments out of the
worst of her family squabbles. But Houldsworth was of the
type that rejoiced in giving the venerable old lady a black eye
whenever an opportunity offered. Nor was he at all likely to
be influenced by the flattery of being taken into Ministerial
confidence, that subtlest of all methods of dealing with the
really dangerous back-bencher.

West decided it would be wisest to be amiable.

"I'm seeing the Home Secretary at six. I'll tell him what
you say."

"Why trouble? It won't be he who decides what he'll say.
Better tell Gleeson. What is he thinking about it all?"

"That I don't know. Must get along now." As Robert
turned on his heel and left the chamber he realized that that
was just the simple truth. He hadn't the remotest idea what
Sir George Gleeson was thinking. Ought he to go to him
with what he already knew? No. Better to have it all out first
with the Home Secretary, even if it did mean upsetting him
by having to tell him of what looked like the disloyalty of
his hitherto faithful Jenks.

CHAPTER XII

The Home Secretary was not in his room when Robert went along there. The Cabinet meeting was evidently not yet over, for the Home Secretary prided himself on his strict punctuality in keeping appointments. He had all the drearier virtues of a public man. Robert remembered that he had promised the Minister to read for him a confidential report that had been prepared by the inspectorate on the conditions in female prisons. He looked among the papers on the Minister's desk, but it was not there.

He proceeded to hunt through the drawers, all of which were kept in miraculous tidiness by the Minister himself. Robert was firmly of the opinion that tidiness in anyone above the rank of a typist was the sign of an inferior mind, but the Minister hated having his papers tidied by secretaries, though he had no objection to Robert's ministrations. It said much for West's dogged loyalty to his Chief that he spent hours tidying papers for the Home Secretary simply in order to put the Minister in the position of having to read papers because he had no excuse for doing anything else.

While he was going through his Chief's private drawer in search of the missing report he came across an envelope file marked "Cabinet Papers. Secret." As any scrap of paper that goes before a Cabinet meeting, even the most routine report, is always marked "Secret" Robert had no hesitation in opening the file. That the Minister gave him the right to do this was one of the reasons for Sir George Gleeson's coldness to West. Sir George was a stickler for the convention of Cabinet secrecy even to the careful destruction of the blotting-paper after a meeting.

As he was carelessly turning over the papers, which did not seem to include the report for which he was looking, Robert's heart gave a sudden leap. He picked up three sheets of House of Commons notepaper, held together by a paper-clip. He took them to the window to examine them more closely. There was no doubt about it. Accurately copied on to those sheets were the list of figures, code-words in block letters, and hieroglyphics over which he had puzzled for hours the previous night. They could only have been copied from the Oissel notebook, and they had been copied by the Home Secretary himself. Robert knew his hand so well. He looked at the notes at the side, also in the Minister's handwriting. They were evidently a rough translation of the coded words, and they related to the loan negotiations. Here was the very information which would have been invaluable to the British Government had they been in possession of it during their negotiations with Oissel.

Robert replaced the papers in the file, put them tidily in the drawer, and went slowly back to the window. His brain would hardly form the words: "What does this mean?" But what did it mean? When had the Home Secretary made that copy? How had he got hold of the notebook? Of course, if he had seen it after Oissel's death, that was a reasonable explanation. But he knew the code— the code that Annette herself did not know, and surely the old man, so secretive about everything, would have cherished the secret of his private code beyond all else. Yet the Home Secretary knew it… and he was no expert. Had he had the Home Office experts on it? But if he had, Blackitt would certainly have known about that.

And then Jenks—but no, Robert felt he couldn't see the Home Secretary just now. He must have time to think. He was gazing gloomily at the view across Palace Yard when the door opened. Robert turned with a start. "Thank God," he said to himself when he saw that it was not the Home Secretary. It was only the Minister's Civil Service secretary, a pleasant lad with a cheerful 'I should worry' air which usually amused Robert. His name was Bertram Briggs.

"The Cabinet meeting is going on for ages yet," he announced casually. "Mortimer has just phoned through. Chief says don't bother to wait. He'll see you after dinner."

He caught sight of Robert's face as he walked to the desk. "Good Lord, West, are you ill? You look ghastly. Can I get you anything?"

"No, thanks. I'm all right. Been overdoing it, I suppose, and this hot weather. I think I'll go on the Terrace and get some fresh air."

"You're helping on the Oissel case, aren't you?" asked Briggs, seating himself on the edge of the desk, and swinging a leg.

"I seem to have tumbled in on it, but I expect you know as much about it as I do." Robert said this casually, but he kept an eye on Briggs to see how he took it. Did he by any chance know anything about the Oissel notebook?

"Not me," said Briggs. "You know what the Chief is like, close as an oyster. You are a favourite, and doesn't that make our Gleeson mad! He's got it in for you all right. Wonder what would happen if you blossomed out as Home Secretary before he retired. Queer thing about politics nowadays, anybody can become anything."

"Thanks, but you might have Houldsworth some day."

"Wouldn't make much difference, Communist or Conservative—the Gleesons run the show. If they are old hands at politics the Ministers don't want to be bothered and leave it to us. If they are new, their inferiority complex won't let them contradict us, so the good old Civil Service lets the puppets play."

"There might be a revolution some day, you know."

"What difference would that make, except that the revolutionaries wouldn't dare to cut our salaries? They would have to pay us twice as much and implore us to go on doing whatever we were doing."

West snorted! "Damn you, Briggs, and damn your smug complacent Civil Service!"

"It isn't smug. It merely goes on doing the job. You politicians think you can improvise government like jazz on a piano, and that if you say a thing in your speeches it will happen of itself. Can't be done. Blessed are the forms and the *questionnaires*, to the umpteenth million of them."

"I'll go and get that drink," said Robert gloomily, and banged the door behind him.

Robert went back to the Terrace to try to think out the implications of his new discovery. A faint mist was rising from the river. The tea-time guests had gone. Only a few determined souls were marching up and down the long flagged pavement in their endeavours to keep down the dreaded weight. Everything was quiet and cool. Westminster Bridge looked solidly reassuring, bearing proudly her never-ceasing traffic. Lambeth Palace with its Saxon stones seemed to murmur its comforting message:

"*And as things have been they remain.*"

Robert, as he leaned over the parapet and gazed down on the swelling waters of the rising tide, was not so sure. The foundations of his faith in human nature were crumbling. Like other young politicians of his period, Robert West never gave religion a thought unless it happened to come up as a political question, some organization wanting money for schools, another church wanting a bill to stop somebody doing something or other. Trained in the conventions of a public school, with its compulsory chapels, Robert had simply absorbed the one guiding principle for his moral life, that there were certain things that certain people did not do. Not all conventions held true for everybody, but a man must stick to what held true for his type. A Cabinet Minister could not do things that might be overlooked in a back-bencher.

What had the Home Secretary been doing? Could it be he who was the moving spirit behind the mysterious murder of Georges Oissel in Room J and the burglary at Oissel's flat, in which Jenks had been shot. There were many missing pieces in this dreadful jigsaw, but would the hand of his own Chief appear in the complete picture?

Should he phone Blackitt to come over for another talk? Instinctively Robert reacted against that. Blackitt was a friendly ally now, but he would have to do his duty, Minister or not.

Should he go in search of Sancroft and talk it over with him? Sancroft was a loyal soul whose discretion could be trusted, but he had an independent mind. His job as a lobby journalist was to jump to conclusions and stick to them. West wanted to talk round the problem and arrive at no conclusion just yet. He was afraid of possible conclusions, especially the one at which the irreverent Sancroft was certain to jump.

Don was the man. They would dine together at the same table again as they had dined on the night of the murder and talk the whole thing out.

When he had telephoned for Shaw, who promised to come over at once, West returned to his restless pacing up and down the Terrace, which was filling now with guests for dinner. He managed to avoid being roped into a party to meet Rosaleen Ray, the new cinema star, who was holding a little court at the Peers' end of the Terrace, and to escape having to fill in at a Colonial Office party to some lawyers and educationists from West Africa.

"It's no use, Rory," he protested to the energetic Under-Secretary who was determined that he should come and be polite to "his coloured fellow-subjects." "I know I ought to come and be amiable, but I never know what to say to people from the Empire except 'It's a good old Empire, isn't it?' And so often they don't think it is. They are sure to feel they are oppressed or that we aren't doing our duty by 'em, and then it gets so awkward. I don't know a thing about exchanging needles for cocoa-beans, so do count me out."

Robert was pointed out to a good many people as he walked up and down waiting for Shaw, unable to settle down to do anything else. The Oissel case was still the main topic of conversation. So far people were being good-humoured about it, and rather resentful of the fuss the Americans were making. The Americans ought to understand that the police were doing their best. But Robert knew, and the Government knew, that this mood would last only over the week-end. Then a debate would be forced, a statement would have to be made, world publicity. Robert groaned at the thought. But that the Home Secretary, rigid, domineering, conventional, should be mixed up in the shady side of such a show—this

Robert found himself unable to believe, but he felt more curious about his Chief than he had been in all the years he had known him. He had taken him as much for granted since his boyhood as he did the statue of Queen Victoria in the square at home. Was the human statue a façade hiding something exceedingly queer?

The lights began to be lit in the Terrace dining-rooms. The hour before dinner on a June night on the Terrace is one of the compensations of an M.P.'s life. No constituents have to be lived up to impressively. It is the time for chosen friends and intimate little parties. Robert, standing with his back to the wall of the Speaker's house, which closes one end of the Terrace, looked down the quarter-mile of flagged walk. The over-ornamented Gothic walls were softened in the twilight. The river had gathered a rich blue from the sunset sky. M.P.s came out for a breath of air. Guests began to arrive. There were several dinner-parties being given. *Débutantes* in long dresses whose velvets and lace swept the old stones gave colour. The rough tweed coats of the miners' M.P.s added a touch of homeliness. It was all so mixed, so English, and so essentially friendly.

Only the windows of Room J remained dark. No party had been given there since the night of the murder. To Robert, miserably conscious of his secret, that darkened room seemed a symbol of the rot under this gay surface life. Things in England were not what they had been when this place was built and Victoria opened it. He felt how little he knew of the world outside his island, and of the great forces that were sweeping into his guarded world. Russia and America, titans of the East and West... and between them the England of tradition, of the old ways, of the splendid past... But if those traditions did not hold good... if there were breaches in the dyke?

Not for the first time did Robert West rage angrily against that public-school education which had given him no clue to this new world. Some of the Labour men, the younger ones, seemed to know what was happening. But was he so very different from the Stuart-Orfords, looking back to a world that had gone, to traditions that seemed to be breaking?

His reverie was interrupted by the arrival of Don Shaw's card. He decided not to take Shaw to the Harcourt room after all. They would dine amid the cheerful racket of the Strangers' Dining-room, the shabby, crowded, smoke-laden room where M.P.s can entertain their guests with the cheapest meal in the West End. "I'm not being mean, Don," said Robert as he explained this. "But I want to seem cheerful while I can."

"Get it all off your chest," Shaw drawled in his soothing voice. "I won't interrupt."

Very rapidly, letting his food grow cold on his plate unheeded, Robert told the whole story as he knew it. Shaw gave no sign of surprise. When he had finished Bob said rather impatiently: "Well?"

"You seem determined to think the worst of your Chief," was all Don said.

"But, Don, hang it all, that's just what I don't want to do, but what other explanation is there?"

"I suppose I have a contrary mind, Bob, so let's go over the points, and I'll try to put a possible case for your Minister."

"Good. That's what I'd hoped you'd do. Well, let's begin with the first point. Jenks, the Home Secretary's man, despite all official regulations is lent directly by him to Oissel."

"That's easy. It was done, you say, to soothe Oissel, who was in no doubt as to Jenks' confidential relation to the Home Secretary. Sir George Gleeson also knew, and had at least sanctioned the innovation, even if he didn't approve it."

"Right," said Bob. "Now the next point. Jenks knows which is the key document, and steals it to have it copied."

"You have no evidence at all that it was being copied for the Home Secretary. In fact, quite the contrary, since he has apparently been able to obtain copies elsewhere. That leaves two questions to be settled—who was Jenks operating for, and where did your Chief get his copy?"

Robert made a note of these two points on the back of an envelope. "We'll come back to those," he said, "but you must admit that it looks queer if Jenks gets the only opportunity he could have had to get the pages copied when the Home Secretary had managed for the first time to get Oissel to break his rule about dining out."

"It certainly gave Jenks his opportunity," said Shaw, helping himself to more potatoes, "but that does not necessarily mean that the Home Secretary deliberately provided it, any more than you did. If Jenks was doing this for some rival group it might have been just a piece of buckshee luck for him."

"And then the next point—Oissel is murdered, his flat raided, and Jenks killed on his return from getting the memobook photographed. Where does that fit in?"

"Well, it doesn't fit into your theory about the Home Secretary. At least, he would be doing things in a wholesale fashion if it did. I come back to my original theory there, Bob, that some other group is operating. Surely you can get information about that."

West shrugged his shoulders. "These big Government loans are carried through so few channels, and in this case the other channels don't seem to have been in the least interested," he said. "I managed to get from Mortimer, the Prime Minister's secretary, that the only other possible group had been tried and simply would not come in. That's absolutely confidential, of course. It would make things look worse for British credit if it came out."

"Then we are left with the fifth and last point," answered Don. "Your finding a copy of some of the pages of the memo-book among the Home Secretary's papers, and in his handwriting. Now where did he get them from? Has he been in possession of the book since it was found on Jenks?"

"It's been locked in Blackitt's cupboard all that time. I know that."

"But *you* had it out for a night—why shouldn't *he*?"

"I'm sure Blackitt would have told me if the Minister had borrowed it."

"Could any other official have got it for the Minister if he specially asked for it? Is there any way you could find that out?"

"I could phone Blackitt. I think I could put it to him quite casually. I'll just go along and do it now."

West was not absent long. When he returned it was with the information that the Home Secretary had asked to look at whatever papers had been found on Jenks. They had been sent to him, and he had returned them in about an hour's time with a note of condolence written in his own hand to old Mrs Jenks, and two five-pound notes to be included when the Home Office sent to her the money that had been found in the wallet. "A perfectly natural thing for him to do, of course, so Blackitt did not mention it to me. It's evident he doesn't think anything of it. But he is emphatic that no Home Office experts have been called in to decode the cipher."

"The queer thing to me," said Don thoughtfully, "is why the Home Secretary should return that notebook when he knew of its importance. Surely he could have kept it in special custody himself if he had wanted, couldn't he?"

"Yes, of course. Especially if he'd had a word with Gleeson. Now why did he send it back and say nothing?"

"Don't you think you'd better see your Minister, and discuss the whole thing with him?" asked Shaw. "There may be a perfectly simple explanation of what looks queer on the surface. In fact, it may be so simple that he himself doesn't see how bad it would look if it came out to the public more or less as it has come to you. If Houldsworth and the Scots Members are on this they may ferret out something of what you have discovered. Fancy all this coming out in Parliament without the Minister realizing the sort of construction that could be put on it!"

"Yes, of course, I must see him," answered West, "but will he discuss it with me? He's damnably touchy if he thinks I'm questioning anything he has done, though he stands more from me than anyone connected with this place. I don't suppose he'll even listen to me."

"Then you'll have to go to some one who will make him listen," said Shaw impatiently. He was growing a little tired of the attitude which both West and Blackitt adopted as a matter of course, that there was something sacred about a Minister of the Crown, and that the vagaries of a rather bad-tempered elderly gentleman must be treated as matters of real importance.

"I'll see him first thing to-morrow morning," said Robert, "and if Gleeson is with him I'll sit on the doorstep and refuse to be kicked off it. If he's going down to his place at Esher for the week-end I'll travel on the running-board of his car if necessary and shout at him through the window. I can't do more than that."

Shaw looked with affection at the handsome head of his friend. "I don't suppose those hectic measures will be really necessary, but get hold of him and make him listen you must.

He seems to me to be calmly sitting on a powder-barrel that may go up at any moment."

"It will take a lot of other things with it, if it does. Lord, what a life, and some folks think that the House of Commons is a peaceful refuge for the aged and infirm! Irak will seem comparatively tame after this, won't it, Don?"

CHAPTER XIII

After Shaw had gone, and as the House was still sitting, West allowed himself to be roped into the fag-end of a party of Murray Grey's which had already been going on for some time in the dining-room next to Room J. Kinnaird was there and waved to him from the other end of the table as he came in. Robert was not feeling particularly convivial, but he was in the mood for drink, and lots of it. He finished the remaining half of a bottle of champagne, and went on to drink steadily what was put before him. The bells rang for the rising of the House, but the party took no notice. It was midnight before the head waiter was able to impress upon the host that his party were positively the last people in the building.

As they went along the corridor the waiters were extinguishing lights behind them. By the time they got out into Palace Yard the remainder of the staff came hurrying by. West lingered for a while by his host's car talking rather vaguely about the business of the day.

Suddenly, as Murray Grey drove away, and West was crossing the Yard, he remembered that he had left his attaché-case in the room where the party had been. To his horror he realized that all the careful notes he had been taking about the Oissel murder were in it. To leave it lying about was impossible even though every one had gone. The one idea in his drink-fuddled brain was that he must retrieve that case at any cost.

With a word to the policeman at the entrance he hurried back into the House, up the stairs, and into the central lobby. There is no place so eerie as the House of Commons when every one has gone. Within half an hour of its pulsating with life and movement it will be deserted, the only lights in the long corridors being the firemen's lanterns on the floor, which make deeper the shadows on the high walls. He felt his way down the stairs to the swing doors which lead to the Harcourt corridor. There was a faint light from the river, then impenetrable darkness. Robert couldn't remember where the switches were, but he thought he could grope his way to Room H, where Murray Grey's party had been held. He wondered if the policeman was kept on duty in Room J all night. Gleeson's orders had been definite that it must not be left, but perhaps with doors locked and the police on guard at the outside entrance that had been considered sufficient.

As he groped his way along the corridor walls there came over Robert the queer feeling that he was not alone. His heart began to beat quickly.

"Are you there? Anyone there?" he said sharply.

There was no answer. Then it could not be the policeman. Even if one was still on duty he would not be standing in black darkness. He walked along a little farther very quietly, feeling for his box of matches. With a quick gesture he struck a light. He was too quick. The head of the match lit, and flew off the stalk. But in its fall for one split second it made an arc of dim light, and by that light Robert saw to his horror a man's boot with a frieze of trouser-leg. Some one was standing not three yards away from him.

"Who's there?" he said again. He had a feeling that some one was moving very silently. He put his fingers into the box to get another match.

"Oh, damn," he said aloud, "that was the only one."

Then he cursed himself for a fool. He had given some one a valuable piece of information by saying that. For some one must be there. That boot had a foot in it.

Sheer fright had sobered Robert by now. Whoever was in the corridor was no friend of his or the police, or they would have spoken. Who were they and what were they, or was there only one? What were they doing in the darkness? Robert felt pretty sure that the clue to the Oissel murder, perhaps even the murderer himself, had been at that moment within reach of his hand, and in the most closely guarded building in London, with police only two hundred yards away. It was maddening.

If he could reach one of the smaller dining-rooms he could get his hands on the light switches. They were all on the same plan as in Room J, which he knew by heart. Feeling his way very cautiously, and with his heart beating to suffocation, Robert made his way along the wall. Any moment some blow might fall from the dark, as mysteriously as the shot that killed Georges Oissel in that empty room.

He got to Room J and stealthily tried the door. It was locked. So the policeman was not on duty. Or had the owner of that boot retreated inside the room? Carefully he groped his way next door to Room H. The door opened as he turned the handle. With a gasp of relief he found the switch and turned on the light. But even with the door open most of the corridor was in darkness. He could see no one. It was he who was illumined, a target for any foe that was lurking in the shadows.

A box of matches had been left on the table. Robert struck a light and walked along the corridor. Of course he would find no one that way. But at least that meant that they were avoiding a fight. He went back to Room H. He must get police while there was still a chance that the owner of the boot had not been able to get away.

As he went back into Room H he almost screamed. A face was pressed against the window. It vanished as soon as he saw it. With a swift gesture Robert switched off the light. He was safer in the dark. He groped his way to the window and cautiously looked out on to the Terrace. All was dark; only the lights on Westminster Bridge twinkled in the distance. He went back to the door and cautiously opened it. A fresh draught of air struck his face. Some one had opened the door that led from the corridor on to the Terrace.

A flashlight was turned full in his face. "Thank God," said Robert. "Where did you come from?" It was a policeman.

"I was on the Terrace when the light in Room H was switched on. I thought it was Room J, and right glad I was to see it was you, sir, but you did look scared."

"You are on duty here all night?"

"Yes, sir. Orders about Room J. I haven't left it before, sir, but I felt awful queer—room going round. I felt I must get on to the Terrace for a bit of air... I..." The policeman made a gesture of grabbing the air, and then collapsed at West's feet.

"Good God!" gasped West. One never expects to see a sick policeman. An awful thought shot through West's brain. Was the policeman drugged? Had some one been trying to dope the watch-dog?

He left the policeman stretched on the floor, while he groped his way to the telephone in the room he had just left. He rang up Sergeant Bourne. No reply. He got through to the police room at the Members' entrance. A cheery voice answered. It seemed like a life-line from a sane world.

While waiting for the police to come Robert went back to the prostrate policeman. He switched the usual official flashlight around and strained his ears. All was deadly still, until he heard the hurrying footsteps of the policemen coming down the stairs. Had the owner of that foot been able to make his getaway? Certainly he had had every opportunity, but he must have known the terrain better than himself. That was one point he must remember to tell Blackitt.

When the police arrived Robert left one with the sick constable, while he and the other searched the kitchens and the dining-rooms. They unlocked Room J and switched on every light in the place, but no one could be seen.

Robert phoned Blackitt at his home in Camden Town and was asked to stay where he was until the Inspector arrived. By this time the policeman who wore an ambulance badge had managed to get the unconscious man round by the liberal application of doses of salt and water. Robert's immediate concern was to keep the night's affair as quiet as possible. Need the policeman be taken to hospital?

"Not he," said the ambulance man, who was giving him a dose of brandy. "Right as rain now. Takes some dope to knock a chap like you over, eh, Robinson?"

Well, thank heaven, that danger of leakage to the newspapers would not happen! West shuddered to imagine the morning papers if news of this night's adventures got out. He hinted at secrecy to the older of the constables. "I shall have to make a report to the Superintendent, sir."

"Yes, of course," said Robert, "but do see to it that nothing gets into the papers. I am sure Inspector Blackitt will be most particular about that."

By the time Blackitt arrived the constable was better, but still shaky, and very worried about having left Room J. He explained that the waiters always left a cup of coffee for him or whichever policeman was on duty there each night. No, he hadn't noticed which waiter had left the coffee this night. It was put on the service shelf outside Room J. He had just drunk it before going into the room, and the cup had been cleared away. After drinking the coffee he had gone into Room J, but had begun to feel ill. No, he hadn't felt ill at once, it came over him slowly. He thought the place might be stuffy, and had decided it wouldn't do any harm to go on to the Terrace for a stroll and keep an eye on Room J from there.

"Did you see anyone about?" asked Blackitt.

"No, Inspector. Mr West and Mr Murray Grey were about the last to go out after their party, and the waiters weren't two minutes after them."

"Had you drunk your coffee before the waiters went?"

"Yes, sir. One of them said, 'Here, hurry up, we want your cup,' so I drank it up quick."

Blackitt and West exchanged glances. "Which waiter said that?"

"It was that little chap, youngest of the lot he is, apple cheeks, I don't know his name."

"That's not the one who served in J," said West. "Was he the one who put the coffee there for you, constable?"

"I don't know, sir. I don't know who did. The young lad took it away, sir, but any of them might have brought it."

"Some more combing in that kitchen is indicated," West said to Blackitt.

"I've done a good bit there already without getting much forrarder, but this takes the biscuit," said Blackitt. "Anyway, we can't do more to-night," and he repeated West's orders to the constables that nothing should be said as yet about the events of the night, except the report to the Superintendent.

After the sick policeman had been sent home and another guard put on the room, West went to look for his attaché-case and was relieved to find it where he had left it.

"That policeman was obviously doped by some one who wanted to get into Room J," he said as Blackitt walked back with him to his flat.

"Yes, and not too well done. I suppose they just wanted to give him enough to send him to sleep while they did what they had to do, so that he would wake up before questions were asked in the morning. They evidently hadn't realized how much a hefty man like Robinson would need."

"It must have upset their plans that instead of going to sleep in the room he'd been able to lock the door behind him and get on to the Terrace, and so keep himself going for a while."

"Yes, probably, but the question we want to know is, whose was the foot that was inside that boot you saw?"

"Well, obviously it must have been some one who knew the run of the place pretty well—a waiter, or perhaps... a Member."

"All your party went out before you?"

"Yes, I think I was the last out with Murray Grey. We all rather went out in a mob, you know... and... er... well, I wouldn't like to swear to everything that was happening just then. We had been drinking all we wanted. Murray Grey isn't one of the House pussyfoots."

"Can you remember who was there, besides Mr Kinnaird and Mr Murray Grey?"

West tried to think. "Honestly, it's all rather a blur, but

we could get a list from Murray Grey to-morrow, or later
to-day, rather."

"But there were some men there who were not M.P.s?"

"Oh, yes, the majority, I should think. There were about
fifteen or sixteen men in the room altogether. But I'm damned
sure that Murray Grey had nothing to do with any monkey
tricks. He's as straight as a die."

"I don't suppose he had. But we mustn't neglect the fact
that here was one obvious way in which people not connected with the House of Commons could be on the lower
corridor long after the House had risen, and when there was
no one else in the building. Now can you remember what
kind of a boot it was that you saw? Was it an evening pump,
for instance?"

"No, it was a man's walking boot. But that doesn't help
much—none of Murray Grey's guests were in evening dress."

"Can you remember if it was a good-looking boot, or
might it have belonged to a waiter, for example."

"There you've got me. I have the vivid impression of a
boot with the edge of a black trouser on it. Only a second,
remember—I couldn't exactly take notes," and West looked
rather apologetic.

"That's all right. You've remembered quite a lot. It might
therefore have been a waiter's or a guest's or some one not
connected with either."

"It might have been a waiter's, but somehow that impression wasn't left on my mind… a more substantial boot than
waiters would wear in the House."

By this time they had reached the narrow street in Soho
where Robert rented his odd little flat. Blackitt paused for
a moment under the street lamp at the corner, to relight his
pipe. Robert, waiting for him, was standing on the other

side of the road about four doors up from the entrance to the narrow stairs up to his flat. He was astonished to see a slender man in a light overcoat, his hat pulled well down over his eyes, walk out from the doorway and pass rapidly along the street.

Robert darted across the road and gripped Blackitt's arm. "Who's that? He's come out of my doorway." With Blackitt at his heels Robert ran after the man, but he had already turned the corner. When they got there they could see no one. The man had vanished into the darkness of the mass of little passages of Soho's back streets.

"Better let me go first," said Blackitt, as they went back to the stairs which led to Robert's flat. "Was he hiding in the doorway, do you think?" For there was a passage at least ten feet long before one came to the heavy door which was Robert's private entrance.

There was no sign on the door that anyone had been trying to force it. The men went carefully up the winding stairs and reached the actual door of West's flat. There were no signs here of its having been tampered with. West opened the door and switched on the lights. The flat was empty, and nothing had been touched.

"Perhaps the man was just sheltering, or taking up a position for the night," said Blackitt.

"Might be," said West thoughtfully. Then he added slowly: "Queer thing, Blackitt, but though I couldn't see his face there was something familiar about that man. I felt as though I'd seen him before, or he reminded me of some one, but I can't think who. It's tantalizing... I... no, I can't pin that recollection down—it was just a momentary feeling of recognition."

"Some one waiting to beg, perhaps, and disappointed at

your not coming home alone?" suggested Blackitt. "Or," he added with interest, "could it conceivably be the owner of the boot you saw in the darkness?"

Robert perched on the edge of the table. "I didn't see his boots, but I feel I know the man. Oh, my God," he added with a desperate irritation, "what a night! Things just at the tips of one's fingers all the time and yet one isn't able to get hold of anything! It's damnable!"

"Make some of that coffee you promised me. Perhaps the connexion will come back to you," smiled Blackitt.

"Good. I'll get this giddy percolator going. I warn you it's liable to blow up, Blackitt, but this chicken needs some strong black coffee. You look in the pink in spite of being yanked out of bed at one A.M. Sign of a mis-spent youth, I fear."

Blackitt grinned from his creaky armchair by the gas-fire, wishing that all his colleagues in the work he had to do were as pleasant to deal with as this cheerful, friendly young politician.

He accepted gratefully the strong black coffee which Robert finally produced. "I wonder," he said thoughtfully, as he stirred several lumps of sugar into it, "whether whoever was in the corridor was really after Room J."

"If they were connected with the Oissel case, surely they must have been. That was the scene of their operations then, anyway."

"Yes," said Blackitt in his slow, deliberate way, "but what my mind has been working on is this. We've all concentrated on Room J. We've assumed that what killed Oissel must have been inside that room. Well, need it have been? I'm beginning to doubt it."

"But the bullet must have been, or else it couldn't have killed him."

"True, but need the revolver that the bullet was fired from have been in that room. That's what I keep worrying round."

"You mean that whoever was in the corridor to-night was trying to cover up some tracks that we haven't found yet?"

"Either that... or he was preparing for a second murder."

"Good Lord, Blackitt... what on earth——?"

"What I feel about this business," continued Blackitt, "is that we've all been going round in a little circle, so to speak. Not looking for the bigger things behind, if you get me."

West, thinking of the notes in the Home Secretary's file, murmured a feeble "Ye... es."

"When we—I mean the police—had to start off with the burglary at Charlton Court, we went through the usual investigations. And there was only one conclusion we could come to."

"What was that?"

"Well, not only that it wasn't a burglary—not in any ordinary sense—but also we became pretty sure that it wasn't any of the usuals. Everything pointed to some one who knew the run of the place."

"Got any theory who?"

"We went through all his customary visitors as you know. Not a shaky one amongst the lot. As respectable as the Archbishop's."

"Kinnaird?"

"I went into his affairs pretty thoroughly, but couldn't get anything on him. Been hit a bit by the slump, but who hasn't? Nothing that his friends couldn't help him through, I gather. And there's no motive in his case. He is practically engaged to Miss Oissel, and was on the best of terms with the old man. No, I've come to the conclusion that we must begin thinking from the starting-point of the loan. I think that's the skeleton in the cupboard."

"Or the cupboard which the skeleton is in," smiled Robert, in spite of his utter tiredness. He was longing for sleep, but now that Blackitt had got his ally to himself he was in the mood to talk.

"And that's where I'm worried about the Home Secretary."

Robert sat up with a jerk, all attention. "Why?"

"Well, I take it this loan business isn't finished?" Robert felt that the Inspector must be guided into safer paths.

"It is as far as he is concerned. He was only in it at all because he knew Mr Oissel personally. Now he is out of it the Home Secretary is out of it too."

"I'm not so sure," said Blackitt thoughtfully. "I wish I knew more about... er... well, how friendly the Home Secretary was with Mr Oissel."

"I don't see what that's got to do with it."

Blackitt knocked out his pipe. "Well, I'm arguing like this, though I don't see my way too clear as yet. There was big money in this loan for somebody."

"Not for the Home Secretary," said Robert hotly, but even as he said it he thought of those notes in the file, and felt rather sick.

"No, but perhaps his friendship with Mr Oissel was stopping some one else having a look in, and his influence may be being used in that way now."

"This is getting all too fantastic, Blackitt, it really is. Are you suggesting with this talk of a second murder that some one is going to put the Home Secretary out of the way in order to get in on the loan? How on earth could that help whoever is responsible for Oissel's murder?"

"Perhaps they expected to get the Minister the first time. How could they know that he would be out of the room while the dinner was going on? A very unlikely thing except for the accident of the division."

"Ye… es, that's true. He wouldn't have been out otherwise, and then there would have been a witness to the murder."

"Or another corpse."

"Or…" But Robert's mind refused even to frame the haunting fear that was growing in it that the only person who could tell how Georges Oissel died was the man who last saw him alive. Blackitt's theory of an international gang was safer anyway. It should be encouraged.

"There is this to be said for your theory, Blackitt," said West. "International rings haven't stopped at murder on a wholesale scale in the past. Wars have been the tools of their trade. I suppose there's no reason why they should stop at going into the retail business, so to speak. My only difficulty is that I don't see how they expect to cash in on the results."

"I'm not accusing respectable financiers," said Blackitt.

"There aren't any," interrupted West flippantly.

"What I mean is that Oissel was a tough customer who hadn't stopped at much himself. He seems to have known as much of the underworld as most. And the Home Secretary knew him when he didn't wear a top hat. These two come together again when one is a Minister and the other a millionaire. But there may be old scores to be paid off. One of them has met the bill. Has what you stumbled on to-night anything to do with putting paid to the account of the other? That's what I'd like to know." The two men sat silently considering this. Then Blackitt rose to go.

"Blackitt, I never expected you to be romantic," said West with an uneasy laugh as he bade his visitor good-night. "Anyway, you look like having *your* hands full."

"I'm glad there's a bit of a move on from their side," replied Blackitt. "It was the stalemate, not being able to get a clue anywhere, that got me down."

When Blackitt had gone West threw himself into a chair. Tired as he was, he had never felt less like sleep. He might gibe at Blackitt's theory, but it seemed to him uncomfortably near the truth. The Home Secretary had something to hide. There might be a perfectly good explanation for those notes in his file, just curiosity when Jenks' papers were brought to him, but the fact that, knowing that the book was Oissel's (as he must have done), he should have sent it back to Blackitt without any inquiry as to how it came into Jenks' possession—this seemed too strange to admit of any completely innocent explanation.

It was still odder to think of the rigid and honoured Cabinet Minister with a wild-cat past. The logging holiday had seemed such a perfectly respectable explanation of his friendship with Mr Oissel, but, as Blackitt had remarked, it had been very much in the pre-tall-hat stage of Oissel's career.

And that boot in the dark. Who had been on the corridor and slipped out into the night unseen? Some one who knew the ways of the House—that was pretty evident. And who was the man who had been hiding in the doorway? Anyway, there was nothing to be done now, but he must see the Home Secretary as early as possible in the morning. Tearing his clothes off somehow, Robert got into bed and slept the sleep of utter exhaustion.

CHAPTER XIV

"Beware of the week-end" is sound advice for any Government which has even the possibility of a crisis in the offing.

When a Minister who has been having a bad time surveys the House, which meets on Fridays at eleven in the morning, generally in lounge suits or tweeds as an indication of the slackening of political attention, he will say to himself, "Praise the Lord, they will have to be quiet for the next two days anyway." But the lazy M.P.s go home to talk to their wives or their club friends, and the energetic ones go and talk to meetings and conferences. If there is even a hint of mystery in the air no M.P. can possibly be expected to refrain from hinting at a 'crisis.' That is why Ministers hate Mondays.

Robert, after the events of the previous night, was determined to see the Home Secretary as soon as possible this Friday morning. He dashed into the Home Office, only to be told by Briggs that the Home Secretary had gone away for the week-end.

"Surely you remember," said Briggs. "He's gone to christen a new ship that his constituents have built."

"Why the hell does he want to go off on a jaunt like that, at a time like this?" said Robert savagely.

"Don't deprive a Minister of his toys, else what's the good

of being a Minister? Don't you like it when the brass band meets *you*? Oh, there's an urgent message from Lady Bell-Clinton. She wants you to ring up as soon as you come in. Shall I get her number for you?"

Robert moodily waited while Briggs fussed about with the telephone. He had screwed up his courage for what was likely to have been an extremely unpleasant and difficult interview, and the Chief he was so anxious to save from the consequences of what Robert thought he must have done had gone off on a joy-ride to christen a ship!

"That you, Robert?" said the gay voice of Lady Bell-Clinton down the phone. "I want you to come down to Clinton Bardsley this week-end. Now don't say you've got another engagement—you've simply got to come."

Lady Bell-Clinton was a very important person, being an M.P. herself and the wife of the Secretary of State for War. Any other time Robert would have hailed such an invitation with joy, but he could not face a house-party just now. He was feeling aggrieved, and rather like the Tommy who asked after his fifth fatigue where was the rest of the British Army. He conveyed this over the phone as tactfully as he could.

"Anything may happen on this Oissel case and with the Home Secretary out of town I feel I ought to be on tap. The Minister asked me to work with Inspector Blackitt, you see." Robert's tone was not entirely free from a certain self-importance. He half expected to be chaffed by Ivy Bell Clinton, but she said: "That's why you must come. Annette Oissel is coming, and she specially asked me to produce you."

Annette had asked for him! The world suddenly looked a much brighter place.

"Then of course I'll come. I want to see her about a lot of things."

"I expected you might," answered Lady Bell-Clinton drily. "I'll drive you down from the House after lunch if you like."

Robert dashed back to Soho to pack his bag in high excitement. Had Annette asked for him because she had more to tell him about the mystery, or—and here Robert felt warm inside—could she have wanted to see him anyway?

Robert was always more amused than awed by the luxury of Clinton Bardsley, largely because the personality of Ivy Bell-Clinton made it so difficult to be awed by anything connected with her. The daughter and heiress of the largest firm of brewers in the world, Ivy Bell had married in Sir Anthony Clinton, a baronet whose family was older than most European dynasties. But she had insisted on the double name; she was not ashamed of her origin, and she had made Clinton Bardsley a lively meeting-place for people doing worthwhile work in the world and who held the most widely differing opinions.

Lady Bell-Clinton took an impish joy in inducing the most extraordinary people to mix together, but the party that Robert West found on this occasion was one of her super-respectable kind. It included a Cabinet Minister with a wife who must surely have been taken to her christening in a robe of black *crêpe de Chine* and old lace; a couple of City men whose wives were not in evidence; a champion lady golfer; and Lord Dalbeattie, a member of the synthetic aristocracy whose peerage had been made for him only six months previously.

West looked with interest at Dalbeattie, whom he had not met before, but whom he had heard described as the Pirate King because of his sensational and successful raids in the world of high finance. Dalbeattie looked so smooth and self-contained that Robert remembered with a smile Ivy

Bell-Clinton's description of him as being like one of those Russian dolls, very solid-looking outside but containing such a surprising number of things when you unscrew them. The unscrewing of Lord Dalbeattie would be a very interesting operation even to an expert like Lady Bell-Clinton.

Annette did not appear until sherry was being handed round before dinner. Robert was at first annoyed to find that Kinnaird was very much in attendance on her, but on second thoughts he was rather glad. He hoped there would be a chance for a further talk with him about Oissel and his affairs.

During dinner Robert felt like a marionette in some queer puppet-play. The small party was marooned round an oval table in the immensity of the Louis Quinze dining-room. In deference to Annette, stately and silent in her black gown, no mention was made of the affair at the House of Commons, though it was obviously the one thing every one except the woman golfer was thinking about. Fortunately Mrs Rockingham's loud voice and endless selection of quite good golfing stories filled in every awkward gap that opened. Lady Bell-Clinton pulled a face at Robert as he opened the door for the retreat of the ladies. It was tiresome to have to go and be a lady in the drawing-room when she wanted to be an M.P. and remain for the talk. The House of Commons unfits a woman M.P. for the smaller observances of the social routine that is prescribed for the Lady Bell-Clintons.

While the port was being passed Dalbeattie turned to his host, the Secretary of State for War, who looked blissfully peaceful, and remarked: "You are dallying along rather dangerously with this Oissel affair, aren't you?"

"I—what have I to do with it?"

"Well, you are in the Cabinet."

"Precisely. Do you expect me to undertake the duties of the police as well? I understand Robert here has turned amateur detective, and from what I can gather from Gleeson"—here Sir Anthony turned to West with his precise little smile—"you are not any too popular with your department because of it."

"But surely you realize," said Dalbeattie, "or some one in the Cabinet ought to, that this business is creating the very devil in the City?"

Sir Anthony turned his mild blue eyes upon his guest. "I cannot see what it has to do with the City."

"Really, Clinton"—and Dalbeattie's voice had an edge of exasperation—"I sometimes think that even Cabinet Ministers might occasionally take a look at the world outside their departmental doors. Everything affects the City. There are all sorts of ugly rumours. The Cabinet is walking blindfold into a first-class crisis."

Sir Anthony Bell-Clinton calmly surveyed the ash on his cigar. "The City likes to have something to excuse a flutter. But this matter is entirely the affair of the Home Office. I have no doubt that the Home Secretary will present a report to the Cabinet when he has anything to report." Then he turned to Philip as one who is tactfully changing the subject and remarked pleasantly: "So the lovely Annette is a very great heiress indeed, from all I hear."

Kinnaird smiled politely. "She tells me that she feels very worried by the responsibility of it."

There was a general laugh at this. "A responsibility that will no doubt be shared very soon," added the other Cabinet Minister. Again Robert had that feeling of taking part in a charade. Every one was saying pleasant little bromides as though they were repeating parts in a play. He glanced at

Dalbeattie. He seemed real. So did Kinnaird. Men up against life. West wondered if he too had that air of puppetry that seemed to be shared by the other Parliamentarians who were present.

When there was a general move to join the ladies Robert found Dalbeattie at his elbow. "Like to come for a stroll?" asked the older man.

"Nothing I'd like better, but will Lady Bell-Clinton…?"

"Oh, that's all right. Ivy wants people to do as they like."

The formal gardens of Clinton Bardsley were drenched in moonlight. "This is the loveliest place I know," said Robert, touched by the amazing beauty around him.

"Yes," said Dalbeattie drily. "I wonder how much longer even the Bell-Clinton income can keep it up. The day of these private white elephants is over."

"It's a damned shame," said Robert hotly. "I mean, they did stand for something that will never be quite the same in the world again."

Dalbeattie looked at him with surprise. "And you've been mentioned to me as quite a dangerous Bolshevik! This environment has produced Anthony Clinton, who is as much use in the modern world as an ivory Buddha. But now about this Oissel affair. Have you formed any conclusion yourself about it? I gather from the Home Secretary that you have taken hold of it. I'm glad some one has."

"Even if only a P.P.S.?"

Dalbeattie laughed. "They have their uses."

Robert hesitated. He felt the strength of Dalbeattie's personality. He was tempted to pour out the whole story, even to his fears about his Minister. But decency forbade. He must see the Home Secretary first. He dare not share his knowledge—and his suspicions.

Dalbeattie misinterpreted his hesitation.

"I am not exactly an outsider in this matter," he said quietly. "I have been advising the Prime Minister on technical matters connected with the loan. I was very much against the Home Secretary seeing Oissel privately."

Robert felt that he must appear to be frank. To let out just a little might be the best way of concealing the bigger secret. "I expect you know more than I do," he said. "All we have been able to find out is that Edward Jenks, the Home Secretary's man who was guarding Oissel, appears to have been double-crossing both Oissel and the Minister. We have discovered that he was attempting to steal certain important documents. At least, the evidence we have points that way. It is not absolutely conclusive."

Dalbeattie stopped in his slow, deliberate walk, and turned to stare at Robert. "The Home Secretary's man trying to steal important documents from Oissel. Good God, man, it's worse than I ever imagined it could be." As Robert had become used to the lesser secret, he was surprised at the effect it had on his companion.

"It's much worse than that," he said to himself, "or it may be." Aloud he said: "Well, the proof isn't conclusive, as I say."

"It doesn't have to be. The suspicion is enough. How many people know even that much?"

"Just the Inspector in charge and myself."

"But surely the Home Secretary… what does he say about it? You aren't trying to sit on this volcano, are you, for some idiotic idea of trying to get kudos out of it?"

Robert was offended, and showed it. "I have been trying to get an interview alone with the Home Secretary for two days, but he has been too busy."

"He would be. He'll be tidying his papers at the day of

judgment. Where is he now? Let's get a car and drive to see him at once."

Dalbeattie made Robert feel that he had been as lackadaisical as the politicians he had been despising at dinner.

"We can't get him this week-end. He's up in Scotland christening a ship."

"My God!" Dalbeattie sat heavily down on a seat. "How does this country get itself run at all? Here is a first-class crisis that may blow the Government out of the water. The Home Secretary's man is involved in a shady side of it, and the Home Secretary is allowed to toddle away to christen ships without being told of it. What the hell do you think of yourself, West?"

Robert was suddenly frightened. Had he been fancying himself as amateur detective without realizing the bigger implications of the affair? This man made him feel like a schoolboy caught with matches and a tin of paraffin. Well, Dalbeattie had better know the worst, and perhaps he could take over the whole damned thing.

"That is not all," he said, almost dreading, yet revelling in, the effect he was about to produce. "Jenks went out to have those papers photographed on the night that Oissel was murdered, and I have found copies of the code in the Minister's handwriting among his files. He knows the code too. He had decoded the words, and the notes were all about the loan." He blurted all this out without stopping. Dalbeattie had gone very quiet.

"Are you mad, West, or are you drunk?"

"I shall go mad, very soon, Lord Dalbeattie, if I think about this business much more. I know you think I've been a fool, but I only found out about the Home Secretary having the code this morning. I tried to see him. I've been trying to get a word with him ever since I found out about Jenks, but I tell you I can't get five minutes alone with him. Gleeson seems never to let go of his hand these days."

"And a good thing too," said Dalbeattie as if to himself. "No, West. I don't think you are a fool—anything but. You seem to be the only person who has seriously tackled the problem, apart from the police of course. They know all this, I take it?"

"Not anything about the Home Secretary. I kept that to myself. They know about Jenks, of course."

"Well, I'm glad you kept this to yourself. You are sure no one else knows?"

Robert felt that he could not destroy the impression he had evidently made on Lord Dalbeattie by attempting to explain about Don Shaw. And anyway Shaw was too absolutely trustworthy to count.

"No. I've told no one else," said Robert. "But I'll see the Minister on Monday. I'll make him see me alone."

"He will see you," said Dalbeattie grimly. "Now we'll get out my car and go and see the Prime Minister."

"The Prime Minister?" gasped Robert. "But we can't do that before I've seen the Home Secretary."

"We can and must. There are bigger things at stake than that old gentleman's *amour propre*. God knows what he has been up to. Had some bright idea of double-crossing Oissel, I suppose. It's like a rabbit trying to put it across a terrier."

"But 'the dog it was that died,'" quoted Robert, as they walked back to the house.

"You're right, West, and a damned intelligent fellow if I may say so. You haven't found out whether the Home Secretary murdered Oissel as a conscientious contribution to the settlement of the international problem, I suppose?"

West laughed. He couldn't help it. He felt so utterly relieved now that he had shared his nightmare with so capable and astute a person as Dalbeattie. Then he remembered the coming interview with the Prime Minister. He found himself hoping that that awe-inspiring person would not be at Chequers, or in any other available spot, and at the same time thrilled with the idea of himself, a mere Parliamentary private secretary, arriving in state with the powerful Dalbeattie for a midnight interview. There is no wine so intoxicating as that feeling of being really in the inside when big events are moving.

Even the irrepressible Lady Bell-Clinton was awed when Dalbeattie sent the butler for her, and told her that he had phoned the Prime Minister, who had remained at Downing Street for a Saturday function, and that he and Robert were going there at once. She was too skilled in the management of men to ask any questions when both of them were obviously tense. She would be the confidante of each of them separately when they had calmed down. Besides, they would have more to tell her then. Lady Bell-Clinton preferred to deal with only one man at a time.

CHAPTER XV

During the long drive back to London in Dalbeattie's Rolls-Royce, Robert was put through a close cross-examination on every detail of the case. Then Dalbeattie was quiet for a time. "I think," he suddenly said, "that the murder will have to be kept separate from the Jenks affair. The Home Secretary does get sudden cranks. I've known him a long time, and he is quite incalculable when he gets some idea in his head. But I still believe him to be as straight as he is stupid. We've got to frighten him into telling the Prime Minister exactly what he has been up to, but the mystery of Oissel's death still remains, and that is what will make it so damned awkward for the Government."

"They don't seem to be very worried about it," said West. "I mean, if it is really going to be so serious they ought to do something about it, oughtn't they?"

Dalbeattie made an impatient exclamation. "I've often wondered, West, what it is that happens to most men—not all, of course—when they get into a Government. All parties seem to catch a low fever. I suppose it is that men get absolutely engrossed in their own departments, and the most difficult thing is to see a show as big as Britain, never mind the Empire, as a whole. I remember when a previous Government was within three days of dissolution and a smashing defeat talking to a Cabinet Minister who was calmly making plans for the following year. He just hadn't heard that there was trouble afoot. It sounds incredible, but I assure you that actually happened. And the man was not a fool, but a really capable Minister."

When the car drew up before the door of No. 10 Downing Street, Robert's thrill returned. He had attended official garden-parties there, and knew the hall and the main office. He had seen the room in which the Cabinet met. But he had never seen the private part of the house. As he walked up the white staircase with its simple green carpet, and the cheaply framed photographs of previous Prime Ministers on the walls, West warmed to this traditional simplicity of English public life. He followed Dalbeattie, who was evidently quite familiar with the house, through the oak-panelled but rather sombre dining-room into the small drawing-room which opened from the end of it. A simple snuggery it had been made by its present occupant. Comfortable chairs in bright chintz covers, a huge official desk, and a few books made all the furnishing of a room which must have heard more important conversations than almost any four walls in the world.

Robert, who was growing nervous and trying hard not to think too much of what was in store for him, was rather cheered when the Premier rose from his armchair clad in a dressing-gown and soft slippers. "I had changed when you telephoned," he said pleasantly, shaking hands first with Lord Dalbeattie and then with Robert, "and I knew you would forgive my receiving you like this."

"It is quite unpardonable to have bothered you at such a time, but you know that I should not have done so had I not felt that the matter was urgent," Dalbeattie replied with formal courtesy, but Robert saw that the two men were on terms of complete equality.

While his companion was explaining in general terms why he had brought West in such a hurry, Robert tried to get used to the Prime Minister in this informal garb, in place of the quite impressive figure who dominated the Treasury Bench in the House of Commons, when Dalbeattie turned to Robert and said: "Now I think you had better tell the Prime Minister the whole story as you told it to me." Robert felt his face go white. But he had gone over every detail so often in his own mind that he was able to give a coherent account of the entire affair from the first letter he had written for the Home Secretary to Georges Oissel to the finding of the decoded notes in the Minister's file.

The Premier was a good listener. He sat back in his chair and listened without moving or uttering a word. As Robert finished he turned to the older man and in an even voice which betrayed nothing of his own feelings he asked: "Well, and what do you think of all this, Dalbeattie?"

"It sounds incredible, but… well, there you are. West isn't a fool. Why ever did you let the man touch those loan negotiations? You know I was against his being brought in—right from the beginning."

"Please. We can't go into all that again. I had hoped the Home Secretary's personal relations with Mr Oissel would be useful, as undoubtedly they were, especially in the early stages of our discussions."

"But what *has* he been up to?"

The Prime Minister smiled a rather weary half-smile. "We must await his explanations. But I am sure that whatever he has done he did with the best intentions."

Dalbeattie laughed grimly. "Oh, these ultra-conscientious folk! They make ten times more mischief than the rogues. And when we are all in the soup he will be quite hurt if some one doesn't move him a vote of thanks. Christening a ship in Scotland he is at this minute, and leaving this powder-magazine behind him. The fuse is timed to explode on Monday. I suppose he will be back for the debate on the adjournment?"

"That's not till eleven," said West.

"It could come on at seven-thirty, and will, if a breath of all this has got out. I hope you have been extremely discreet, West," said the Premier.

"I can assure you I have not told a soul, sir." Again Robert's conscience pricked him about Shaw, but, thank God, Don was all right—and what a blessing he had not said a word to Blackitt!

The Prime Minister knocked out his pipe on the hearth. "Personalities, personalities, my God, what a problem they are!"

Robert had a glimmering of pity at that moment for this lonely man, for any man whose position raised him so far above the common run and yet left him with no means but his own wits to deal with the warring personalities around him. Sensitive to atmosphere, Robert felt that these two men wanted to be alone. They had to face the gathering storm. Queer that though he had never met Dalbeattie before dinner on this very night, he felt glad that the Premier had him at hand when such a crisis had to be faced. He rose and said deferentially to the Premier: "If that is all I can do, sir, perhaps if I went now…?"

"My man will drive you back to Clinton Bardsley," said Dalbeattie. "Tell him I will stay in town to-night. He can come back for me to-morrow."

"It will be long after midnight by the time I get back. Perhaps it will be rather rough on Lady Bell-Clinton to go down now."

"She will never forgive you if you don't."

The Prime Minister looked up in alarm. "Do you think he had better go there, Dalbeattie? Lady Bell-Clinton means well, but it might be very difficult for West to keep his own counsel about all this, if she were determined to know."

Dalbeattie smiled. "West looks as though he knew how to deal with a pretty woman. It will cause less comment if he goes. Think out a good yarn while you are driving back, West, for you'll have to tell Ivy something. Do you think you could manage to have a talk with Kinnaird during Sunday without, of course, giving a hint of anything we suspect about the code? I'm curious to know what his real relations were with Oissel, and whether Miss Oissel is going to accept him."

"Is that wise?" asked the Premier nervously. "Secrecy is above all essential until we have seen the Home Secretary. West might be pumped by a clever man like Kinnaird without his knowing it."

Dalbeattie smiled encouragingly at Robert. "The lad seems to have done pretty well so far. I think he can be trusted."

Robert went out to the waiting car with these words ringing in his ears, and on the long drive back he pondered on the problem, which is really the central problem of all government, of why it was that the forceful personalities like Dalbeattie, men who are born to be leaders of men, are so seldom found in active politics. He would like to be under Dalbeattie in a hard fight. He thanked his stars that he had had the impulse to trust him with that confession in the garden after dinner.

It was nearly two o'clock when Robert reached Clinton Bardsley. Every one had gone to bed except Lady Bell-Clinton and Philip Kinnaird, who had sat up with her. They came across the hall as soon as they heard the tyres ground upon the gravel of the drive.

"I would like to think that it was devotion that made Philip sit up with me, but I fear it was only curiosity," laughed his hostess as she took Robert into her own little sitting-room, the one spot of unconventional comfort in the vastness of the place. Robert was grateful for the hot coffee she prepared on an electric heater, and for the pile of sandwiches that had been left for him.

"And now you are going to reward us by saying that it is all too confidential for you to say a word. But do tell me this. How *did* the Home Secretary murder poor Mr Oissel?"

Robert laughed. He had made up his mind about his line as Dalbeattie had advised. Since Kinnaird was here, and Annette would presumably have told him about Jenks, it might be interesting to try out his reactions.

"And could you really be trusted not to say a word to anyone?"

"Goodness me, young Mr Robert West! I was in Parliament while you were still in a prep. school."

"Then you have been long enough there not to quote age as a proof of wisdom," teased Robert. "The point is, as I expect Miss Oissel told you, Kinnaird, that we are not quite easy in our minds about Edward Jenks."

"No, Miss Oissel has told me nothing. She is the soul of discretion, as you know."

Robert was amazed. Wasn't Kinnaird on such intimate terms with Annette as he had hinted, or did that reserved young lady keep her confidence even from those nearest to her? Had he made a mistake in telling Kinnaird so much?

"Our evidence is not conclusive," he said, trying to lead

away from the scent. "The only reason why it is so confidential is that Jenks stood in such a special relation to the Home Secretary. We can do nothing until he returns on Monday." Kinnaird's face showed no special interest.

"I wonder if he thinks I am just making this up for Ivy's benefit," thought Robert, "or whether he is really unconcerned."

Kinnaird begged another cup of coffee. "Haven't the police any theory as to the burglars who shot Jenks?" he asked.

Robert was anxious to keep the conversation on safe generalities. "Of course, Lord Dalbeattie will be able to help us a lot there. He is inclined to the theory that some pirate group in the City might have had something to do with it. Seems rather fantastic to me, England not being America; we ought to put a tariff on gangsters if the U.S.A. starts exporting them."

Dalbeattie had said nothing of the kind, but Robert thought it was a neat invention and a safe one. He was rather surprised at the effect it produced on Kinnaird.

"I think Miss Oissel ought to be told if Lord Dalbeattie is taking a hand in her affairs," he said angrily. "I can assure you that his intervention will not be welcome to her."

Lady Bell-Clinton blew several little smoke-rings from her cigarette. "It's not exactly a private affair of Annette's, is it, if British securities are falling, and there is going to be a Parliamentary crisis next week? I am glad you confided in Dick Dalbeattie, Robert. I feel safe when he has got anything in hand. Now we won't worry you with any more questions. Up to bed, both of you."

Robert had the impression that Kinnaird would have liked to stay behind and talk to him alone, but Ivy Bell-Clinton firmly prevented that by laughingly driving the two men

before her up the stairs, and playing the anxious hostess as
she saw them to their rooms. Robert undressed very slowly,
thinking of this new complication. Dalbeattie had not hinted
that he had any special knowledge of Kinnaird or the Oissels.
He had merely asked Robert to try and find out whether the
engagement of Annette to Philip was likely to take place.
Was Dalbeattie interested in Annette? There was a Lady
Dalbeattie—Robert vaguely remembered seeing pictures of
her in the sporting illustrated papers—so Dalbeattie could
not himself be a candidate for Annette and her millions.
Then why should Kinnaird be so furious that Dalbeattie
was interesting himself in the matter? And on what a slight
thread that interference had hung, a mere chance emotion
in the garden in the early evening—Robert's fear of being
alone with his tremendous secret! But was it a chance? Robert
wondered whether it was really Annette Oissel who had asked
that he should be invited to Clinton Bardsley, or had it been
on Lord Dalbeattie's initiative?

CHAPTER XVI

Summoned by a telegram marked "Government Absolute Priority," the Home Secretary arrived at No. 10 Downing Street punctually at ten o'clock on Monday morning. Though he had travelled all night and had driven straight from the station, he was as perfectly groomed as though he had just left his own bedroom.

The Prime Minister did not receive him in the snug sitting-room where he had talked to Robert and Lord Dalbeattie, but in the formal office set aside for his official use. No one who had seen them sitting facing each other would have imagined that the Home Secretary could have been guilty of even an indiscretion. He was far more at his ease than the Prime Minister. The Home Secretary fitted into the life of official England as a hand into a glove. There was scarcely a period since the days of Queen Elizabeth when some member of his family had not borne high office in the State. Neither Whig nor Tory, Conservative nor Liberal, Governments had been complete without their name. None had so far joined the Labour Party, a fact which made it difficult for the Home Secretary to believe that that party could continue to exist.

It was incorrect to say of such assured eminence that he had 'won' his position in the Cabinet. Rather had he marched by well-signposted stages to the place which was obviously his due. In the public mind he conferred stability on any Government he entered. But recently there had been a disturbing element in his world. Very regrettably, as he considered, certain newspapers had been encouraging the low craft of the caricaturists.

These fellows had seized with joy on such magnificent copy as he provided. That heavy face, that high collar, that air of heading a procession if he merely walked down a street, had been used with deadly effect by one famous cartoonist as the very symbol of Governmental pomposity.

Another was building a reputation by poking his fingers through the imposing façade. The public now knew him by an impish nickname. To millions who had never seen him he was familiar by the utterly incongruous name of "Flossie," bestowed on him in bitter irony during a savage onslaught by Michael Houldsworth, and now invariably used in every cartoon in which he appeared.

Yet, such is the habit of the British public, the average man and woman liked him none the less for being able to laugh at him. "Flossie" did mean something in the life of that period.

But the Prime Minister was not so easily absorbed into the everyday mind of his time. The public was not quite sure of him because he, elusive, incalculable, was never quite sure of himself. He held his present high position not by qualities of decisive leadership, but because of the very absence of those qualities. To some degree he reflected the lack of purpose of his period. It was counted to him for a virtue that he could answer any question and leave the questioner soothed, but completely in the dark as to what he meant. Yet not even his irritated enemies could deny the personal charm of the man. In public he was an expert at stroking ruffled feathers, whether of a Parliamentary opponent, a foreign nation, or a hostile public meeting.

The colleagues who worked nearest to him and his own personal friends saw a different side of the man. He had a temper which could take full revenge in private for the self-control needed for his official *rôle* of public soother.

As the two men greeted each other the Home Secretary said: "I hope it is really important. You know how I hate travelling at night. The doctor has warned me… my heart…"

"I think you will find that the matter is of sufficient importance to warrant your immediate attention," was the quiet reply.

The Prime Minister sat down at his desk. The Home Secretary lowered himself with dignity into the armchair by the side of it. He tweaked the knees of his trousers, carefully crossed his legs at a correct angle, and leant back with his fingers pressed together in an arch, like a judge in chambers prepared to consider a statement about to be made to him.

The Premier looked at his Home Secretary with some irritation. Yet he, the man who was never quite sure of himself, could not help being impressed with such complete self-assurance. That was why the Home Secretary had been more in his confidence than any other member of his Cabinet. It was incredible… could he really have done it?

"What have you been doing in the Oissel case?" he asked.

"The police have the matter in hand. Gleeson is keeping his hand on the case. Scotland Yard has put its best man, Blackitt, in charge of it. Robert West, my Parliamentary private secretary, you know, has done quite a lot of work in connexion with it, and very satisfactorily, I believe. I cannot see how much more could be done, but if you like I will see that a report is prepared for the Cabinet on Wednesday."

"You know that there is to be a debate on the adjournment this evening?"

"Ah, yes. West managed to have it postponed from last Thursday. But it will be possible to make a non-committal statement, especially in view of the fact that the inquest is to be on Thursday. In that sense the affair is really *sub judice*, so I doubt whether it is in order to raise the question at all."

"What the Labour Party will raise may be only too much in order," said the Premier looking at his colleague sternly.

"Indeed," replied the Home Secretary, apparently unimpressed.

The Prime Minister leaned forward. "Will you please tell me what part you have played in this affair."

The Home Secretary did not meet his eyes. "I have told you, unless you want me to go over the whole circumstances of the dinner once again. You have had my statement about that."

That shifted glance decided the other man. The Home Secretary had something to hide. His self-assurance could be punctured. The man-who-was-never-quite-sure-of-himself was going to get considerable joy from doing it.

"Some further information has been brought to my notice since you left London," he said suavely.

"I shall be interested to hear it." A slight mist seemed to pass across the other's face.

The Premier kept silence for a few seconds. Intensely sensitive to atmosphere, he could feel the rising uneasiness of this man whom he had always secretly hated even while they worked together as colleagues and friends. It was an exquisite moment. Then, because he was a fine actor who never held a pose a second too long, he changed from Caesar Borgia to the practical man of affairs. It was these lightning changes of attitude that made him so formidable an antagonist, so distrusted a colleague.

"Perhaps I had better just tell you what has been put before me. I have no doubt at all that the explanation is a perfectly satisfactory one, but I must know where we are before I meet the House."

"Certainly," said the Home Secretary. His face was a little grey.

"The information that I have is this—that your confidential man, Edward Jenks, who was in attendance on Oissel, was found with Oissel's private notebook in his pocket—the notebook in which he kept the details of his most confidential transactions. It has been ascertained that during the time Oissel was dining with you at the House of Commons, Jenks had been out of the flat and had had the written pages of the notebook secretly photographed. It has been further discovered that a copy of Oissel's memoranda relating to our loan negotiations is in your private file, in your own handwriting, and with the notes decoded."

The Home Secretary sprang to his feet. "This is intolerable. Do you mean to tell me that the police have been given access to my private file of Cabinet papers?"

The Prime Minister was rather taken aback by this fury of indignation where he had expected collapse. He did not want to bring in West's name, or not at present. "That has been discovered by accident," he temporized, "an accident which may prove very fortunate for the Government and for you. But do you admit that these are substantially the facts?"

The Home Secretary sat down again in the armchair. From habit he assumed the same pose, but he did not tweak his trousers at the knees. The Prime Minister felt master of the situation. Forgotten for the moment was the crisis into which the whole Government was likely to be precipitated. He was enjoying the sense of power, of mastery over this representative of the old families which had flouted him, over the man who had assumed the *rôle* of his special adviser in the Cabinet, over all the old order which he hated even while he led it. In the rich voice of a professional evangelist leaning over a penitent he said: "Won't you tell me exactly what you have done, so that I can help to put things right?"

He overdid it. His tone stung the pride of the man before him. The Home Secretary rose to his feet, a little unsteadily. He addressed his Prime Minister as he would have addressed a meeting of company directors.

"My action," he said slowly, but deliberately, as a man choosing his words for an important pronouncement, "may seem somewhat unusual. It may even be misinterpreted. I shall take effective steps to relieve the Government of any responsibility for it. But my conscience is clear. I did not act without thought. I did what I considered my country's best interest demanded. I..."

The Premier came off his own pose, irritated beyond bearing by the elaborate posing of the other.

"Sit down, man," he said, "and tell me what you have done. There will be plenty of opportunity for justificatory speeches afterwards."

The Premier's businesslike tone completely punctured the Home Secretary. He sat down hurriedly, and looked at his colleague like the muddle-headed elderly gentleman he really was.

"I am afraid I have blundered very badly," he said pathetically.

By no artistry could he have done a better thing for himself than by this revelation of his utter helplessness. The Prime

Minister was no bully. It was strength he hated, not weakness. No living thing that placed itself at his mercy had ever cause to regret it.

"Now, don't get worried," he said in his more usual friendly tone. "There's nothing so bad that there isn't some way out. If you will tell me everything, without keeping anything back, then we can consider what is to be done."

The Home Secretary evidently found some difficulty in beginning. He moistened his lips with his tongue. The Premier noticed this. Himself almost a teetotaller, it hardly ever occurred to him to offer drinks except at meals. Now in his real desire to help the Home Secretary he remembered his omission. "Have a drink? I believe Mortimer keeps some whisky in the cupboard here."

His guest accepted gratefully, and helped himself to a generous supply. Comforted by the familiar feel of the glass he began: "It is difficult to explain, and I fear it will sound incredible, but I do want to assure you that I didn't plan all this. It just seemed to happen, and then this atrocious murder upset everything." He paused.

"Yes, go on," said the Premier, who had got himself well under control.

"I did not think of anything else when I lent Jenks to Georges Oissel, except of keeping him in a good temper when he refused to have a Scotland Yard man, and when Gleeson insisted he must have some protection. Gleeson thought it a good idea when I suggested Jenks. You do realize that, don't you?"

"Perfectly. It seemed to me an admirable arrangement when you told me about it."

"Well, then," continued the Home Secretary, gaining encouragement, "you remember—let me see, it was a week last Thursday, how terribly time flies!—you remember the meeting with Oissel when we were at an absolute deadlock, when we couldn't make out whether the provisos he insisted on putting into the loan agreement were bluff to force better terms out of the Government or whether they were meant seriously by his group. And you suggested that I might meet him in some informal way, and see if I could find out what were his real minimum terms."

"Yes, I remember," said the Premier, beginning to wonder to what extent he was to be involved in this fantastic affair.

"Well, it was then that I decided to ask him to dinner at the House the following Monday. As you know, it was very difficult to persuade him to come. He declared he never left his rooms at night, but I assured him everything would be all right with Jenks there."

"Good Lord, man, you actually said that to him, and then used Jenks to steal his papers. What could you have been thinking about?"

"My country," said the Home Secretary simply. He was not posing now. "I assure you that the thought never entered my head when I persuaded Oissel to come to dinner and told young West to make all the arrangements. But when I began to think of how I should talk to him—he was not an easy customer as you know—my mind kept coming back to that notebook to which he was always referring. I remembered that Georges always had an atrocious memory. Had to make notes of everything, and he always made them in code. We had worked a code out one summer when we were logging together. I wondered whether he used the same one still." The Home Secretary paused and took another sip, looking at the Prime Minister as an apologetic schoolboy might look at his headmaster.

"And then?" asked the Prime Minister. His tone was even, and betrayed nothing of what he was thinking.

"Well, I can't quite explain how, but it suddenly occurred to me that if I could have that notebook for a few minutes we should probably find in it all we wanted to know—that is, if he was still using the same code, which I thought quite likely. Georges never altered things he had grown used to."

"So you brought in Jenks?"

"I did not like doing that, but it could not have been managed without. Of course there was the possibility that Oissel might have the notebook on him when he came to dinner, but Jenks told me that he usually locked it in his desk with his other papers."

"Didn't Jenks seem surprised at the Home Secretary, of all people, making such a proposition to him as that he should steal papers he had been sent to guard?"

Even a worm would have turned at the iciness of that tone, and the Home Secretary was not a worm. By the mere act of confession he was beginning to regain his usual self-assurance.

"My dear Prime Minister," he said with a suspicion of a smile, "you and I have been responsible for the administration of Secret Service funds for a long time. Is all this so much worse than many things that you, and I, and every other occupant of our offices have been responsible for at some time or other?"

"But you yourself, you, a Cabinet Minister, to be directly involved! It was incredibly stupid."

"Perhaps—unwise, certainly—but it is an interesting question whether the acts we vicariously sanction are the more moral because we do not directly participate in them."

The Prime Minister began to feel that his colleague was

gaining the advantage again, the last thing he intended should happen.

"We cannot have a philosophical discussion about the virtues at this moment. Jenks was apparently quite willing to help in these proceedings."

"Jenks was at one time a valued member of our Secret Service staff. When I explained that the information contained in that notebook would save his country many millions of pounds he merely regarded the matter as an ordinary piece of the Secret Service work he had done for years. I left all the details to him, of course. It was he who suggested having the pages photographed. And, of course, but for the burglary the plan would have worked perfectly. We should have had the information which would have given us the whip hand with Oissel, and no one would have been any the wiser. I trust that those burglars, when the police find them, will get the punishment they so richly deserve."

The Prime Minister threw back his head and laughed. "Flossie" was priceless. He had committed the most unpardonable piece of folly, he had outraged every official British tradition. If the facts were suspected not only the Government, but the Party, were irretrievably ruined, and there he sat, a pillar of the Established Church and the Established Everything Else, shocked at the wickedness of the unknown burglars.

"I am glad you take it like that," said the Home Secretary, partly offended, partly relieved.

"How am I to take it? I hope I shall soon wake up and find that it is all a nightmare. I have never heard of anything so fantastic. And what do you imagine is to be done now?"

"My duty is perfectly plain. I shall go into the witness-box at the adjourned inquest and simply tell the whole truth, taking the whole blame myself, and completely exonerating the Government. Naturally, I will place my resignation in your hands before I leave you this morning."

The Prime Minister looked at his colleague with a return of his former respect. He was not whining for secrecy. "Flossie" would face public execration as he had faced and conquered angry election crowds. Could he pull it off? For a passing moment the Premier wondered whether after all that might not be the best way out. Then his own instinct, which was always against publicity, reinforced his conviction that not even "Flossie" could get away with a story like this. No one would believe that he, as Premier, had not known something about it. Then there was this awkward business of the murder. How was that to be explained? No, the utmost secrecy must be maintained, but that might be difficult if the Home Secretary suddenly developed one of his mulish fits.

"Whatever may have to be done finally," he said slowly, "you must do nothing in a hurry, and nothing without consulting me. I want you to promise me that now."

"Certainly I promise to consult you. That is the least I can offer."

"Then before we decide anything I propose to consult Dalbeattie, telling him what you have told me."

"Lord Dalbeattie! What has he to do with it?"

"Dalbeattie knows everything except what you have told me of your own part in the affair. And he suspects something of that. He is absolutely to be trusted, and has been in some tight corners himself. Frankly he is my one hope."

"But if he knows, how many other people do?"

"No one. Not even the police know anything about it. But you must leave this to me now, otherwise the Party will be dragged through the mud. No protestation by you could save our prestige if all this became public. Think of the headlines in the Opposition Press."

The Home Secretary dropped his head into his hands. "I never thought that I should reach the stage when a revolver offered the only way out," he said brokenly.

"For God's sake, man," said the Premier, gripping his shoulder in real panic. "You must not do anything of the kind. I shall not allow you out of this room until you give me your word not to do that. We should be in a worse mess than ever."

"Very well. I will do what you think best."

The Premier was touched by the weary tone of the older man. "Dalbeattie is here," he said. "I asked him to come along for consultation. I will see him in my sitting-room. Why not lie down on the sofa here for a bit and rest? All this strain after an all-night journey is no joke." With that charm he knew so well how to use, the Premier put his guest on the couch and went in search of Dalbeattie.

CHAPTER XVII

While the Prime Minister and the Home Secretary were having their interview in the Cabinet office, Robert West, who had been asked to come to Downing Street at half-past ten, was shown into the Premier's sitting-room, where Lord Dalbeattie was sitting writing at the big desk.

"Ah, that you, West? Good morning. Have a chair and the morning papers. The Home Secretary is still with the Premier."

"He arrived, then?" said Robert. "I wondered if he would alter his arrangements. He hates doing that more than anything."

"You did not see the telegram," was Dalbeattie's dry remark as he turned back to his work.

The little room was very still. The wonderful view across the Horse Guards Parade was softened by summer rain. A small bright fire burned in the hearth. A quiet English interior that except for the view from the windows could be paralleled by thousands of similar comfortable homes. But Lord Dalbeattie did not seem to fit into this restful comfort. Bob took the opportunity of studying him. Quietly dressed in a blue lounge suit with a black silk tie, reading documents and occasionally making notes upon them, the man seemed to radiate energy though his body hardly made a movement. Robert felt the intensity of his concentration.

Sitting back in the armchair, quietly smoking, Bob speculated about the forces of which Dalbeattie was one of the central and directing powers, as colossal a figure in his own financial sphere as Georges Oissel had been in his.

What were the men like Oissel and Dalbeattie going to make of this England, which Robert through school and university had been trained to think was the centre of the universe, governing itself by its own elected Parliament. Dalbeatties and Oissels held the power now. To them and their like, whatever their nationality, England was but an incident, a set of statistics. The scope of their interests was international. Yet if they were in politics at all they belonged to the same party as Colonel Stuart-Orford, though what was their common interest with that pathetic survival, with his D.S.O., his Croix de Guerre, tributes to a personal valour for which there seemed to be little room in the world that the Oissels and the Dalbeatties were creating?

Dalbeattie was a whole man, he exhaled virility, but poor emasculated cripples like Georges Oissel had as much power. The new world they were creating, the world of bonds, and debts, and mortgages, massive industry, and wild speculation, was bringing with it a new set of traditions, a new standard of values, as it had brought new art and music, the jazz band, the mass-production cinema.

Dalbeattie had finished his work. He put the documents into a large envelope, sealed it, rang for an attendant, and ordered the package to be taken immediately to his private office in Victoria.

"Sorry to have been so occupied," he said as he took the armchair opposite Bob, and lit a cigarette. "It is an old habit of mine. I never go out without some work that I have on hand. I earn my leisure that way. Now tell me what you were thinking about when you were looking at me so solemnly."

Robert was rather startled that he had been noticed, but why waste words in conventional excuses when there was a chance of talking to a man like Dalbeattie?

"I was thinking that you and Oissel were the real revolutionaries. I saw that unemployed march which was being broken up by the police last week. And then our dear old frightened middle classes think that those poor chaps are the revolutionaries to be afraid of. And you, who can skin us by a simple inflationary operation, are regarded as the really safe and respectable people."

"I understand that I have been called the Pirate King in Parliament," replied Dalbeattie with a smile, "and the name would certainly have suited Oissel at one stage of his career."

An idea struck Robert. "Do the Pirate Kings have their little wars, and is Oissel one of the casualties?"

"That is an idea I am working on, and I have some information which bears out that theory. But we must hear what the Home Secretary's story is first. Surely they can't be much longer now."

The house phone rang. Dalbeattie answered it. "The Prime Minister is coming now," he said.

Robert walked to the window, and stood there until the Premier appeared. He looked nervous and anxious.

"Shall I go, sir, and wait somewhere?" asked Robert. The Premier glanced at Dalbeattie. "I don't think so, do you?" said his lordship. "He knows enough about the position to be told the rest, and we may want him."

"Very well," said the Premier, sitting down at his desk. Speaking very rapidly, and in a tone which betrayed his irritation, he repeated the Home Secretary's story. "And," he said in conclusion, "he wants to go into the witness-box on Thursday and confess the whole thing."

"That will be a pretty mess," snorted Dalbeattie. "The Caillaux trial will be as nothing to it. It will be played up abroad as an English Dreyfus case. Can't you see the French papers! Imagine the front pages of the Hearst Press! He'd better take a revolver to himself before he does that."

"He has suggested that already," said the Premier. "I have made him promise to do nothing of the kind."

There was silence in the room. The Premier sat at his desk with his head in his hands. Dalbeattie sat on the arm of the chesterfield chewing the end of a cigar. Robert stood with his back to the window. Each of them was picturing what the Home Secretary's confession meant—an international crisis, a financial panic, unavoidable dissolution of Parliament, the ruin of the Party, and all because one muddle-headed elderly gentleman thought he was clever. The retribution seemed almost comically out of proportion to the intention behind the offence.

It was, of course, Dalbeattie who spoke first and took command of the situation. "We can isolate the problem of the Home Secretary. He must go home and have influenza. Otherwise he will cause suspicion by his woebegone air. Then we can tackle the mystery of Oissel's death and the burglary at his flat. They may have been quite separate occurrences or they may hang together. One thing is certain—if we can track down the cause of those, or even one of them, we can screen the Home Secretary's little flutter completely, and he can quietly resign on the grounds of ill-health when the sensation has died down."

The Prime Minister looked up eagerly. "Yes, of course,

that is the best way out. The Home Secretary had nothing to do with the death of Oissel. His man apparently died in defence of Oissel's property. If we can find the murderers then nothing need come out at all."

"If we can," thought Robert, "but can we?" Aloud he said: "And the adjournment debate to-night?"

Here the Premier was on his own ground. "As the Home Secretary will be absent through illness, I will take over that. I can pass word to the Opposition through the usual channels that we are on the verge of important discoveries which ought not to be jeopardized by publicity. They will keep their own people quiet. But we must have some sort of statement for the inquest, Dalbeattie."

"When is that?"

"It was adjourned till Thursday," said Bob.

"Then we have three days," said Dalbeattie. "I'll join West in his amateur detection. I had better keep an eye on him, Prime Minister, or he will have the entire Cabinet marched to the gallows."

The Premier smiled. "That will be a practical application of the old Cabinet joke that if we don't hang together we shall hang separately. But I am very grateful to you, Dalbeattie. Shall I have a word with Gleeson?"

"How much does he know already?" said Dalbeattie turning to Robert.

"No one ever knows how much he knows," Bob answered gloomily.

"The perfect civil servant! I think I had better see him myself. Perhaps if you told him that the Home Secretary was ill," he said, turning to the Premier, "and that I was taking an interest as I knew old Oissel, it would be sufficient until I can have a talk with him."

"Good. I will do that. Now I must say good-bye. A deputation has been kept waiting half an hour. But I look to you both to get the Government out of this mess."

Robert felt that the mystery was as good as solved as he went downstairs behind Lord Dalbeattie, with whom (oh, joy!) he had been coupled in the farewell of the Premier. The awful tension of the week-end was over. Surely Dalbeattie could not fail… but if he did?

"I think I'll stroll over and have a look at the mysterious Room J," said Dalbeattie as they stepped out into Downing Street. "No"—as Bob made a movement—"I am not expecting to find anything there. But I hate mysteries. They annoy me."

Robert felt that he ought to apologize for the poor old Parliament that had insisted on having a mystery although it ought to have known that Lord Dalbeattie did not like them.

The rain had cleared and the sunshine was breaking through the clouds as they walked across Palace Yard together. To avoid unnecessary stairs Robert took his companion in through the Speaker's courtyard and under the arches that lead to the House of Lords.

Dalbeattie looked about him with curiosity. "Do you know, I've never been round here before! I always use the Peers' entrance. Curious place, this. It looks as though a regiment of murderers could be stowed away here without being seen."

Robert laughed. "I've always said that there were plenty of opportunities for murder in the House," he said. "There are ventilating shafts, and queer passages, and odd corners where bodies could lie hidden for days. But the maddening part about our mystery is that it has happened in the least mysterious part of the House of Commons, far away from all these passages. There just is nothing here but an ordinary big dining-hall, a straight corridor, and these small dining-rooms leading straight from it. Here is Room J—you can see for yourself." The policeman on duty at the door was the Constable Robinson who had been the victim of the Thursday night incident. "Better again?" asked Robert pleasantly. Then he suddenly remembered that he had not told Dalbeattie that part of the story yet.

"Quite all right, sir, thank you," replied the policeman as he opened the door for them. "Inspector Blackitt has been in not so long ago, sir. He told me to tell you he would like to see you if you came along."

Dalbeattie walked into the small oak-panelled room. "Shut the door," he said. Robert obeyed. "Where was Oissel sitting."

"At that end of the table, opposite the door. At least, that was where the Minister left him, and as he was very crippled he was unlikely to have moved about much. Still, he might have done."

"Haven't the police tried to trace the trajectory of the bullet?"

"Blackitt was on to that at once, and got the experts on to it, but the bullet had made such a mess it was impossible to decide. It had hit a bone, and shattered it pretty badly. Besides, the poor man had tumbled off his chair, and it was difficult to know just how he had been sitting."

"And the bullet?"

"It was of the same make as the ones in Oissel's own revolver, same size and all that. It could have been fired from his revolver, but Blackitt has convinced us that it wasn't."

"Then whoever fired that bullet knew enough of Oissel and his possessions to use the same type of bullet."

"Unless it was pure coincidence. They were both of English make and standard pattern."

"How many people knew this dinner was being held?"

"From our side, only the Home Secretary and myself. I did what correspondence was necessary, not the office."

"The kitchen staff—wouldn't they know? Did they know it was for Oissel, or did you just order the dinner yourself?"

Robert considered this new suggestion. "I don't think I made any particular secret about it," he said thoughtfully. "There wasn't any need. The Home Secretary did not want it in the Press, but the kitchen staff here are pretty good about that. They don't talk to the Press. The manager is pretty severe on them if they do."

"Did the manager know that the guest would be Mr Oissel?"

"Yes, he certainly did. I told him as I had to order special food for him."

"Good, then we will talk to the manager."

The manager of the kitchen department came readily to meet them. He was particularly anxious that the affair should be cleared up, for one of his best dining-rooms was out of commission meanwhile. He had been offered a big fee for the use of it from Members who wanted to enjoy a macabre sensation, but he was under orders that it must not be used, and the policeman still on duty at the door to prevent the entry of unauthorized persons was an unpleasant reminder of the tragedy to all his other diners.

The manager, however, was quite definite that he had told no one of the identity of the Minister's guest, except the waiter to whom he had passed on Mr West's special instructions. "Then let us see the waiter," said Lord Dalbeattie.

"That poor waiter has been bullied and browbeaten out

of his senses," said Robert, while they were waiting for the manager to bring him. "But the police have not been able to shake him in one detail of his story."

"Sounds suspicious," said Dalbeattie casually. "The innocent are seldom as well primed as that."

But Dalbeattie could make nothing more of the waiter than the police had done. The man was obviously tired and nervous. The manager explained that the police had been at him so often that he was sleeping badly and was very worried. But he could tell no more than he had said at the inquest. Every second of his time between the Home Secretary's departure and the sound of the shot was accounted for. Dalbeattie out of sheer pity for the harassed man slipped him a pound-note.

When they were alone in the room again Dalbeattie examined the narrow windows with their heavy hasps, the solid panelling, the little cupboards, even the floor, and the well-fitting heavy door. Not a mouse could have got into that solidly built room except through the open door. Robert judged this a good moment to tell him the story of Thursday night. Dalbeattie whistled.

"Then they were either trying to cover up tracks or get something that had been left behind. I suppose that is Blackitt's theory?"

"Either that, or even that they might be planning a second murder—the Home Secretary, for example."

"Well, that might be a useful bit of work at this juncture," grinned Dalbeattie. "But we can't hope for that. I'll see Blackitt this afternoon. Then perhaps we might explore Oissel's flat at Charlton Court. But it seems to me that the main clue must lie hidden here. Meanwhile what about a spot of lunch?"

"Would you care to lunch with me here?" asked Robert greatly daring.

"Excellent idea. Will keep me in the Commons atmosphere—that is, if you will promise to let me out alive. How do I know that you haven't sworn a lethal campaign against all financiers, and that you did not murder old Oissel yourself?"

"I shall begin to think I did shortly," laughed Robert, as they walked together into the Strangers' Dining-room.

"Who is that pretty girl?" asked Dalbeattie as they took seats.

"That's Grace Richards, the M.P. for Stepney East."

"Socialist, of course?"

"Yes."

"So you know her fairly well? She seemed to smile on you very warmly."

"Quite well," said Robert rather uneasily, wondering whither these questions were tending.

"Then why not rope her into your detective job?"

"She has helped me a bit," said Robert puzzled, "but what could she do specially?"

"Put her on to that waiter and the kitchen staff. Ask her to talk to the stillroom maid who was making the coffee that the waiter went to fetch. A girl like that could do it without putting them on their guard. Ask her to find out tactfully if there were any strange waiters on that night."

"But the police have already done that. Blackitt I know has cross-examined every member of the staff who was on duty."

"The police are no match for a really highly trained servant, especially one accustomed to holding his or her tongue in a place like the House of Commons. I learned that fact in a very costly way when I was trying to get a divorce. My wife knew it, and I paid for the lesson."

Robert looked with fresh interest at Dalbeattie. He couldn't remember any *cause célèbre* in connexion with him. Had the divorce come off? In that case the Lady Dalbeattie of the illustrated sporting papers was no obstacle to his paying attention to Annette Oissel.

"You think you can find something out from the Charlton Court side?" asked Robert, politely changing the subject. After all, you can't ask a man if he got his divorce in the end. But he wondered whether Dalbeattie's purpose in his suggesting work at Oissel's flat was to provide an excuse for being near Annette. Couldn't he worm himself in on to that? Robert felt a queer ache when he thought of Annette as she had sat that night before dinner in the hall at Clinton Bardsley.

"Well, it seems to me that the only fruitful line, if we can't get in front of the murderer and see where his bullets came from, is to get behind him. We must find out who had sufficient hatred against old Oissel to be willing to take the risk of murdering him, and frankly the only person I know of is Annette Oissel herself."

"Annette!" Robert's face went white. "But that is preposterous. She told me herself how generous he had been to her, how little he required of her in return."

"You saw her the morning after his death. Was she very upset?"

Robert remembered her coolness and self-possession, and then, in her own flat that evening her gay gown, her willingness to come to tea on the Terrace that day despite the conventions of mourning.

"She is so very reserved, of course, she always is," he said in defence. "But she couldn't. It seems incredible. People don't do things like that."

Dalbeattie helped himself to cheese. "Your Home Secretary, for example. Incidentally"—and he chuckled—"it will be an amazing situation if the net result of our joint endeavours to find old Oissel's murderer is that we shall have to decide whether Annette or the Home Secretary is to be thrown to the wolves."

"But why should Annette want to murder an old man whose money she was going to get anyhow, and who certainly does not seem to have stinted her when he was alive?"

"It's a queer story, and both Annette and her grandfather are queer people. They are Basques, really, a wild folk. Old Oissel came from the Basque village of Itaxxou and badly wanted Annette to marry the local grandee. It was the dream of his life. Annette simply would not look at him. She told her grandfather to leave him the money and let her earn her own living. The battle had died down for a time during these loan negotiations. But Annette was to accompany the old man to Pau for this new rejuvenating treatment, and I suppose she expected that the old struggle would start again."

"But she could have left him without murdering him. Why, the jewels she was wearing when I called at her flat would have kept her for years if the old man had never given her another penny. It's absurd."

"But Basques aren't like that. They don't just go away quietly. Theirs is a dagger and rope history. Now"—as Robert made an impatient movement—"I'm not accusing Annette of planning the murder. I'm simply saying that as far as I know the old boy's circle, Annette was the one who had had most provocation and, if she wasn't found out, had most to gain."

"I don't believe it. I shouldn't believe it if she told me so herself. She is too fine, too essentially civilized, she…"

"Has she got you that way too? Oh, Annette, what scalps

you have hung at your belt! I've yet to meet the man who could resist that slow smile of hers, and those eyes. Now I could tell you a few stories about her that…"

"I don't want to hear them!" In his fury Robert had completely forgotten where he was and had jumped to his feet, to the amazement of the bewigged lawyers lunching at the next table and the startled surprise of Grace Richards, who had been watching their table with interest all through her own meal.

Dalbeattie rose too, his nonchalant manner pulling Robert to earth and covering up his action. He motioned to the waiter. "No, sorry, Lord Dalbeattie. This is my lunch."

"Oh, yes. Pardon me, I couldn't pay here of course." He waited at the door, while Robert went through the formalities and joined him. He put his hand on the younger man's arm.

"Now I didn't want to upset you, and you can forget what I said if you want to do so. Annette won't be inconvenienced in any way. I shall see to that. But it is no use trying to unravel a mystery like this unless you are prepared to face every possibility, and keep your own emotions out of it. Find the truth, and then let your feelings dictate what you should do with it. That seems to me the only common-sense way. Better we should find it out, if there is anything in what I say, than that Annette should find herself in the hands of Inspector Blackitt. Don't you agree?"

"Yes, of course," said a rather crushed Robert.

"Good. Then go and see what you can do with Miss Richards."

Dalbeattie left Robert with a hearty handshake and apparently with a job of work to do for him, but the younger man had an uneasy feeling that he had been told to go away and play with Grace Richards while his elder took the business seriously in hand.

But he could not face Grace just yet. He went on to the Terrace, the haven of so many worried men. If all the troubles that are dropped over that parapet into the Thames were tangible things the river would overflow regularly.

He walked slowly to the Peers' end, where his privacy was less liable to continual interruption than in the stretch reserved for members of the Commons. So many hearty fellows think that an M.P. walking by himself must be feeling lonely, poor chap, and chummily hail him to join their more festive group! The House of Commons can be almost as lonely as a desert, but it is difficult to be quiet in it.

Leaning over the low wall and looking down at the river, West felt every nerve in his body quivering. Even to himself he had never admitted the intense emotional effect which the sight of Annette caused in him. He had told himself that he was excited and over-strung because of the excitement of the murder and his worry about Jenks and the Home Secretary. He knew now what nonsense all that had been. He was in love with Annette Oissel, hopelessly, desperately in love with her. And Annette was in danger. Of course it was absurd that she could be guilty, but if Dalbeattie thought that of her, others less friendly to her might think it too. People could be arrested on suspicion. Annette's beauty and elegance in a police cell—it was an intolerable thought. His mind raced on to other possibilities. He found himself staging wild attempts at rescue in which somehow Annette was to be taken off in an aeroplane to some marvellous South Sea Island, where he and she…

"Are things really as bad as you look?" said a cool, fresh voice.

Robert was startled out of his reverie and came back slowly as a man awakening from sleep.

"I'm sorry, Gracie. Was I looking fierce?"

"Fierce? You looked as though you were just about to bite some one's head off. And you were gripping the top of the parapet as though you would pull it down like Samson. Dare I ask what is the matter?"

"Of course. As a matter of fact I was just coming to look for you. I want you to help me again."

"Not poor Michael? It's no use, he won't be done out of his adjournment speech to-night. I could only do that once."

"Oh, that does not matter. The Premier is taking that on himself. Houldsworth won't get much change out of him. Besides, we've put the leader of the Opposition on to steamroller him. That's all fixed up," said Robert firmly, trying to give an impression of confidence he was far from feeling.

"Then what is the trouble? I thought you dreaded a debate above all things?"

"We did then. But now we are getting things ready for the inquest on Thursday, so it's easy to get out of saying anything to-night. But this is the point. What we are afraid of now is that some one, I can't tell you who, but some perfectly innocent person is going to have a bad time to prove that they did not do the murder unless we can find out certain things before Thursday."

"Oh, what a rotten shame! Of course I'd like to help to stop that."

Robert was thankful that he had got her thus far, otherwise he had been afraid that at the mention of her making inquiries among the staff she would toss her head and declare that she did not propose to do the policeman's job of spying on workers. He felt he could hardly blame her if she did take that line.

"Well, it's come to this. We've followed up every clue, and

Lord Dalbeattie—that is the man you saw me lunching with to-day—is convinced that there must have been some one in and about the Harcourt room or the kitchens that night who hasn't been traced. The police have made inquiries, but they can find no trace of anyone. Dalbeattie isn't sure about the waiter, and he has the odd idea that the stillroom maid who makes the coffee might know something if only some one she wasn't afraid of could approach her. There may be nothing in it. It is only the slenderest chance, but unless we can find out something by Thursday there may be a very grave miscarriage of justice."

Robert had taken the right line. He saw that. She would have been completely unimpressed by the difficulties of the Government, and had she had the slightest idea of what the Home Secretary had done she would have been the first to force publicity. But the idea of some innocent person facing a charge like this appealed to her.

"Leave that to me," she said quietly. "I know the women cleaners and the women in and around the kitchens. I often go and talk to them. I'm sure that if there is anything they know they'll tell me."

"Gracie, I'm more than grateful, and when you know the whole story, and you shall, every word of it, then you'll see that it was worth while helping with this."

They stood for a moment, their eyes held. Perhaps it was the turmoil in West's own heart that caused Grace's sudden flush. She dropped her eyes.

"Sorry to interrupt and all that, but can one of you provide a match?" said a familiar voice. Grace looked up startled into Sancroft's cheerful face. "Oh… er… sorry," she said, "I'm just going," and she turned and walked quickly away.

"Did I really interrupt a tender interlude?" asked Sancroft as Robert produced a lighter. "If so, I'm sorry."

"Of course not. Don't be a fool. I was just asking Gracie if she would do something for me on this Oissel case."

"Mmmmm!" Sancroft mocked.

"For God's sake, Sannie, don't be an ass. The one place I know where a man can be good friends with a woman without either the banns or the divorce court being assumed is the House of Commons. It's too much to hope that it will stay like that long, but you needn't start the rot."

"Far be it from me," said Sancroft. "Anyway, Grace is as capable of looking after herself as most. It's about the Oissel case I want to see you. That is, if you feel you can discuss it with a humble journalist after consorting with Premiers and financial magnates."

West felt a little conscience-stricken. He had not been able to keep in touch with Sancroft, but his acute brain and level judgment might be as useful to Annette as all Lord Dalbeattie's driving-power. Robert now could think of the problem only in terms of Annette and her safety.

"I'm sorry, Sannie," he said. "But you know what it can be like. The Minister has been as stubborn as a mule, and I've had to help him when the others got furious with him." As a sudden effort at a completely misleading explanation that was rather neat, and Robert had the grace to feel slightly ashamed of himself.

"That's all right. If you are in deep water I don't ask for confidences. You know where to find me if you want me. But I'll just bring my little scraps of news and lay them at your feet like a good dog."

"You make me feel a beast, San, but I'm pledged to the hilt to keep mum. But if you have any news for God's sake let us have it, for we've precious little."

"Well, I've just got this from our City man. I don't know

if Dalbeattie knows. But Kinnaird was in much worse difficulties than was thought. He has been selling short and the settlement was due to-day. The few people in the know did not expect him to meet his liabilities."

"And has he?"

"Yes, and it's Oissel stock that has helped him to do it. Miss Oissel must have pulled him through."

Robert stuck his hands very deep into his pockets, and clenched them tight. He managed to say in fairly even tones: "Have you any idea how long Kinnaird has been rocky?"

"That's difficult to say, of course. His resources have always been assumed to be pretty considerable. But he's been speculating pretty heavily of late, and got on the wrong side of the market. It's rather a wonder that Oissel didn't advise him, seeing that Kinnaird was sweet on his daughter. Oissel has been making enormous sums out of the recent currency changes."

"But how have you got to know this, Sannie? Dalbeattie didn't say a word about it. Surely he would know?"

"The settlement, of course, only took place to-day, but it's quite common property by now. Nothing unusual about that, of course. But the fact of how shaky he really was is a secret that has been very well kept. I got to know because our City Editor's brother is, or was, Kinnaird's confidential clerk. He's sacked him recently. I'd asked our man to get to know anything he could about anyone connected with Oissel in any way, and he passed me on this tip to-day."

West stood very still, trying to fit this news into Dalbeattie's theory. It fitted only too well.

If Annette wanted to marry Philip Kinnaird, and if that marriage was being prevented by the stubborn old grandfather, and if Kinnaird had told Annette about his financial difficulties, was it outside the bounds of credibility that Annette had determined to get rid of the wretched old man, and use the millions she would inherit to save her lover from financial ruin and social disgrace?

Thinking of Annette's proud head, the reserve of power suggested by her slow graceful movements, the strength of will expressed in the set of her jaw, added to the wild Basque temperament which Dalbeattie attributed to her, was it an impossible thing for her to have done?

Off his guard in Sancroft's familiar presence he turned to him fiercely and blurted out his thoughts. "Why shouldn't she? Why should the old and the rich thwart the lives of young people? There's too much of it—love and happiness sacrificed to greedy old people."

"Is this a general statement of some new philosophy, Bob? Back to the cooking-pot for the old men of the tribe, eh? Or did that bright young granddaughter pop Grandpa in the soup, so to speak?"

"Good Lord, Sannie, what have I said? I mean..."

"You know, your nerves are going to bits, Bob, my lad. All this secrecy, and keeping things from your best friends, isn't in your line. You know it's all right with me. Why have I to keep saying that? Is Miss Oissel suspected of having a hand in the death of her grandfather?"

Put as bluntly as that, instead of in the romantic veils of thwarted love and Southern temperament, it made Bob realize afresh the implications of the theory. "No," he said, "it's too absurd."

"But some one has thought of it! *You* have been thinking of it from what you said just now."

"Well, er, Lord Dalbeattie put it forward as a possibility—Basque temperament, you know."

"Basque my eye and Betty Martin," said Sancroft roughly. "Bob, you're going all romantic about this girl. She has only come into your ken these last few days, but as a journalist I've known of her for at least five seasons in London and Paris. She's as luxurious as a Persian cat and as extravagant as a peacock. The sort of life she has been leading saps nerve and decision. I don't believe she could plan a *coup* like this in what must have been very elaborate detail. And why the burglary, when she had the keys to her grandfather's flat, and was his regular hostess?"

"But if she wanted to marry Kinnaird and old Oissel wouldn't let them marry?"

"And what difference do you think a marriage ceremony would make to those two?"

At the implications of this sneer Robert went red and then white. He turned, without speaking, to the parapet and rested his head on his hands.

"I'm sorry, Bob, but I've been making inquiries. Annette Oissel is notorious. Kinnaird is only one of her queue."

"Then why should she put up so much money to save him from a smash?"

"He is the reigning favourite, and as such I imagine he can have what money he wants. It would not make a great deal of difference to the Oissel fortune. But she's no Lady Macbeth even if she does look a bit like one at times. I would wager my last shilling that she had nothing to do with her grandfather's death... Besides," Sancroft continued, "why should she come to you the very morning after to insist that it could not be suicide when the papers were giving out that it was?"

"But if she knew that it wasn't suicide, could there have been a better way of putting the police off the scent?"

Sancroft laughed. "Well, of course, if you are determined to prove that the poor girl is a murderess..."

"Oh, go to blazes, Sannie! We've got to find the facts. Then we can decide what to do with them afterwards."

"A highly moral sentiment from the Parliamentary private secretary to the Home Office. Ah, well, the lovely Annette is not my concern, thank heaven! But my opinion is that you're drawing the circle too narrow in keeping it round the people that Oissel associated with in London. However much Annette might have wanted to get rid of her grandfather, and frankly I don't believe she did, how could she have staged that mystery in Room J, and why should she go to so much trouble?"

"Then whom have you in mind?"

"I think you have to go deeper into Oissel's past, Bob. Dalbeattie might be able to help there. We've all assumed that Oissel's death had something to do with the loan. But it might not have had the remotest connexion with it. Don't you remember quoting to me some remark of Kinnaird's to the effect that Oissel hadn't as many rivals as he might have had if so many of them had not died first? There are some grim possibilities in a life like Oissel's. Have you talked to Kinnaird at all?"

"Well, no, it's been rather difficult…"

"Rivals for the lady's favour, you mean? I think Kinnaird is pretty well established there at present, Bob, unless of course Mademoiselle thinks that the time is ripe for a change."

West said nothing.

"Sorry, Bob. I don't see why you shouldn't have a turn with Annette Oissel if you want to. It would at least be an exciting interlude. But as my wretched editor expects some copy by four o'clock a spot of work seems indicated. So long!"

The Terrace was filling rapidly for the tea-time scramble. West remembered wearily that he had promised Donald

Shaw to get him in for the debate. He had better go up and collect him. As he moved through the groups of Members, their relations, and their constituents, he felt his arm held.

"One moment, Robert."

He looked down into the vivacious face of Lady Bell-Clinton.

"Sorry. I have some one waiting for me. Do you want me?"

"Yes, just a moment. Your guest can wait." Lady Bell-Clinton pulled him into a seat beside her, and though the table at which she sat was full of her guests she managed by turning her shoulder to isolate herself and West.

"Robert, I want you to do me a great favour—well, two favours."

"You know if I can…"

"Of course. Now the first one is that I want you to come to dinner to-morrow night… That all right?"

"I'm not much in the mood for dinners and I'm busy on this Oissel case. The Premier has asked me to keep in touch with Lord Dalbeattie. If he wants me…"

"Dick is coming too," interrupted Lady Bell-Clinton, "and Annette, and Philip Kinnaird."

"Then of course I shall be delighted."

Lady Bell-Clinton was touched by the grey misery in Robert's face. "Is it hurting very much, Bob—Annette, I mean?"

Robert looked at her startled. Had Dalbeattie told her?

"Annette has that effect on men. I've seen several good men made utterly wretched by her, and she can do it without lifting a finger."

"But the other favour?" said Robert, rather relieved that Lady Bell-Clinton suspected no more than a hopeless love-affair.

"I want you to get permission for me to hold my dinner-party in Room J."

Robert stared at her in amazement. "But that's impossible, Lady Bell-Clinton, and, forgive me, but it seems hardly decent. I'm sure that the police would not allow it, at least not till after the adjourned inquest."

"You don't think I'm just sensation-seeking, Robert, do you?"

Robert remained silent. It was evident that he did, and disapproved strongly.

Ivy Bell-Clinton leant forward and said in a rapid low tone, "I can't explain here. I don't want to be overheard. But I've consulted Dick Dalbeattie and he approves. I have a feeling that I can wrench the mystery out of that room, Robert, and I want to reconstruct the circumstances, sit where Mr Oissel sat, and see if I don't have an inspiration. I believe I will. Madame Paloma told me I was psychic."

West smiled. He knew Madame Paloma, the latest Society pet who was managing to extract large sums of money by clever spiritualistic stunts. Robert had been to one or two of her *séances* with Ivy Bell-Clinton, and had been interested in the ingenious flattery of the whole performance.

"If you feel that there is hope in that line, why shouldn't you and I, or you and Lord Dalbeattie, go and sit there quietly? But a dinner-party, and Oissel's granddaughter among the guests—I mean, well, what would people think?"

"No one need know. I'm not proposing to announce it in *The Times*."

"How could you do a thing like that without having every lobby journalist outside in the corridor? Things are on tiptoe about this Oissel case. The Government may be broken on it yet. How could such a party avoid becoming the first-class Press sensation of the week?"

Lady Bell-Clinton was not used to having her pet notions opposed like this. "I shall have that party, Bob, if I have to have it at midnight when every one has gone home. I feel I can help, and it's not right of you to stop me."

"I'm not stopping you. I am just telling you that I don't think you could get permission. But if you like I will phone Lord Dalbeattie, and see what he thinks."

"Good. Then it will be all right. There will only just be the five of us, unless you want to bring the Home Secretary. Do you think he would come if I asked him?"

"Heaven forbid!" said Robert fervently as he made his escape.

CHAPTER XVIII

West secured an "Under the Gallery" ticket for Donald Shaw. These are the most coveted seats in the House of Commons. Originally intended for experts interested in some particular bill, this little pew under the Distinguished Strangers' Gallery holding barely a dozen is open to the guest of any M.P. provided that there is room in it, which is not frequently. Curiously enough, in spite of the easy equality that prevails now in the House, though women may sit as Distinguished Strangers and occupy the seats reserved for Colonial legislators, and though they may occupy the corresponding seats in the Civil Service box, this coveted little pew on the floor of the House of Commons, not particularly reserved for anyone now, is rigidly barred to any woman, though she may be the expert in charge of a bill.

Women M.P.s might try to abolish this absurdity, but the House, which in the past years has swallowed whole strings of new camels, would die in the last ditch in defence of some antiquated gnat of a custom.

The great advantage to the favoured visitor is that his M.P. host can sit on the bench below him, and point out the sights of the place. Donald Shaw, who was frankly thrilled at being so much 'in' the House as to be almost 'of' it, was intrigued by the complete informality of an assembly that to the outsider represents the central power of a great Empire.

Members turned their backs on the unfortunate man who was speaking, talked in loud tones, read order papers, got up from under his nose and walked out, yet the debate went on. Only when the conversation threatened to drown the voice of the speaker did some of his supporters call "Order, order," which usually produced a lull for about three minutes.

"I should die of fright if I had to try to make a speech to people who made it so clear that they didn't want to hear me," said Don.

"It's not quite as bad as it looks," said his friend. "If a man is any good he gets a hearing. And anyway Hansard reports it verbatim, so he can tell his constituents that he said all that. Queer-looking lot, aren't we?"

Don looked round with interest. "I've never been in the House before, but I motored through England when I was home last. There was a General Election on at the time, and I remember looking at all the candidates' portraits on the walls, and thinking that they were quite a good-looking lot."

"Oh, if we looked like the portraits on our election addresses, the House of Commons would be a beauty chorus," grinned Robert.

"It looks rather like a stage set to me," said Don. "The Speaker, and the three men in wigs in front of him, and the big table, and brass boxes, and the rows of you on each side—it could be put on the Drury Lane stage as it is."

"And that's what is the matter with the whole show, Don. It simply isn't real. We've all been brought up to believe that this place is the supreme power in the State. Well, it isn't, and then every one kicks the M.P.s because they can't do the impossible with an instrument that really has very little power compared with the forces outside."

"But if you pass a law here, we have got to obey it."

"The point is who decides what laws we shall pass. Not our parties. The party sham dissolved at the last election. There are big forces fighting for mastery outside, Don. At the best we are only the scoring machinery. At the worst we are the cover on the safety-valve. The one hope is that we may not be shut tight at the wrong moment."

"You mean there may be a revolution?"

"Oh, there's a revolution on now, on since the War. We don't have barricades in Britain, not being a theatrical people. But don't you feel, since you came back, the tug-of-war that's going on?"

"Tug-of-war rather expresses it. One side gaining a bit and then being pulled back. Is the House of Commons the rope?"

"It's hardly all that—one strand in the rope certainly. But the tug is going on everywhere, in the factories and the mines, on the ships, police and unemployed demonstrators, the two sides in any big strike."

"And who's going to win—the Socialists?"

"There you are, you see. Being English, you immediately put the struggle into political terms. The same struggle is going on within each party. It's bigger than politics, it's the Stuart-Orfords against the Huxleys and the Rutherfords, the displaced man in the labour queue against the latest machine, the man of the old ruling class against the force of the masses demanding bread. He can't give it them. He doesn't know how. And he can't get away by explaining that the bread isn't there, because they are told by the Press that it is being burned by producers who don't know what to do with it. It's the New Order coming to birth, Don, and it's taking a damned long time about it."

"Why not help it? Hasn't some one got a plan? Surely the figures are known?"

"Plan!" said Robert bitterly. "There are scores. Then the old struggle starts again over each plan. No, there's nothing to be done that I can see. Let 'em fight it out, and then the victor will have to produce a plan, I suppose. It's a grim prospect, all the same."

A House messenger came along the bench, and handed West a note.

"It's from the Premier's secretary," said Robert, reading it. "This debate is fizzling out, and the adjournment is coming on in a few minutes, so you won't have to wait as long as you thought. I'll have to slip back on to the P.P.S. bench. See you afterwards."

Shaw watched the good-looking young man as he crossed the floor, bowed to the Speaker, and took his place on the second Government bench. He felt rather hopeless about a world where the young men like Robert West, with brains and a high sense of duty, the men who ought to have been burning with new ideas, eager to displace the old, simply shrugged their shoulders in bitter helplessness and said: "Let 'em fight it out and see what happens." But surely, he thought, even as a registering machine the House of Commons was worth while. Suppose there were no registering machine until the tension got too strong and the whole social structure collapsed. "No," said Don to himself firmly, "I may be old-fashioned, but I shall still continue to believe in the House of Commons."

The House began to fill rapidly. The news of the adjournment debate was on the electric indicators. The Premier came in. Michael Houldsworth rose to speak. There was a quiver of expectancy.

Houldsworth was a precise speaker with a rather metallic voice. He and the Premier were old antagonists. They had measured swords often.

"I shall be told, in fact the intimation has been conveyed to the Opposition leaders through the usual channels, that it is impossible for the Government to make a statement, that the adjourned inquest is on Thursday, and that meanwhile the matter is *sub judice*. I am not interested, Mr Speaker, in how a certain unfortunate gentleman died in this House."

"Then you ought to be," shouted Members from the Government benches.

"I have no doubt the gentleman's friends will supply all the sympathy necessary," said Houldsworth quietly.

There was an uproar. The front Opposition bench was shocked. The Premier looked pained. Points of order were raised all over the House. Could a guest of this House and a dead man at that be insulted in this way?

The Speaker rose. The tumult was stilled. Looking at neither side the man with the quiet voice from under the heavy canopy said that he hoped due respect would be paid to the dead. Don was impressed. It was like the voice of an oracle.

Houldsworth continued, having stood quite unmoved by the uproar. He secured a hearing by saying that he meant no disrespect to the dead, he did not want to bring Mr Oissel as a man into the discussion at all. The questions he wanted to ask were incidental to the murder, and had no connexion with police matters that would be discussed at the inquest.

Then in a brief but deadly speech which lasted but ten minutes Houldsworth stuck his needles into the Premier. Why had the Government observed such secrecy about this loan? Had any other financiers than the Oissel group been invited to co-operate? There was talk of secret provisos. Had Oissel made such provisos? Had the Government accepted them? Were they consistent with the dignity of this House? What was the present state of the negotiations? Had the terms stiffened as much since Oissel's murder as the Stock Exchange rumoured? Why did the Government maintain such obstinate silence while British securities crashed? Was there any truth in the rumour that the U.S.A. had threatened financial reprisals? Did not the Government realize the seething volcano beneath them? Never had a House of Commons witnessed such utter ineptitude, such slothful ignoring of the dangers of the situation. Was English credit to crash while a young and insignificant Parliamentary private secretary was allowed to run around and amuse himself by playing the amateur detective?

Houldsworth sat down amid general murmurs. That last sentence had somewhat spoiled the effect of his speech. Lady Bell-Clinton looked across at Grace Richards and observed in her high mocking tone, "That's because of you." The House can be unbelievably cruel, and men stung by Houldsworth's manner and his deadly questioning took revenge by laughing at Grace's furious red cheeks. "The female of the species is more deadly than the male," Shaw's neighbour in the box quoted to him as they both looked at poor Grace with sympathy.

The Premier rose smiling. The laughter had dissipated the atmosphere caused by the middle part of Houldsworth's speech. He was sure of himself in the House now. He began by expressing his sympathy with Miss Oissel, the lady to whom the heart of every gentleman (a slight emphasis on the word) in this House would go out in chivalrous feeling. He sympathized with the Home Secretary bearing the treble strain of the loss of an old friend and an honoured guest, of departmental responsibility, and responsibility for the detection and punishment of the murderers. Every one with any connexion with the event was mentioned and separately sympathized with. When he spoke of the kitchen staff, of its devotion, of its indignation at the tragedy, the golden voice roused even the Opposition to approving murmurs. He had remembered the workers who were so often forgotten. Only Houldsworth's face remained set in its grim lines.

By the time all these sweets had been handed round, the House was in a proper mood for the Premier's statement that the American Embassy were giving the fullest co-operation to His Majesty's Government, that the fall in securities was the result of disreputable attempts to take advantage of an old man's tragedy, and that strong measures would be taken by the Government to deal with the situation.

The Member who had raised this debate had attacked the police, continued the Premier. He paused a moment, and then said in his silkiest tones: "Perhaps the honourable Member does not like the British police." The House roared with laughter. The slight emphasis on 'honourable' and 'British' had been exquisite in its insult, for Houldsworth was a strong supporter of Soviet Russia. But the police were not in the habit of announcing their discoveries or their theories in order to please certain impatient gentlemen of the Opposition, especially when they had reason to believe that their efforts were soon to meet with success.

The House went absolutely still. Every Member on the benches, every Pressman, the public in the galleries, hung on his next words. When the House does that it is the most flattering, the most dangerous moment in a politician's life. What orator, when he has brought this critical, restless, bored audience to such a pitch dare deflate it by an anticlimax? The Prime Minister when he rose had intended to be at his foggiest, his most non-committal. It would have taken a less sensitive, a less impressionable man to have resisted the lure of that crowded, listening House.

He looked round them, happy in his mastery. It was not his part, nor was this the place, he said, to reveal what the police knew. That must be done at the coroner's court. The inquest stood adjourned until Thursday. Was that too long for certain honourable gentlemen to wait? In their anxiety lest the truth should be known before their names appeared in the papers must they try to force a premature statement which could only hamper the men who were bearing so grave a responsibility?

The House rustled its opinion of Houldsworth, who was not often caught at a disadvantage. But he remained quite calm amid the general disapproval. Commendation by his political foes was the last thing Houldsworth desired. The golden voice went on to hope that the House would continue its trust in the men at the helm, and as Premier he thought he could promise, if they would restrain their impatience, that if not by Thursday, at least by some early date, the British police, the most admirable in the world, would have brought the miscreants to the bar of British justice, the fairest in the world, and all would be well if England to herself remained but true.

He sat down amid roars of applause. The golden voice had triumphed again. The Speaker put the resolution of adjournment perfunctorily, and the Members poured out of the House laughing about Lady Bell-Clinton's score over Houldsworth and Grace, happy as schoolboys who are unexpectedly allowed to leave school early.

Robert West's furious expression prevented anyone chaffing him. A man who started it retreated hastily, for Robert looked as though he would knock him down. Grace had left the Chamber as soon as the motion was put, escaping unnoticed in the hubbub. West could not very well ask any of her own party where she had gone. Houldsworth had disappeared also. Had he gone to comfort her? Damn the fellow! And damn Lady Bell-Clinton—why could she never avoid saying the first thing that came into her head? Robert was genuinely fond of her, and respected her real kindness of heart. Why must she do these things which laid her open to such fierce hatred?

Remembering that he had to rescue Shaw, who had been decanted with the other occupants of the "Under the Gallery" pew into the lobby, Robert pushed his way out of the Chamber, but was held by Lord Dalbeattie, who had just come down the staircase from the Peers' Gallery.

"Have you a minute?" he asked Bob. Then, seeing the young man's unhappy face, he said: "Whatever possessed Ivy to say that?"

Robert shrugged his shoulders. He could not trust himself to answer.

"Has she asked you about this dinner-party?" said Dalbeattie.

"Yes," replied Robert. "It is, of course impossible. Equally, of course, if you want it, it can be managed, but in that case you had better have a word with Gleeson yourself. If he gives permission I don't suppose that the House authorities will raise any objections, but they won't like it, and I'm not coming anyway."

"Oh, yes, you are," said Lord Dalbeattie firmly. "To be just to Ivy, the dinner was only a passing fancy of hers, but I have taken it up and I want it carried through. I want to see the room under the conditions it was that night, and with the same waiter."

"Then why don't you and I dine there alone together? It would be nearer the conditions of the Oissel dinner than a party."

"But Annette and Philip Kinnaird want to be there, and Annette has some claim. I would like her to come."

"Then there is no necessity for Lady Bell-Clinton."

Dalbeattie laughed. "Poor Ivy. She deserves to be left out, but it will be a terribly dull dinner without her. You really must forgive her... Will you make the arrangements with the manager? We'll dine as late as possible, say nine-thirty. Keep it as dark as you can, of course. We shan't be able to prevent the Press getting to know something is on, but we can avoid any preliminary announcements. Has Miss Richards found out anything, by the way?"

"She hasn't had much time yet. And we can hardly expect her to be helpful after this evening, can we?"

"Oh, she'll get over that. After all, there is nothing unflattering to a woman in having the number of her admirers announced to the world. Have a word with some of the Pressmen. They are very decent about incidents like that. It will be kept as a House joke."

CHAPTER XIX

Tuesday was a terrible day for every one remotely concerned with the Oissel case. The Prime Minister had been gracious on Monday evening, delighted with the success of his speech, surrounded by people offering congratulations for having smashed Houldsworth, never an easy feat. The papers on Tuesday morning reminded him of the price he had now to pay. His hints that something vital would be known and would be produced at the adjourned inquest on the Thursday had put the House of Commons completely in his hand and avoided any further debate. No M.P. would risk making a fool of himself, as every one insisted that Houldsworth had done, by forcing the debate before the inquest. But if that promise were not fulfilled, if the police had nothing at all to say, if a further adjournment had to be asked for, then the position would look ugly indeed.

Already rumours had begun to fly round that the Government knew more than they would say. A widely read morning paper had begun to hint that perhaps powerful people were being covered. Its leader on Monday morning had been headed "OUT WITH THE TRUTH!" Another paper threw the headline across its front pages "IS SOME ONE BEING SHIELDED?" and had denounced political interference with the police. These rumours had been scotched by the Premier's speech. Tuesday's papers praised the Premier and poured wrath on "notoriety seekers" whose impatience might hinder the police at the very moment of triumph. Michael Houldsworth had a thoroughly bad Press, and the Premier as much adulation as even he could swallow over one breakfast. But the hero of the occasion left his egg and toast untasted as he suddenly realized that there remained just fifty-two hours before those promises had to be made good, and that he had not had the slightest foundation for one of the hints that he had given.

It was then that Downing Street woke up. Secretaries hung on the telephones and called up every one they could think of. The police head of Scotland Yard had to listen to the Premier over the telephone until his head buzzed. "Damn it all," he said. "Why can't he let me see him instead of talking a solid half-hour through the phone?"

Sir George Gleeson was sent for. The great civil servant entered the Premier's room magnificently, intending to make even him understand that the police could not have amateurs like Lord Dalbeattie and Robert West brought in to interfere with their work. He was not now dealing with "Flossie," however, but with head of the State, made desperate by a crisis likely to overwhelm them all. When Gleeson went out from Downing Street an hour later his own panic was as great as the Prime Minister's. He nearly embraced Lord Dalbeattie, to that gentleman's astonishment, when he arrived to secure Gleeson's permission for the dinner in Room J. He not only gave permission with the utmost warmth, but he accepted the invitation to it, which Lord Dalbeattie, not expecting this kind of reception, had thought it tactful to offer. But if Lady Bell-Clinton had suggested even a spiritualistic *séance* that morning, she would have found a stout supporter in the awe-inspiring Sir George.

Robert was glad when the day wore on towards evening. He had brought his dress clothes with him, and changed in the room downstairs which is sacred to such rites. A large square room has little curtained cubicles for the changing operations, and as the barber's shop on a ship is a good place to hear the latest news about the number of knots that day and the latest scandals among the passengers, so the man who presides over the barber's department of the House of Commons knows as much as anyone of the gossip of the moment.

West had left his bag with the head attendant and went down to find everything put in readiness for him. The taps in Number I bathroom had been turned on.

"I thought this bathroom had been given over to the women M.P.s," said Robert.

"They don't use it much, sir. Shy of coming down here, I suppose, sir. But it's the best bathroom. Miss Richards came in the other day, sir, and I told her that Mr Gladstone had taken baths in this very bath. There weren't so many bathrooms here in those days."

"I hope Miss Richards was properly impressed?"

"Well, sir, of course it's very nice to have ladies here, I'm sure, sir. It must be nice for the gentlemen. But somehow ladies don't seem to be as much impressed about things as they used to be, do they, sir—I mean the young ones don't?"

Bob laughed. "Perhaps Miss Richards was a little embarrassed at the idea of taking a bath after Mr Gladstone?"

"No, I don't think so. It would take a lot to embarrass a young woman these days, meaning no disrespect to Miss Richards, sir. Have you got all you want, sir?"

"Yes, thanks. I'll come along to you for a shave afterwards."

"Oh, yes, sir—Lady Bell-Clinton's dinner in Room J? It's a queer place to enjoy oneself in, sir, isn't it, if you'll pardon my saying so?"

So the bath attendant knew all about the dinner he had tried so hard to keep a secret. But how could anything be kept a secret from the staff of the House of Commons? Of course every one from the women cleaners to the Sergeant-at-Arms knew all about this dinner, as they had known about the Home Secretary's dinner to Mr Oissel. A highly intelligent trained staff with long years' experience of the ebb and flow of the tide of Members who drift through their hands could not be expected to be blind and deaf when it suited the authorities that they should be.

"We are not dining there to enjoy ourselves," said Robert. "We are going to consider what might have happened that night. We rather don't want it talked about. Perhaps you would mention that to your staff."

"Oh, yes, sir. My staff never talk." ("Don't they!" thought Robert.) "But, sir, I've often wondered why more people don't get murdered in this place when you think of the opportunities."

"Indeed," said Robert, his attention very much on the alert. "What opportunities?"

"Of course, sir, I don't mean that anyone wants to murder M.P.s, but it would be easy enough to slip past the police if anyone did. I mean, sir, all these workmen that are continually in the building. Some one could dress up like one, and no one would ever know if they wore the uniform."

"I suppose it might be done," said Bob thoughtfully.

"Well, if you've got all you want, sir, I'll leave you, sir."

As the door clicked behind the attendant Bob sat on the

edge of the bath. Was this a possibility? Had the assassin been in the building disguised as a workman. He knew Blackitt had had the notion that some one might have been there disguised as a waiter, but no trace of such a man could be found. The manager of the kitchen department and all the waiters had sworn that they knew each other too well for that to be possible, and as no big dinners were held that night no extra staff had been engaged. But a workman was different. He would not be known to the waiters, and would not be noticed by them. But it was nine o'clock at night. A workman who was not on the ventilation staff, all of whom were old employees, would have been noticed wandering about the Harcourt corridor at that unusual hour. Blackitt had questioned every member of the ventilation staff, who go round at intervals to look at the thermometers and open shafts. But every one of these had satisfactorily accounted for his movements.

And yet that boot in the dark. Some one had been in the corridor then, and but for the accident of Robert's returning for his case his presence would never have been known, even though a policeman was on duty. Had some one access to the kitchens, who was being assisted by some member of the kitchen staff? Every clue seemed to lead back to that. Lord Dalbeattie might have hit on the best idea when he had suggested Grace's inquiries. And the accomplice might be some one they had never thought of... the owner of that boot in the dark.

Bob splashed in the bath, thinking that he knew something of what Tantalus must have felt when the things he wanted just eluded him. The solution was hovering near. He felt that very strongly. There were only some forty-two hours now before the inquest. But the answer remained maddeningly out of reach.

A policeman was still at the door of Room J when Robert walked along there. The room had not been unguarded for an instant since the crime. The constable opened the door for Robert. Sir George Gleeson, Lord Dalbeattie, and Philip Kinnaird were already there.

"Sherry or cocktail, Robert? We are the punctual sex, it seems. Ah, there's Big Ben just striking the fatal hour as it did that night."

"Yes, it only wants a nine o'clock division to complete the 'noises off,'" said Bob. The door opened and Lady Bell-Clinton came in, still wearing the plain black day frock she always wore in the House of Commons.

"I haven't changed," she said in her high, gay tone. "Some one has to look after the old country while you men make yourselves look pretty. And what a beauty chorus! I shall be in the audience to-night. I caught a glimpse of Annette as I hurried down. She looks marvellous."

The door was flung open, quite impressively, by the constable on duty. "There now, what did I tell you?" laughed the hostess. Annette as she stood for a moment framed in the oak doorway certainly did look marvellous. She wore a long, perfectly cut gown of rich white satin in an oyster shade that caught the lights as she moved. A cleverly cut Chanel scarf of blue satin draped one shoulder. Her only ornament was a sapphire clip on the front of her dress, an *ensemble* which heightened the effect of her white skin and those unusual dark blue eyes.

"Surely I am not the last?" she said smiling.

"But of course you are. Such an entry must be the climax," said Ivy Bell-Clinton irrepressibly. She was fond of Annette, but felt that she badly needed some one to laugh at her, a task which no male on her horizon was likely to perform.

"Now then, Dick, this is your death's-head feast. How do we arrange ourselves?"

Dalbeattie had evidently planned that. He took the seat at the oval table which faced the door, the place at which Georges Oissel must have sat. "The waiter tells me that there was, of course, a smaller table in then, but that obviously would not do for us. Will you sit at my right, Ivy, Annette on my left, then Sir George next to you, Ivy? West, you are next to Miss Oissel. Kinnaird, you will be left without a lady."

"I shall have to be content with looking at them."

"Philip was intended to be at the Court of King Edward, one of Lady Warwick's young bucks, you know, but he got born too late."

"You told me that Dick Turpin was my *rôle* last time we met!"

"I don't know what is your true *rôle*, Philip, but anyway you are much too good-looking to be let loose among us poor impressionable women. Dick, I hope this is going to be a thoroughly extravagant dinner."

Annette Oissel turned to Robert. "Why do you never come to see me? You haven't been since that awful day after my grandfather died."

"I can't tell you how much I should have liked to have come, but I didn't want to intrude."

"I want to see more of you, but I suppose you are so busy on this affair."

"Well, we are trying hard to find something to tell the court on Thursday, and I have been on it all the time since I saw you."

"Such a waste of time," said Annette pensively.

"But you wanted us to find the murderers, you said."

Annette shrugged her shoulders. "Yes, of course, I was

upset that morning, and very indignant that the papers
should say Grandpère had killed himself. Nothing would
have annoyed him more. But he is dead. People know he
didn't kill himself. Nothing will bring him back to life. Why
should the living waste their time trying to find how he died?
What good will it do anyone now?"

Robert looked at her astonished. Why this change from
her attitude that first morning? Or was she really only concerned about it not being thought that the old man was a
suicide. But if she knew the truth, would not the suicide
theory have been so much more convenient? Had she been
trying to put them off the scent? But even now she had not
spoken as though she were worried about the affair. She had
simply suggested it was an annoying waste of time to have to
bother, rather as one would say: "Oh, don't trouble to bring
in the garden chairs."

"Then I shall expect you to-morrow," said Annette lazily.
"Would you like to come for a cocktail about five?"

"Unless I'm absolutely tied up on this business I'd love to
come. If I can't I'll phone."

"Oh, don't trouble to do that," drawled Annette, "just
come when you can. I shall be at home all the evening."

Robert felt the blood racing through his veins as he
turned back to the general talk, which thanks to Lady Bell-
Clinton's merry chatter had warmed up considerably. As Lord
Dalbeattie had said, it would have been a dull party without
her. Small and fair and plump, she was the complete contrast
to Annette, as her radiated energy was equally different from
the impression of reserve power which any sensitive person
could feel was hidden under the younger woman's stillness.
Robert was sure that Sancroft had misread Annette completely. Whatever the life she was leading, however luxurious

and softening her environment, this woman was the blood and bone of old Oissel. She was probably as capable as he had been of planning big to get her own way.

Completely absorbed by his thoughts about her, utterly happy in her nearness to him, Robert did not attempt to take much part in the conversation that flowed round the table. He did, however, notice with some amusement how they all, except Annette, watched every movement the waiter made.

"Of course the waiter knows we are watching him, and the poor devil is bound to drop something soon," thought Robert, "and then every one will assume that it is his guilty conscience.—That waiter must be some lad to stand up to all he's had to face this last week." This last remark was made in an undertone to Annette.

Her large blue eyes met his own for a moment. "But I think that applies much more to you. I think it is wonderful that you do so much and keep so calm when every one seems to be making such a fuss."

Said as Annette said it, that remark completed Robert's subjugation. He glanced at Philip Kinnaird to see whether he had noticed and was resenting Annette's interest in himself, but Kinnaird was discussing the financial crisis with Gleeson and Dalbeattie.

"You got out of your difficulties rather well, I hear," said Lord Dalbeattie.

Robert thought this was a somewhat untactful remark, but it did not embarrass Kinnaird. "Yes, I nearly got caught—the last crash was rather unexpected. But fortunately Annette was able to come to the rescue."

Apparently there was no secret among these people about Kinnaird's financial difficulties, at least his recent ones. Dalbeattie had expressed no surprise when Robert had passed on the information as to his previous shakiness which he had obtained from Sancroft.

"Every one is shaky," Dalbeattie said casually. "None of us knows from hour to hour what is going to happen. The biggest men may be caught out by one error of judgment just now."

"I think this Stock Exchange gambling ought to be stopped," said Sir George Gleeson in his most magnificent manner.

"What, a Bolshevik in the Home Office! Shame, Sir George, no wonder there are all these goings-on in Parliament when the Home Office itself begins to talk like that," said Lady Bell-Clinton in tones of mock-horror.

"Of course, the whole system is absurd," said Lord Dalbeattie. "Much of it is just roulette played on a world scale. But you can't take all the interest out of life."

"Especially when you're talking about putting down blood sports. What is a fellow to do?" asked Kinnaird.

"Go gunning for grandfathers," answered Ivy Bell-Clinton unexpectedly.

The whole party roared with laughter, but Robert, watching Kinnaird, saw that though he laughed the retort had taken him aback. Sir George continued:

"I should have no objection to the Stock Exchange system if it were being run frankly to give punters a flutter under proper control. But taken with the seriousness that it is now, when Governments rock because of some preposterous rumour that is started the Lord knows how, and whole towns sink into poverty and unemployment as a result, then it's a wonder to me how sensible men tolerate and even defend such a process. I know Miss Oissel will forgive me when I say that it's no wonder some men at the top get shot. I can't understand why there isn't a widespread demand from the people that a stop should be put to the whole thing."

"Don't know what's happening to 'em," commented Lady Bell-Clinton. "That's why we are allowed to have such a very good dinner at Dick's expense."

The waiter served coffee, and the door closed upon his final ministrations. The group went suddenly silent. Every one felt embarrassed except Ivy. "Well," she said, "and what is expected to happen now?"

Lord Dalbeattie lit his cigar with some care. "The party isn't quite complete yet, my dear. There are two or perhaps three guests to arrive."

"Not for dinner surely?"

"I had hoped they would have been able to come for dinner, but as they were working on the new clues they said they would try to be here by ten o'clock."

"New clues—but how exciting!" exclaimed Ivy. "Have we to wait for a grand *tableau*, 'The Murderers Produced,' or are you going to tell us about it beforehand?"

"Not long to wait now, Ivy. And there may be nothing to tell. But it seems to be our only chance of finding anything."

A silence fell on the party, the sort of thick, stifling silence that comes in a *séance*. Each in turn tried to break it, each felt the words die on their lips unspoken. Annette sat like an ivory statue. Ivy felt that she must shriek lest the ghost of the murdered man appeared. They sat only for a few minutes, but each one felt it to have been hours when there was a knock at the door. It was opened by Inspector Blackitt, who held it open while Grace Richards walked in, followed by Sancroft. The Inspector followed them in and closed the door behind them.

Dalbeattie rose, but the others remained seated, still under the spell of that awful silence.

A chair was pulled to the table for Grace. The two men found seats for themselves—the Inspector by the wall, Sancroft by perching on the edge of the service table.

Lady Bell-Clinton's hostess instinct helped her back to normality. "Well, I hope you have some news, for another disappointment would be more than we could bear."

Grace looked at Lord Dalbeattie. "We have some news," she said. "We think we are on the track of the man who caused Mr Oissel to be murdered, but there is still the missing link of the revolver."

"We shan't be long in finding that, I think," boomed the deep voice of Inspector Blackitt. "It's only a matter of..."

At this point the whole company, tense with nervous excitement, nearly jumped out of their skins. The division bell suddenly began to ring. "Oh," screamed Lady Bell-Clinton, her overwrought nerves finding the outlet her self-control had denied them this last half-hour.

West and Kinnaird made for the door to go upstairs to vote. Grace suddenly stood up blazing with excitement. "That's it, Inspector! Oh, what fools we've been! That's it!"

"By God, you're right!" said Blackitt, while Sancroft dashed to the door. "Let's get a ladder."

CHAPTER XX

"We must vote," said Kinnaird quietly to West. "The solution will keep till we come back." West hardly heard him, and no one noticed his going. Every one made an excited group round Grace except Annette, who quietly lit another cigarette. "What's the matter, what's the matter? Do tell us," said Ivy Bell-Clinton, her self-control almost completely gone. Sancroft and Blackitt returned with the ladder.

"Where's Mr Kinnaird?" said Blackitt sharply, looking at the group.

"He's just gone upstairs to vote," said West. "He said he would be back immediately. I ought to have gone, but I couldn't leave this now."

"Damn!" said Blackitt. The others stood in amazement while he picked up the phone. "Get me through to the Inspector's office… That you, Bourne. Don't let Mr Kinnaird leave the building. Warrant? No, of course not. Just keep him, or ask him to come to Room J, will you?"

Sancroft by this time had got his step-ladder against the wall, and with a screwdriver was working at the small grating that contained the division bell. These little square gratings, inconspicuously near the ceiling, are familiar objects in every corridor and most rooms of the House. They hide the bells that fill the building with their clangour when a division is called.

"Here it is, Blackitt! Look!"

"Let me look too," exclaimed Lady Bell-Clinton, and insisted on being the next to go up the ladder. She gasped. "It's here." Ingeniously fastened, with its muzzle pointing at the heart of anyone sitting in the chair at the head of the table, was a revolver.

"But how could it have gone off by itself?" asked Ivy Bell-Clinton as she stepped gingerly down the ladder and made way for the polite but impatient Inspector. "That's easy," said Blackitt, as he examined it carefully with a flash-lamp. "There's a broken contact here. It must have been fixed so that the first stroke of the division bell that night at nine o'clock released the contact and pulled the trigger. Damned ingenious, but, my God, why did we never think of pulling out this grating, when we tapped every panel in the place?"

Lord Dalbeattie went up to have a look. "Ingenious as you say, Blackitt, and all the merit of simplicity. I suppose I must have seen this grating every time I have come back to look round this room, and it never occurred to me that it could hold anything but the bell."

"By Jove, Blackitt," said West excitedly, "that's what the man in the corridor was here for. The policeman had been drugged so that some one could get that revolver away. And if they'd managed it we should have been done."

"It's a good thing that we kept a guard on this room," Blackitt replied. "Else whoever put it there would have been able to make a complete getaway."

"And who did put it there? Not...?" Lady Bell-Clinton looked at Annette, but could not frame the name. The telephone rang. Blackitt picked up the receiver. "What, not in the House?... And his car there in the yard... but he must be here... Search everywhere... you can't have done. Well, keep a watch on every exit." The Inspector replaced the receiver and looked at Annette. She might have been a statue with her dead white face, and the heavy satin moulding her limbs like drapery in stone.

Blackitt said nothing to her. He hurried from the room.

Lord Dalbeattie turned to Sancroft and Grace. "Now perhaps you will tell us what has happened, but a glass of wine before you begin——" Grace waved away the proffered glass, which Sancroft cheerfully accepted. "It's just like Inspector Blackitt to go off on his duty, when he should be here to get all the praise," she said. "He really is splendid. I've done nothing except under his orders."

"But what have you done, what has happened?" asked Lady Bell-Clinton impatiently.

Grace stiffened. She had a score to settle with her lively antagonist. Lord Dalbeattie patted his friend's hand warningly, and encouraged Grace with a look to proceed.

"Well," she said coldly, the eager enthusiasm gone from her voice, "when Bob, I mean Mr West, asked me to find out what I could, I had a talk with Inspector Blackitt first."

"Sensible girl," commented Lord Dalbeattie. "Most women would have wanted to do the thing on their own."

Under this encouragement Grace lost a little of her stiffness. "He asked me to talk specially to one of the cleaners whose daughter was keeping company with Cedric—that's the waiter for Room J."

"Cedric! How romantic!" gurgled Lady Bell-Clinton.

Grace ignored the interruption, but Lord Dalbeattie felt that the tide between the two women was rising rapidly.

"And then?" he asked with a smile.

"I soon found it would be hopeless to talk to her in the House or near it. All the kitchen staff are furious about the whole affair. They think it reflects on them, and the police have put their backs up to such an extent that they will say nothing themselves and keep a sharp look-out to see if anyone is prowling round asking questions."

"Shielding some one?" This from Sir George Gleeson.

"No, I don't think so. It was just their clannishness and the feeling that the service has been let down. Well, I thought of an idea to get this woman talking without her suspecting anything. I couldn't have her in my rooms—I am in digs—so I asked her to come to Mr Sancroft's rooms this evening to dust all his books. I told her I arranged this sort of thing for him."

"And do you?" cooed Lady Bell-Clinton.

Grace's eyes flashed. Dalbeattie came again to the rescue. "Ivy, you simply must not interrupt. Go on, please, Miss Richards."

Grace turned her shoulder to Lady Bell-Clinton and addressed herself with burning cheeks exclusively to Lord Dalbeattie. "We got her talking while she dusted the books. Blackitt had told me that they could find nothing against the daughter. She wasn't spending more money or anything suspicious like that. But while the mother was gossiping away quite unsuspectingly she happened to mention that when Cedric married her daughter he was going to leave the House of Commons and set up as an electrician. Mr Sancroft asked if he knew anything about electricity, and she said: 'Oh, yes. He's a dab hand at anything with wires.' Well, that seemed to be a new slant on him. So, as soon as we decently could, we left her to go on with the work and came down here to meet Mr Blackitt."

"And was that a clue?" asked Sir George.

"Blackitt and I had discussed the theory of a concealed revolver," Sancroft took up the story. "The difficulty was where, and who could do it. This information gave the clue that Blackitt wanted. He had been suspecting Kinnaird for some time, but had kept it to himself. He told me that when I gave him some news about Kinnaird's finances."

No one dared look at Annette except Ivy Bell-Clinton, who went and stood near her in a protecting attitude as though to defy the entire police force of Britain to touch her friend. "And what next?" asked Dalbeattie when the moment's silence had become more than anyone could bear.

"We waited in the manager's room until Cedric had finished serving your dinner," continued Sancroft. "Then Blackitt sent for him. This dinner had simply broken his nerve. He must have had a nerve like iron to keep going so long. But as soon as he saw us he guessed all was up. Blackitt just said quietly: 'How much did Mr Kinnaird give you to fix things,' and he broke down completely and cried like a child."

"It was awful, Lord Dalbeattie," said Grace. "I don't think he meant any harm, but Mr Kinnaird got hold of him... I mean... oh, I'm sorry," looking at Annette.

"I don't believe it. I don't believe Philip would do such a thing," said Lady Bell-Clinton stoutly. "You can't take a waiter's word against Philip's. It is monstrous... all these Socialists too. You don't believe it, Dick."

"Do be quiet, Ivy," said Lord Dalbeattie. "How has he been able to stick to his job all this time? One would have thought he would have tried to get away."

"He couldn't," said Sancroft. "Blackitt has all along been convinced he knew something. Though the police hadn't a shred of evidence against him, they've never let him out of their sight. His one hope of safety lay in keeping his head, sticking to his story, and trying to brave it out. Cedric had no producible evidence against Kinnaird—it was all the other way. He tried once to come to you, Bob tells me, but Blackitt was with you."

"Then he was the man in my doorway," said West excitedly. "I knew there was something familiar about the cut of his jib. Was he the man whose boot I saw in the corridor?"

"No, that was Kinnaird, I gather. But Blackitt has got all that out of him. Cedric was in the kitchen at the time, and got Kinnaird away. You were probably pretty near death yourself that night, Bob."

"But you have only the waiter's word for all this," persisted Lady Bell-Clinton. "And you admit that the waiter has no evidence against Mr Kinnaird. Besides, how could he persuade the waiter to do such a thing?"

"He got the waiter his job here—oh, no, nothing to do with this—two years ago. He was giving him another chance. Cedric would have been serving a pretty stiff prison sentence if it had not been for Kinnaird," said Sancroft, "but that is not the only evidence Blackitt has against Kinnaird." Sancroft was utterly indifferent to the feelings of Annette, who had sat through all this like a statue. Every one else, even Grace, felt that the situation was becoming intolerable.

There was a feeling of relief when further revelations were interrupted by the return of Inspector Blackitt. His face was set and stern. He walked to where Annette was sitting and stood looking down at her. Annette did not move even an eyelid. Robert found himself staring fixedly at the curve of her breast. He was near to tears. What did it matter about Kinnaird? But she—was she to be mixed up in this... was Blackitt going to arrest her? Blackitt had known more than he had told him then. "Annette, Annette." He felt that they must all hear the beating of his heart. He wanted to choke Blackitt before the Inspector could say what he had come to say.

"Miss Oissel," said the Inspector grimly, "this building has been searched from end to end, and Mr Kinnaird is not in it. Have you any idea where he is?"

"Not the slightest," said Annette. She moved no other muscle than her lips.

"And of course she would not tell you if she had," said Lady Bell-Clinton indignantly. "I never heard of such a thing."

Inspector Blackitt looked at Lord Dalbeattie. It was obviously impossible to continue any cross-examination of Miss Oissel while the gallant Ivy was in the room. "Ivy," said Lord Dalbeattie very gently, "I think if you took Miss Richards with you and gave her some dinner… and perhaps Mr Sancroft would like a bite too… they have been working hard and haven't had any, you know… then we can just have a talk with Annette and see if there is any way we can help."

"Help Annette!" snorted Lady Bell-Clinton. "You want me to leave the poor girl with all you men while you put her through a third degree about the man she is in love with." The indignant lady remembered all the speeches she had ever made about the justice of having a woman present when the police took evidence. Was she to be beaten off the ground just when she could help her friend? Lord Dalbeattie, who could read her like a book, and whose influence over her was immense, went to her and put his arm on her shoulder. "Ivy," he said very gently, "you must trust me. I will see that Annette isn't bullied, but it is better that you go now, and take Miss Richards with you."

It was useless to protest further. Lady Bell-Clinton swept from the room, and Grace and Sancroft followed her. She left them in the corridor without a word. "All the same, she would be good stuff to have beside one in a scrap," said Sancroft as he watched her pass swiftly down the corridor. Grace was almost in tears. To see Robert West lost in utter adoration of Annette Oissel had been hard. Sancroft suddenly realized what was the matter. Without another word he slipped his arm through hers. "Sandwiches, my dear. Let's go to the bar."

Inside Room J Robert was thanking his stars that he had not been ordered out too. He felt that he would have raised a riot rather than have left Annette, but of course... he couldn't. His helplessness made him feel faint. Would Annette's self-control last out?

Now that he was no longer irritated by Lady Bell-Clinton, Inspector Blackitt's tone was more kindly. "Mr Kinnaird is your *fiancé*, isn't he, Miss Oissel?"

"He is my husband," Annette answered. "I understand that English law relieves me of the necessity of answering further questions about him."

There was dead silence. Each man could hear his own breathing. West, Gleeson, and Dalbeattie had almost unconsciously drawn together. Blackitt still stood slightly bending over Annette, a symbol of the dreaded Law.

Annette rose and faced them all. Was her amazing control breaking? Her lower lip trembled a little. "But yes, I will tell you," she said suddenly. "You shall hear the other side before you hear more evidence against him. I have loved Philip ever since I left school. There have been other men... but it was always Philip I really loved. At first he was a friend of my grandfather and I just a girl. But he began to love me... I made him... and then when he wanted to marry me my grandfather hated him. He had always wanted me to marry that wretched marquis. But Grandpère knew he couldn't break me. He didn't try—not directly. He was never unkind to me... but he thought he could break me through Philip. He pretended to be reconciled to the idea of our marriage. That did not deceive me—I knew him too well. He never changed. I warned Philip, but he would not believe me. Grandpère helped him to make his fortune... and then when he had got his confidence thoroughly——" She stopped. No one spoke. "Grandpère broke him," she said.

Robert felt dizzy. Those three words spoken like that sounded like an execution. Annette continued slowly: "Philip was desperate, but he thought it was his own fault. No one was so clever as Grandpère. He led him on. No one is so reckless as Philip. Then my grandfather got him into the position where he forged securities, and Grandpère got them into his own hand. Oh, I know he shouldn't have done it—Philip, I mean—but he was just desperate. He felt he dare not tell me. If only he had, I could have dealt with my grandfather in my own way."

Annette paused again. Lord Dalbeattie put his arm round her shoulders and gently forced her back into her chair. "Oh, my dear," he said softly, "why did he not come to me?"

"Why didn't he—but it was me he should have told. I was never afraid of Grandpère. But you know Philip. He is as proud as Lucifer. And Grandpère told him that he would tell me that unless I married that wretched marquis he would denounce him and he would have to go to prison."

"But if you were already married to Kinnaird——?" Sir George Gleeson's tone implied his amazement.

"Yes, but I was a minor when we married, and Philip thought that if he was in prison and I knew the worst, I would be made to consent to a divorce and would have a terrible time with my grandfather when he knew we had married without his consent."

"Well, I suppose you would have had a bad time," said Sir George sympathetically, feeling that English fathers were really much the best, after all.

"Nonsense," said Annette impatiently. "I tell you I was never afraid of my grandfather. Every one thought him an ogre, but he never said an unkind word to me in his life. He was bluffing. If only I had known, if only Philip had given me the least idea, I would have called that bluff quickly enough, and he would have had to put things right for Philip."

"Then why didn't you tell him of your marriage yourself?" asked Lord Dalbeattie.

"Because I was a silly romantic fool. Because I loved the adventure of playing round with other men, and having that secret all the time. But I only loved Philip, though he used to get so jealous."

"I begin to be very sorry for Philip between your grandfather and yourself. He must have had the devil of a time," said Dalbeattie.

Annette's lovely eyes filled with tears. "I realize that now. Between us, we pushed him over the edge. He loved me to desperation, and I played with that love. I maddened him at times. And all the time there was Grandpère pressing him and threatening him. He relied on Philip's shame to prevent him telling me… as it did, until too late. Grandpère pressed just too much. Philip decided that there was no hope for him or me unless he could get hold of that evidence against him. He knew that the papers were kept at the flat—the papers that would incriminate him. He had to steal them. It was he who arranged for the burglary at the flat, but he hadn't intended Jenks to be shot. He was very upset about that."

"But why murder Mr Oissel? Couldn't he just have stolen the papers?" asked Sir George.

"But then, of course, my grandfather would have said what the papers were that had been stolen, and suspicion would have fallen on Philip at once. I think Grandpère would have been glad if Philip had done that. It would have put things right with me as far as he was concerned. Philip realized that. He was crazy with rage and fear... and started drinking heavily. If only I had had the slightest idea what was worrying him... but he told me nothing... He came less and less to Clarges Street... he had been practically living there, of course, as much as he dared without Grandpère suspecting us. And I thought there must be another woman... and set out to make him jealous. It was dreadful... and Grandpère watching and waiting... Oh, Philip..."

Sir George Gleeson, standing in the shadow against the wall, dug his hands deep into the pockets of his jacket. Utterly cold and efficient civil servant as he thought himself to be, at that moment he wanted that old devil to be alive again that he might smash him with his own fists.

Robert's eyes were fixed on the large tears that still hung on Annette's lashes. Would they fall? Would she break? He could cheerfully have shot all his companions at that moment just for a second to comfort her. He felt no jealousy against Philip Kinnaird. He understood dimly something of the torture he had been through.

"Did you know anything about the... er... plot, before your grandfather was murdered?" asked Inspector Blackitt, who resented the emotional atmosphere this woman was creating, and wanted to get at the stark truth.

"Oh, of course not. How I wish I had! I didn't see Philip that night... I was at a dance. He had phoned. The police were waiting when I got back. He knew they would be and did not want to compromise me… I mean by his being there at all. I phoned him the next morning, and asked him to go with me to the Home Office. He did not know what I was going to say. He dared not say anything when I raged in the car at the impertinence of the police for daring to say that my grandfather had committed suicide. And he knew that his only hope was that the death should look like suicide. He had planned it for that. And he was driving with me to the Home Office to wreck his plan, for all he knew. And he did not say a word. Oh, Philip, Philip——" Annette's voice had sunk to a moan. Robert looked desperately at Dalbeattie. "Need this vivisection go on?" he said in a low tone.

"We must get the truth, or we can't help her," Dalbeattie whispered back. And it was true. Gleeson might have shown mercy, but Blackitt was the embodiment of Impersonal Law.

"But has he confessed to you?" Blackitt asked quietly.

"Is that fair, sir?" interrupted West, appealing to Dalbeattie, who silenced him with a gesture. The truth had to be known—better that they should know it first. Annette seemed to feel that too, that here were the only friends who could help, and that they must know everything.

She was silent a moment, then: "It was the night after the inquest had been held… He came to me that night… he realized from Inspector Blackitt's evidence that the police were not deceived, that they did not accept the suicide theory as the papers had done. And that night he broke… He realized what it would mean to me, the slow dragging out of the truth, that even his suicide would not save me, might make me look an accomplice when it was known that I was his wife, and that I inherited the fortune. He told me all."

Those four words—and three men realized what the telling must have been. There would be no reproaches from

Annette. At that moment she would have been at her best, and Kinnaird would have understood what he had gambled with and lost—driven, desperate, reckless Kinnaird.

Inspector Blackitt's voice seemed indecently businesslike when he broke the silence with: "He had planted that revolver himself? He had meant it to look like suicide?"

"Yes, and it was I who made it all so easy for him, I who unconsciously gave him the idea. I told him about the dinner, laughed with him about Mr West's letter of apology that the Minister would have to leave him for the nine o'clock division. And he had got the waiter Cedric his job. It all worked in so well. Cedric fixed the revolver when he was on early duty. He just locked the door. He had an excuse if anyone wanted to come in, but no one did. No one saw him. If the police guard had not been kept on, he would have got the revolver away afterwards without anyone knowing it had been there."

"Cheerful thought how easily such things can be done in the House of Commons, just because no one expects they will be," said Gleeson to Dalbeattie in a low tone.

"But how did he expect it to look like suicide?" said Lord Dalbeattie. "How could he be sure that your grandfather would take his revolver?"

"He knew Grandpère well enough to be sure of that, especially when Grandpère knew beforehand that he was to be left alone even for a few minutes. And he had challenged Grandpère to hit a target only the day before when they were motoring with me. I was driving. That worked easily enough. Grandpère was proud of his shooting. They each fired their revolvers once at a mark on a tree. Grandpère scored. He was as pleased as anything about it, and just put the revolver back in his pocket. That was all Philip wanted, of course. He and Grandpère seemed quite good friends that day. Why should I have suspected anything?"

Silence again. Sir George Gleeson felt his sympathy with Kinnaird waning somewhat. It had been a pretty cold-blooded plot, whatever the provocation—not like shooting a man in anger.

"And the notebook?" asked Lord Dalbeattie, who knew what he wanted to get out of all this. Once clear the Government, and there might be some hope of helping poor Annette.

"Oh, the notebook! At first I thought that that was what the burglars had been after. When I knew the truth, then I kept working at that, because I wanted to turn attention from the papers that Philip had arranged to be stolen. I guessed from Mr West that the Government had something to hide there. And when I realized what I had done—by going to the Home Office and making a fuss about its not being suicide—I thought it would put the police off the scent. As it did, you must admit."

She said this so pitifully that West agreed heartily. "Of course it did! Bunkered us completely," he said. Good God, he thought to himself, what must she have felt like when she realized that she had probably helped to put a rope round her lover's neck—what pluck she had shown!

Annette pitiful, Annette pleading and tender, would have melted a harder heart than even Sir George Gleeson's. Blackitt, whose sole interest was in a professional job well done, began to be afraid of the effect of those wet eyes. He had to find where Kinnaird was. Dalbeattie and West would only be concerned that the Cabinet could now be cleared. The expression on Sir George's face showed that even he would not be too reliable an ally at the moment. He must bring this girl to the point quickly, so that, as a sensible detective, he could get on with his job of bringing murderers to justice without being hampered at every turn by friends of Cabinet Ministers, and powerful Society women like Lady Bell-Clinton.

He tried to continue his cross-examination. "And where is Mr Kinnaird now, Miss Oissel?"

Lord Dalbeattie glanced significantly at Sir George Gleeson, who nodded slightly.

"I think that is all we can expect of Miss Oissel to-night, Blackitt," said Dalbeattie. "After all, Miss Oissel has given the police a lot of help by her statement. It has cleared the Cabinet completely, and that is the really important matter at the moment. As Mr Kinnaird's wife she could have refused to say anything. I think we must not trouble her further. Perhaps to-morrow——"

Annette rose. She leant on Robert's arm. "Thank you, Lord Dalbeattie. If Mr West will take me to my car..." Each man there, except the practical Inspector, wanted that privilege, but they stood aside as Robert lifted her scarf from her chair and put it on her shoulders. Together they walked from the room.

An adjournment debate that had followed the last division was finishing as they went along the corridor. The bells began to ring as the House rose. Down the corridors came the shouts of the policemen, the last call of the Parliamentary day: "Who goes home? Who goes home?"

Annette halted at the entrance. She looked up at Big Ben. "Philip has gone home," she said very softly. "The police forgot the river."

To see more Poisoned Pen Press titles:

Visit our website:
poisonedpenpress.com
Request a digital catalog:
info@poisonedpenpress.com